COMANCHERO ATTACK!

The ground rumbled as hundreds of Comancheros kicked their horses into action, charging straight at the settlement.

"Dragoons to the south side!" Gavin ordered. "Stand ready and wait for orders!"

The enemy was barely fifty yards away and closing fast.

"Cock your pieces!" Gavin shouted.

With the Comanchero army at twenty yards, the soldiers could see the battle lust in the eyes of their enemies.

"Aim . . . Fire!"

Smoke, flame, and ball ammunition blasted outward, plowing straight into the half-breed attackers. Men and horses screamed and tumbled to the ground, quickly soaking the prairie with their blood. The survivors turned and rode back out of range to leave at least a dozen dead and maimed scattered less than ten yards away from the defenses.

"Reload!" Gavin shouted, then turned to his second in command, who said, "least now they know we can bite."

PATRICK E. ANDREWS
COMANCHERO BLOOD

ZEBRA BOOKS
KENSINGTON PUBLISHING CORP.

This book is dedicated to my uncle and aunt
ED AND RUBY ANDREWS

ZEBRA BOOKS are published by

Kensington Publishing Corp.
475 Park Avenue South
New York, NY 10016

Zebra and the Z logo are trademarks of Kensington Publishing Corp.

First Printing: June, 1993
Printed in the United States of America

Chapter 1

Winter moved in fast during that short fall of 1854 at Fort Leavenworth in Kansas Territory. The cold swept down from the north in an invisible curtain of murderously frigid air. The cruel weather locked the prairie in a long season of windswept sleet storms and howling blizzards that dumped weighty blankets of snow across the plains country.

The soldiers at the post settled in for a long, dreary winter's routine, a monotonous life dominated by guard duty and only the most necessary of fatigue chores. One of the least popular of these tasks was going to the Missouri River to saw out cakes of ice, which were invaluable in the hot summer months. To make the ice last as long as possible, it was kept in the post icehouse, insulated by sawdust collected during construction work conducted during warmer times.

In the stables of the dragoon regiment, the horses spent most of the time in confinement. The animals' natural energy was pent-up, finding release only in carefully orchestrated exercise sessions that consisted mostly of being led around in circles by trotting soldiers. This could only be done during rare moments of winter stillness when the roaring winds quieted down for brief periods.

The human element suffered, too, during off-duty hours because of the confinement. Violent outbreaks of brawling in the barracks by the bored, weather-imprisoned troops was accompanied by long bouts of drunkenness by equally jaded officers.

Noncommissioned officers pulled rank to have their bunks moved close to the squadroom stoves, causing disgruntled privates to occupy the draftier areas near windows. The one advantage to winter as the army saw it was the large drop in the desertion rate. Not many soldiers, no matter how discontented, would risk their lives by attempting an escape from the military in weather that could freeze a man to death in a horribly short time.

Out in the open country, the Comanches, Pawnees, and Southern Cheyennes huddled in their lodges, the tribal warrior-hunters unable to venture outside for any great length of time. The Indians lived off the dried buffalo jerky taken during the previous summer. Now and then one of the tribes' many stray dogs was allowed to move into a lodge to enjoy a generous feed of scraps for a period of time. The grateful curs were unable to fathom the change from receiving kicks and angry shouts to good treatment and affection. The animals, showing their canine gratefulness with wagging tails, did not realize they were being fattened up to provide fresh meat. The usual end came from an unexpected blow across the dog's skull to end its short life. Then the women of the tepee skinned and butchered the animal, thus breaking the monotony of dried buffalo.

There wasn't much else to do in the lodges. The young children played with handmade toys, the old folks told legends of the tribe's mystic past, and warriors relived battles and dangerous hunts with long-winded descriptions. At night, the lusty younger men and their women spent long periods wrapped together in buffalo robes. This guaranteed many births nine months hence.

Winter did finally go away, but it wasn't until April of 1855, after the final cold blast caused ice to form on the thick buffalo grass. When those last crystal bubbles melted and dripped down to the deep, dark prairie dirt, balmy breezes began to play across the open country. Meadowlarks appeared in their mysterious way to sing and make their nests as other wildlife, long gone south, returned to the land in their annual migrations.

Indian warriors could now venture out, not to fight the white men or other tribes, but to track and make the first kill of buffalo. The tribes people hungered for fresh meat and the gamey taste of raw liver from the freshly slain bison. Dog meat was all right for a while, but when it came to real eating, only the buffalo would suffice.

Fort Leavenworth, too, had its own way of greeting the warmer weather. Now the sergeants and corporals moved their bunks back to the breezier areas of the barracks by the windows. Yet they weren't the only ones to take advantage of the gentler clime. Several soldiers, fed up with army life, deserted and headed east to the sanctuaries of their home states, where there would be no more howling prairie winters to confine them to the less-than-gentle discipline and routine of a frontier military station. Also, back home, there were no scalp-hunting hostiles waiting to end a soldier's life in a lightning-quick raid or cleverly laid ambush.

One member of the U.S. Army who also welcomed the spring weather was Lieutenant Gavin MacRoss of the dragoon regiment. He was a slim six-footer with sweeping blond sideburns and a well-trimmed moustache. The young officer, a bachelor in his late twenties, was a favorite of all the young ladies at both Fort Leavenworth and the nearby town where he constantly received invitations to soirees and other social events.

While enjoying feminine company, he was an officer who had willingly gone into military life in the wilds of the frontier. What he craved the most was excitement and plenty of activity.

Gavin had almost been driven crazy by the long months of confinement to quarters. He was anxious to get away from boring garrison duty and head out into the field. He knew well that when the Indians had filled their bellies with fresh meat and satisfied the gastric yearnings built up over the winter, they would soon turn to their usual warmaking and plundering.

People who were well-acquainted with Gavin MacRoss knew he was no ignorant rookie with an unrealistic attitude toward Indian fighting. He was a veteran of three years of warring against the plains tribes, and the warrior's heart was something he had in common with his adversaries.

But the military still thrived on routine, and it was Gavin's unhappy duty, assigned to him by his company commander, to see to it that his dragoon unit greeted the coming summer with a vigorous cleaning as the debris dumped on the post by wind, sleet, and snow was swept away. Damaged buildings needed repair, the horses had to be properly and fully exercised to be shaped up for the coming campaigns, new recruits arriving in levees from back east had to be trained, and there was always the monotonous, ever-demanding paperwork without which an army could not feed, clothe, or count its soldiers.

Gavin worked with his company's first sergeant in the orderly room that served as the administrative center of their unit. He was able to but occasionally glance through the windows at the wide-open wilderness that beckoned so longingly to him from the prairie to the west of the post. His only break from that wearisome chore came when it was his turn to serve as officer of the day for twenty-four hours and take command of the post guard.

The evening's guard mount was an established, formal ceremony that included the regimental band's performance. The affair was quite a magnificent sight and always attracted an audience of soldiers as well as civilians from town. Everyone liked the music and the sight of the blue-and-yellow uniforms of the soldiers as they went through the ritual of relieving the old guard and posting the new.

After the pomp was done and everyone had drifted away to other evening pastimes, Gavin, the sergeants and corporals of the guard, and the sentries settled in for the chore of guarding the post. The long night dragged by with a couple of inspections of posts, and Gavin then had breakfast with his company commander and his wife. They were Captain and Mrs. Francis Hanover, a middle-aged couple whose children had moved away to live their own lives. They looked upon Gavin somewhat as a son and saw to it that he was given the opportunity to enjoy a good meal now and then.

After a good feed of potatoes and eggs with the Hanovers, Gavin returned to the guardhouse to sit out the rest of his shift. He had just begun to doze off with a fresh newspaper only a couple of months old, when a call from Post Number One at the front gate was passed from sentry to sentry back to the guardhouse.

"Corporal of the Guard! Post Number One!"

The corporal on duty, a tough old soldier named Steeple, started to respond, but Gavin interrupted him.

"Finish your coffee, Corporal," he said. "I'll see to this."

"I thank the lieutenant," Steeple said gratefully.

"If I sit around much longer, I'll start gathering dust anyhow," Gavin said. He hooked his saber into place on his belt and set his cap on his head, walking from the building across the parade ground to where the sentry on duty at the gate waited. He took the man's salute, asking, "Now who's calling on us, soldier?"

"It's a small wagon train out there, sir," the guard explained.

"The first of the season," Gavin said, happy at this further break in the routine. He opened the door in the large gate and stepped through. A wagon train of a dozen vehicles stood in an orderly row with a man sitting on the seat of each one. Women, all wearing kerchiefs on their heads, and a lot of kids were riding the wagons as well. Every one of them was dressed rather strangely. At least, their attire was not in a fashion familiar to Gavin MacRoss.

"Where's the wagon captain?" Gavin asked loudly.

A large, older man with a thick gray beard stepped forward, holding out his hand. "The leader of this group, that is me," he said in a thick accent. "I am Vladimir Aleksandrovich Valenko. Most pleased to be meetink vith you, I am sure."

"How do you do, sir," Gavin said. "I am Lieutenant MacRoss of the U.S. Dragoons." He looked at the well-made wagons, impressed by their sturdiness. "Your group is the first to arrive here at Fort Leavenworth."

"Ha!" Valenko said with a loud laugh. "Is because ve Russians do not be bother vith the cold. Ewerybody else on the trail, they vaitink for the varm veather, but to us it already wery varm."

Gavin was slightly nonplussed with the man's mixture of "v" 's and "w" 's. "So, you are from Russia? Would that be all of you?"

"Each and ewery one," Valenko said.

Gavin began walking down the line of wagons, taking a close look at both the vehicles and their occupants. Most seemed humble sorts, who removed their hats and bowed to him. When he reached one wagon, the young woman on the seat caused him to stop and stare.

She was a beautiful honey blonde in her late teens. Her bright blue eyes were cast down in a properly shy way, but she did steal a glance at the young officer every moment or so.

"Is my daughter Natalia," Valenko said. He indicated Gavin. "Is army lieutenant by name of—forgiff, please. I am forgettink your name."

"MacRoss," Gavin said with a smile. "Lieutenant Gavin MacRoss at your service, Miss—" He laughed. "Now I forgot *your* name."

"Valenko," the Russian said. "Our name is Valenko."

"How do you do, Lieutenant. I am most pleased to make your acquaintance," Natalia Valenko said in perfect English.

"She had tutor back in Russia," Valenko explained. "English fellow, very delicate and small. I think he like to read books better than do active thinks."

"I've heard of fellows like that," Gavin said, unable to keep from looking at Natalia as he fell in love with her.

Another Russian, this one a slim, morose-looking fellow with large, dark and sensitive eyes, came around the wagon. He stopped in front of Gavin. Unlike the others, he neither bowed nor doffed his cap.

Valenko said, "This is Basil Karshchov, my assistant. He is also the fiancé of my daughter Natalia."

Gavin's heart broke then and there. But he forced a smile and offered his hand. "How do you do?"

"I am pleased to be making your acquaintance," Karshchov said.

Gavin allowed himself one more delicious glance at Natalia; then he became official. "There is a campground you can use just to the north, Mister Valenko—"

Karshchov interrupted. "He is not a mister. He is Count Valenko, a nobleman."

"I see," Gavin said. "Well, I must remember that. I don't believe I've ever met a member of the nobility before."

"Of course," Valenko said.

"Well, Count, after you've settled in—"

Again Karshchov interjected. "He is addressed as Your Grace."

"Fine," Gavin said. "Your Grace. I would be pleased if you would come back to the fort and register with us. The army must keep records of immigrant groups passing through."

"I be back most qvick," Valenko promised.

He wasted no time in turning and shouting orders in Russian to his party. They all immediately reacted, preparing to move out as Valenko and Karshchov motioned them the direction in which they were to go.

Gavin returned to the guardhouse and dispatched Corporal Steeple to the gate to wait for Count Valenko. Then he walked toward post headquarters to arrange for the registration of the wagon train of Russians. On the way he met his company commander's wife, Mary Hanover.

"Our first immigrant train has arrived, Mary," Gavin said. "They're a bunch of Russians, and the head man is an honest-to-God count. Count Valenko, and you call him Your Grace. At least that's what one of his men told me."

"A member of the nobility!" Mary exclaimed. "Why, we've not had such elegant callers in all the time I've been out here with Francis."

"Well, you have one now," Gavin said. "Excuse me. I must hurry to headquarters so they can be properly registered." He continued on his way with fleet but wonderful images of Natalia Valenko dancing in his

12

mind. A quick notification to the sergeant major was all it took to get a proper desk and registration log set up.

"I never expected any of 'em so quick, sir," the sergeant major said. "I figgered the first of 'em would be showing up in a month or so."

"These fellows evidently don't worry much about cold weather," Gavin said. He checked his pocket watch. "The head men should be here soon."

They had less than a quarter of an hour to wait before Count Valenko and Basil Karshchov came through the front door with Corporal Steeple. The count was gracious as he answered the questions posed to him by the sergeant major. The information he gave was not so unusual for a wagon train.

"Is fourteen vagons ve got," the count answered the first question.

"How many adult males and their marital states, please, Your Grace?" the sergeant major asked. Gavin had already told him the proper way to address a count. Such things were of the utmost importance to sergeants major.

"Is tventy-fife men," Count Valenko said. "All marry, but not this man and me. I am vidover, but he engage to ved vith my daughter." He went on, anticipating the next questions. "And ve got tventy-two vifes and four young ladies and four young men too young to be marry. Then ve got thirty children altogether."

"Thank you, Your Grace," the sergeant major said. "What is your destination, please?"

"Ve got place out on prairie in Kansas Territory," Valenko said. He pulled some documents from a leather pouch he wore. "Is map vith the place marked. Also here is paper for your commander. Is special from my government."

Gavin noted the official document the man had pulled from his pouch. "Excuse me, please," he said,

13

taking it. He saw it bore a seal and the address of the Imperial Russian Embassy in Washington. "I will be pleased to present this to our post commander."

"I thank you, Lieutenant MacRoss," Valenko said. He laughed. "You see? Your name I remember."

Gavin nodded with a smile. He went to the adjutant and was given permission to speak directly to the post commander. This was Colonel William Benton, an old campaigner, who had been through just about everything a field-grade officer could experience—or so he thought. The letter set him back.

"Damn me, sir!" he exclaimed after wading through the pompous and lengthy wording. "Damn me, sir!" he repeated.

"Yes, sir?" Gavin said.

"This is a direct request that we grant military escort to this wagon train and all its people led by Count Vladimir Aleksandrovich Valenko out to the spot in the middle of the Kansas prairie where they have decided to establish themselves."

"Are we obligated to do that, sir?" Gavin asked.

"Since this request is countersigned by no less than Major General Winfield Scott, I would say we are more than obligated, Lieutenant. We are *ordered* to do so," the colonel said. "Damn me, sir!"

"Yes, sir," Gavin said.

"Adjutant!" the colonel hollered. "Adjutant! Come in here immediately!"

The post adjutant, a harried and nervous captain, presented himself expecting the worst. "What is wrong, sir?" he asked in a resigned tone.

"Wrong? Wrong?" the colonel exclaimed. "Damn me, sir! We must provide an escort of troops for those Russians out there."

The captain sighed. "Is that all, sir?"

"It's unusual as hell, by God!" the colonel exclaimed.

"I've never had a letter from the commanding general of the U.S. Army telling me to do something like this. Next thing, he'll be sending me notes about washing barracks windows. Damn me, sir, he will! At any rate, we must provide an escort."

"Yes, sir," the captain said. "Whom shall we send, Colonel?"

"We'll send—" He looked at Gavin. "Send him, by God! He's the closest. Put him on detached duty immediately and provide him with some troops."

"How many, sir?"

"A section," Colonel Benton said. "From his own company." He glared at Gavin. "What is your company, mister?"

"I am in Captain Hanover's A Company, sir," Gavin answered, knowing that his commander would be fit to be tied when he learned an entire section and lieutenant would be detached from him.

"See to it," the colonel said, shifting his eyes back to the adjutant. "Dismissed!"

The pair saluted and left the disturbed colonel. When they returned to the front office, they found Mrs. Mary Hanover and several other officers' wives hovering about the pair of Russians. When Mary saw Gavin, she hurried over to him.

"Oh, Gavin!" she exclaimed. "I have invited His Grace and Mister Karshchov to dine with Francis and me at our home. The count's daughter is attending as well. I hope you'll come."

Once more, Gavin thought of Natalia Valenko. "Yes, Mary," he replied. "I think I might be able to make it."

Chapter 2

Mrs. Mary Hanover, wife of Captain Francis Hanover, had scored a social coup because of the absence of the wife of Fort Leavenworth's commander.

Under those circumstances, since Mary was married to the post's senior captain, she had no other equals among the other officers' wives. The only lady outranking her was Mrs. Colonel Benton. But that august person was back visiting her family in Philadelphia, which meant that Mary was the senior lady of Fort Leavenworth.

It was a position from which she intended to milk every advantage and boon. Even though the situation was only temporary, it gave her the undeniable right to play hostess to Count Vladimir Aleksandrovich Valenko and his daughter Natalia. This she did, inviting them to dine with her and her husband in their quarters. Courtesy and custom, of course, required that she invite a few other people, but she kept the guest list down to the absolute minimum. Mary Hanover was not one to share the limelight.

But she did include Lieutenant Gavin MacRoss in her hastily printed invitations. She'd always had a maternal affection for the young officer who was a lieutenant in her husband's company, and an unmarried officer living in bachelor quarters. He filled the void in her life created when her own children had married and moved away.

The festivities began in the late afternoon with guard mount. The entire garrison, in dress blue uniforms, was drawn up, and the band played the appropriate music. The usual onlookers from the post itself, a few visitors from town, and some of the people from Count Valenko's wagon train attended the event. The latter, quiet and subservient in conduct, stood off to one side by themselves as the soldiers went through the ceremony.

Gavin, as the outgoing officer of the day, was at the center of the formation, exchanging information with the incoming officer in accordance with the ritual. Out of the corner of his eye, he could see Natalia Valenko watching as he went through the ceremony of being officially relieved from duty. Even knowing that the young woman's fiancé also watched did not keep Gavin from making particularly colorful and fancy flourishes with each sweep of his saber. He stomped his heels and paraded ramrod-straight, in perfect step with the martial music. Immediately, after marching off, he went to the party group and joined them.

Count Valenko had not bothered to dress up for the occasion, which disappointed Mary Hanover. Natalia, however, wore a very pretty dress that was obviously expensive. All the women standing nearby eyed her attire, marveling at the pattern and material.

The moment Gavin stepped up beside Francis and Mary Hanover, the count rushed over to greet him with an approving smile. "Is wery smart you are lookink," he said. "I know somethink of army ways. I have been in the serwice of the czar. I was subaltern in Nishnij-Novgorod Infantry Regiment. But not for too long was I there. My dear father died, and I vas made to return

17

home to take over estate. But you, Lieutenant MacRoss, are most—how is it said?" He looked at his daughter, asking, *"Kak boenya nazivayitsa?"*

Natalia Valenko smiled at Gavin. "My father says you are most military."

Gavin smiled and allowed himself a long glance at the girl. Then he looked back at the count. "Thank you, Your Grace. That is most flattering."

"But in Russia, ve march like this," the count said. He began parading around in an exaggerated goose step, swinging his arms. He burst into his old regiment's song, his voice booming over the sound of conversation. The crowd around him suddenly stopped talking to watch the old man's antics.

Valenko laughed. "I have too many years, and I am forgettink much."

"Not at all, Your Grace," Gavin said. "You look most soldierly."

"You are nice young man, Lieutenant," Valenko said.

Mrs. Hanover felt herself slipping away from the center of attention. She immediately beckoned to her guests and announced, "Come! Come, everybody! Let us retire to our quarters." She grabbed the count's arm and led him off. Basil Karshchov and Natalia followed with the other invited party-goers bringing up the rear. Gavin walked with Captain Francis Hanover, the both of them resigned to the fact that the company commander's wife would be dominating the entire evening.

The Hanovers lived in one of the better houses on officers row. Originally designed for commanders and staff of field-grade rank, the lack of majors on the post made it available to the Hanovers because of the captain's seniority earned with a dozen years in grade. They had a large parlor, a dining area, kitchen, and two bedrooms on the second floor of the frame structure.

A soldier orderly in a white jacket, the regular maid,

plus two more hired in the town of Leavenworth made up the party's serving staff. When the crowd of a dozen people entered the house, the soldier, a veteran dragoon trooper named Paddy O'Hearn, immediately began walking among the guests. He carried a tray from which he offered drinks to the party-goers.

The count looked at the filled glasses that were presented to him. "Is no wodka here?"

"Beg pardon, sir?" O'Hearn asked.

"The drinks, you don't got the wodka?" the count asked. "I don't vant Svedish wodka; I vant Russian wodka."

Natalia helped out. "My father would like to know if you have any Russian vodka available."

"Sure and I don't know what that is, miss," the soldier said with an apologetic smile. "What I got here is bourbon whiskey straight outta Kentucky. Although I do prefer the Irish product meself."

Natalia gently chided her father in Russian, telling him there was no vodka available, and that he should be gracious by drinking what was offered.

Count Valenko laughed. "Is good. I drink the American vhiskey!" He grabbed a full tumbler.

O'Hearn offered, "I have some water here to—"

The count downed the entire glass in two quick swallows. Then he grabbed another and quickly drained it. Then yet another. "That is good." He took a fourth and winked at the soldier. "You don't forget about me, eh? Come and see I don't get dry, eh?"

"Yes, sir, that I'll do," Paddy O'Hearn said, moving on to the other guests.

Gavin had edged off to one side of the room to wait for an opportunity to speak with the count. He timed it so that Natalia would be with him. The moment the young woman, at the side of Basil Karshchov, stood by her father, the officer walked up and presented himself.

"Your Grace, I am pleased to inform you that I will be in charge of the escort taking you out to your new settlement."

"Really?" the count said. "I think that is wery nice."

Basil Karshchov hadn't failed to note the quick glances Gavin had been casting in Natalia's direction. He spoke coldly, saying, "I hardly think it necessary."

"I ask for soldiers vith letter from the Imperial Embassy," Valenko informed his future son-in-law.

"But we Russian men are quite capable of protecting ourselves and our families," Karshchov argued. He glared at Gavin. "And our women."

Gavin nodded his agreement. "I'm certain you are, sir." He took a sip of his bourbon. "You speak excellent English, like Miss Valenko."

"I am a graduate of the university in Petrograd," Karshchov said. Then he added almost insolently, "Philosophy and languages."

"I see," Gavin said, feeling very unwelcome. "That is very interesting. Well, excuse me, please."

After that he was in no mood to join into any conversation with anyone else. Once more he withdrew from the crowd, going to a quiet corner to sit down. His company commander joined him, giving him a nudge in the ribs.

"You seem quite taken by that young Russian lady, Lieutenant," Hanover said.

"She is engaged to that fellow standing with her and the count," Gavin said.

"Ah! A lost cause, hey?" Captain Hanover said. "Will you be willing to settle for her friendship on a platonic level?"

"I think not, sir," Gavin said. "That wouldn't be a good idea, I'm afraid." In his mind he warned himself about trying to promote any familiarity with Natalia Valenko. Such conduct would only earn him embarrassment and rejection. "At any rate, I doubt if I'll see her again after this escort mission."

Following a carefully timed half hour of socializing, dinner was announced. Everyone trooped into the dining room, where they found cardboard name tags sitting on plates. This was another thing Mrs. Hanover had arranged. She knew a commissary sergeant who had beautiful handwriting. The man had done a skillful job of writing out the guests' names for the lady's party.

Everyone stood behind their chair. Mrs. Hanover, smiling, said, "I hope our fare is not too rustic for you, Your Grace. I must apologize for it, but you must remember we are far, far from civilization here."

"It is vonderful!" the count exclaimed. "And smells so delicious, too. Vhat have ve?"

"We shall begin with an onion and sage soup," Mrs. Hanover said. "The main course is broiled sirloin, garden vegetables, and brandied peaches. There is fresh bread from our post bakery, and for dessert we will enjoy apple pie. It is made from dried apples, I fear."

"I am certain it vill be a great meal!" the count said.

"Please, everyone, sit down," Mrs. Hanover invited.

The gentlemen seated the ladies, then settled in as the small squad of maids began serving the soup. The diners began breaking down into small conversations. That did not please Mary Hanover. She asked in a loud voice, "Tell me, Count Valenko, whatever prompted you to leave the czar's court and seek a place to live in the American wilderness?"

"Oh, my dear Mrs. Hanower, I vas not at court," Count Valenko said. "I vas at my estate to the north of Moskva." He took a sip of soup, then set the spoon down. It was obvious he had been asked to speak on a subject on which he loved to expound. "I am here because of my philosophy, Mrs. Hanower. It is my belief that man's salwation can come only through the simple life. Ve must all be peasants!"

"Oh, interesting!" Mrs. Hanover exclaimed. "Please enlighten us as to your beliefs, Your Grace."

As Count Valenko spoke, Private O'Hearn constantly kept his glass filled with bourbon. The others around the table marveled at how much the Russian could consume without showing the slightest effects of the strong liquor. O'Hearn, as an Irishman who could do himself proud in a saloon, was bound and determined to hit the man's limit and even go beyond. He kept pouring, and Valenko kept drinking and talking.

The count told of his days as a young lieutenant in the czar's army. He had been posted far to the south in the mountains of the Caucasus. Without much to do, he turned to reading books of all kinds. One writer in particular, by the name of Sergei Sakachov, caught his attention. The man, like Valenko, was of the nobility, yet he had discovered what he considered the true meaning of life by observing the serfs on his family's large estate. Gradually, he built a log cabin and lived among them, eating the same food they ate, sharing in their labors, and making love to every willing peasant girl he could find. Sakachov claimed that he had truly reached the zenith of man's existence through adopting this simple, rustic life in which all complications, other than sickness and death, were cast aside. Rolling in the hay with fleshy peasant girls not only pleased the physical senses, it turned up the inner spirituality of a man as well.

The count's loud and candid remarks on the sexual activity caused the ladies to blush and the men to grin at each other.

Valenko went on, telling of how his military career had been cut short by the death of his father. He returned to his own family's extensive properties to administer the rather large operation. It was a difficult and demanding life, filled with countless irritations and attention to detail. He married, had a daughter, and was widowed as the years dragged on in an existence he learned to hate.

On one particularly difficult occasion in dealing with the selling of the season's grain harvest, Valenko suddenly remembered the book he had read by Sakachov. He went to his old army things and searched it out. It took an entire evening and all night to once more consume the rambling but strong message the writer had placed in the pages of the tome.

The next day was spent in deep thought and reflection. That evening, Valenko reached a momentous decision. He sent for his younger brother to take over the estate. It took several months to make a permanent turnover. Meanwhile, Valenko made arrangements to have his daughter Natalia stay at the main mansion and continue her education with her English tutor.

Count Vladimir Aleksandrovich Valenko was about to change his life completely around. The first step was to have a log cabin built out where the serfs lived and worked. It was a majestic structure in comparison to the huts the peasants called homes, but it was simple and strictly functional with no extra decoration or luxury. Large and bare with a sleeping loft on one side, it was furnished with simple tables and chairs, a couple of cupboards, and a fireplace that served for both heating and cooking. The count even tended to his own needs, including sewing torn clothing, preparation of food, and keeping his cabin clean.

The peasants, at first, were leery of the landowner who suddenly moved in to live with them. But gradually, as he joined in their labors, they accepted him. He attended festivals, weddings, and other social events the simple people had. Like the writer, he began to bring lusty peasant wenches up into his sleeping loft, settling in between their plump thighs and rooting away inside their muscular bodies, working the girls and himself into sweaty spasms of pleasure on even the coldest nights.

But he found the long winter darkness that lasted twenty out of the day's twenty-four hours a source of irritation. After all, he could only make love so many times to pass away the endless evenings. Finally, sitting at the table in front of his fireplace, he began to write his own book. He told of reading Sergei Sakachov's works and bringing the subject matter into his own life. He scribbled away for three years before the manuscript was complete. When finished, Valenko sent it to a friend of his in the publishing business in Moscow.

Several months passed before a reply was sent. His friend informed him that the work held no commercial value, but it might be read within the world of academia. The man suggested that Valenko have it published at his own expense, and it could be distributed in various university bookshops where it could attract at least a bit of attention.

One of the readers who first got hold of the work was a young university professor by the name of Basil Karshchov. This impoverished intellectual was a temperamental, sensitive man who taught a couple of classes on philosophy. He was very taken in by Count Valenko's own outlook and experiences. Karshchov wrote to the nobleman and received a reply. This began a year's correspondence that ended with the professor leaving his teaching post and moving in to join Count Valenko in his cabin.

They followed their shared doctrine as Karshchov became a devoted disciple. Hours of discussion that included long binges of wenching and vodka guzzling dominated their lives. They reached the conclusion that Russia was a bad place in which to live the pure life. After all, the presence of the czar and other trappings of civilization were constantly about. It was then that they hit upon the idea of going to the wilderness of America to establish their own self-sufficient farming community that would evolve into a utopia. Getting the people to populate the place was no problem. The serfs on the estate belonged to Valenko by law. He would pick out a few families to bring along with them. The estate held plenty of money to pay for the venture, and there would still be enough left for his brother to carry on the family operation.

Preparations began immediately. Count Valenko's nineteen-year-old daughter was brought into the program. Karshchov had already fallen in love with her. When it came time to leave, he broached the question of her marrying him. Valenko quickly agreed, thinking it wonderful that his right-hand man would be the father of his grandchildren.

The serf families chosen for the venture were called together. When it was announced they would be leaving their homeland forever and would never return, they remained impassive and obedient. After all, these were people who were required to give up at least one son per family for thirty-years' service in the czar's army. Being illiterate, they could not correspond with their soldier boy. Unless he came home or another returning to the village had news of a battlefield death or the loss of life through accident or illness, they might never know his fate.

Supplies were purchased as a lively correspondence with the Imperial Embassy in the United States was begun. Because of the practicality, all wagons, animals, tools, and equipment would be purchased in America. On the appointed day in late spring, the entire group headed out for the Baltic Sea to catch the sailing ship for the land where they would establish their colony.

Count Valenko finished his story—expounding his own sexual prowess with willing, passionate serf women—and tossed off another glass of bourbon.

"Fascinating!" Captain Francis Hanover exclaimed despite a frown from his wife. "So you are going to establish a community out on the Kansas prairie?"

"Oh, yes. That ve vill do," Valenko said.

"Is this to be a religious settlement?" Mary Hanover inquired.

"No," Valenko replied. "It is purely for personal philosophy. My people vill build church or not build church as it pleased them."

"Do you have a name for your new town?" the lady asked.

"Ve goink to call our new home Nadezhda," Valenko said. "Is Russian word." He let O'Hearn fill up his glass again.

"What in the world does that word mean?" Mrs. Hanover asked.

Natalia answered, saying, "In English, Nadezhda means Hope."

Chapter 3

The double rank of dragoons stood at ease in front of Sergeant Ian Douglas. Each man was armed with a Sharps percussion carbine, a saber, and a Colt .36 caliber revolver. The latter was a special issue, only given out prior to going to the field. In addition to the weaponry, the men also had haversacks, saddlebags, and blanket rolls. This equipment sat on the ground beside each trooper. The field gear gave undeniable evidence that duty outside the garrison was in the immediate offing for them.

A pair of corporals, by the name of Steeple and Murphy, stood at the right of each rank. This was the proper position for these junior noncommissioned officers because the five privates beside each made up their squads. Both squads formed the section commanded by Sergeant Douglas in Captain Francis Hanover's dragoon company.

It was early morning, and the coolness of the night held on as the men waited patiently for the military protocol to begin. Douglas pulled the handwritten roster from his pocket and slipped on a pair of magnifying spectacles. He quickly glanced up to see if any of the dragoons were grinning at his poor eyesight. The sergeant was very sensitive about having to use the glasses.

The faulty vision that plagued him had been brought on by the passing of time. Douglas was in his late forties, but looked much older after twenty-three years of hard frontier army service.

"Corp'ral Murphy!" Douglas yelled out.

"Here, Sergeant!"

"Corp'ral Steeple!"

"Here, Sergeant!"

"Anderson!"

"Here, Sergeant!"

He went on down the list calling out the names of privates Belken and Carlson.

"Costello!"

"Yeah, Sarge."

Douglas slowly pulled off his glasses and glared at the dragoon. "What was that you said?"

"I said I was here, Sergeant," Costello said. He was a small, slow-witted man with a decidedly unpleasant appearance caused by a ferretlike homely face.

"No you didn't, Costello," Douglas retorted. "You said 'Yeah, Sarge.' "

"I don't remember," Costello said truthfully.

"You said it not more'n fifteen seconds ago," Douglas pointed out.

Costello shrugged. "I don't know what I said, I guess. That's why I don't remember."

"Well, you'll remember when we get back and you pull ten days extra duty," Douglas said. He replaced his glasses and went on calling out Evans, Fenlay, and O'Hearn.

"McRyan!"

"Yeah, Sarge." Private Jack McRyan was an insolent braggadocio whose face seemed to have assumed a permanent smirk. Small and very thin, he was Costello's mental opposite. McRyan displayed a gap-toothed grin as he returned the noncommissioned officer's stare. He

28

and Dennis Costello palled around together in a manner of speaking. Actually, Costello followed McRyan's lead, which generally meant trouble for the both of them.

"So you're in love with Costello, are you?" Sergeant Douglas asked.

"I ain't thought about it," McRyan said with his usual smirk. "How's come you ask?"

"Well, now, I figgered you loved him if you wanted to share them ten days of extra duty with him," Douglas said. "Which is what you're gonna do."

McRyan looked over at Costello and blew him a kiss. The other dragoons laughed.

"That's thirty days, you son of a bitch!" Douglas growled. "Want to try for more?"

"No, Sergeant," McRyan said, knowing he had gone far enough with the angry noncommissioned officer.

Douglas went back to the roster, finishing up with Rodgers and Walker. He slipped the paper back into his pocket and replaced the spectacles in their case, putting it in with the list of the soldiers' names.

"You all know we'll be escorting the wagon train of Russians out to its destination about sixty miles from here. We shouldn't be gone more'n a couple of weeks," Douglas explained. "I'm sure most of you are as glad at this chance to stretch your legs as I am after that godawful winter in garrison. Lieutenant MacRoss will be in command. He's waiting for us over at the stables." He looked at the corporals. "Have your squads gotten their full issue of rations, equipment, and ammunition?"

"Yes, Sergeant!" they answered in unison.

"And weapons," Corporal Steeple quickly added.

"Any man jack short o' anything is gonna be a miserable bastard out there on that prairie," the sergeant warned. Then, without waiting for further comment, he took a deep breath, bellowing, "Section, atten-*hut!* Right face! Sling arms! Secure your gear! For'd, *ho!*"

The section marched out of the company's cantonment area and crossed the parade ground, heading toward the post stables. Of the thirteen soldiers, six were professionals. Each career man was a veteran of long service with the exception of Paddy O'Hearn, who was halfway into his second five-year hitch. The remaining members of the squads each had less than two years of service, and most of them could not be counted on to reenlist. But that was the least of the army's problems with them. Many, if given the chance, would desert at the first opportunity.

A couple were simple, trusting lads who were serving the colors because of sweet talk from lying recruiting sergeants who painted a picture of army life featuring fancy uniforms, easy duty, good pay, and plenty of admiring girls. Others, like McRyan and Costello, had been given the prescribed choice of army or jail by judges.

Sergeant Douglas marched them around to the rear of the stables and took them to the portion used by their company. He halted them in front of Lieutenant Gavin MacRoss. Gavin strode up to the front of the formation of dragoons and took the sergeant's salute.

"Sir," Douglas said. "First section all present'n accounted for."

"Thank you, Sergeant," Gavin said. "I see they are ready for the field."

"Yes, sir," Douglas reported.

"I'll speak to the men," Gavin said. This brought another exchange of salutes, and the young lieutenant then addressed the assembled soldiers. "This is the season's first foray out into the field," he told them. "It may not be an especially exciting one, but I promise you'll enjoy this chance to get away from Fort Leavenworth, if only for a couple of weeks. It will also be an excellent chance for you new men to get your first glance at this wild prairie country of Kansas Territory. We also have a secondary assignment of mapping the area between here and the new settlement. Do you have any questions?"

"What's the chances of meeting up with some Indians, sir?" Private Carlson asked. He was a farm boy from New Hampshire who showed the potential for developing into a fine soldier. "If we do, d'ye think we might have a battle with 'em?"

"We'll be alert, but I don't think we'll have any trouble in a group this big," MacRoss said. He liked to have troops eager for some action, even if they were ignorant of what they were wishing for. "But that doesn't mean we can relax. Keep your eyes peeled for hostiles."

"Yes, sir!" Carlson answered enthusiastically.

Gavin turned to his second in command. "Sergeant Douglas, get the men mounted up and ready to move out."

The sergeant immediately put the order into motion. The men were able to quickly saddle and bridle their horses as well as correctly strap on the saddlebags and blanket rolls along with the other gear. Although the winter had been confining, many hours had been spent in the stables practicing the proper manner of preparing the horses to go into the field. The men, rookies included, were very efficient. Most of that expertise had been developed under Sergeant Douglas's angry shouts and from the toes of his boots.

In less than a quarter of an hour, the small column with Gavin MacRoss at the head cantered through the main gate and turned toward the campground where the Russian immigrant train awaited them.

As they rode up, the troopers noticed the puzzled expressions on the settlers' faces. Finally, Count Valenko's voice boomed out, "Oh, is you, Lieutenant! Ve did not recognize you as soldiers!" He looked closely at them. "Vhere is your uniforms, eh?"

Gavin laughed. He didn't realize that the customary field dress used by the U. S. Army on the frontier would hardly qualify as military attire by foreigners.

"We are very practical," he said. "Buckskin clothing, civilian hats, and kerchiefs are very handy items to wear. I'm afraid our usual uniforms wouldn't stand up much in the field."

Valenko shrugged. "Only military thinks I am seeink is your carbines, sabers, and boots. Maybe your horse saddles and all that, too. Othervise, you are lookink like bandits."

"I'm afraid you are right, Your Grace," Gavin said. He dismounted and pulled a rolled-up document from the top of his gauntlet. "I've taken the liberty to work out the best route. I suggest we head south for the Kansas River and follow it to where it meets with the Republican. If we turn to the northwest at that point, we are but a short distance from where you plan to settle in."

"Thank you much for your kind adwice," the count said. "I am sure you know vhat is best way to trawel."

Gavin glanced at the wagons. "You seem to be ready to go."

"Yes. We leaf now, *nyet?*"

"As you wish," Gavin said. He turned and gestured to Sergeant Douglas. "Put out a couple of scouts, flankers, and a rear guard. Then have the remainder of the men split on each side of the wagon train."

"Yes, sir!"

"Make sure there're a couple of the experienced men out on the point and tell them to head for the junction of the Republican and the Kansas," Gavin added.

"I'll see to it, sir," Douglas said. "That'd be the job

32

for O'Hearn and Fenlay." He rode back to where the soldiers waited to make the assignments.

Count Valenko strode rapidly toward his wagon at the front of the train, shouting in Russian and gesturing in excitement at his people. They responded immediately, jumping up on their vehicles to await the order to move out.

Gavin rode to a position beside the count's wagon where he could stick close. As he reined up, he noticed a rather stout, blond woman sitting on the wagon seat beside the nobleman. She was young and wide-faced with plain features and a pair of large breasts pushing against her peasant blouse. She sat on the wagon seat in a mannish, bold manner with her knees apart under her skirt. The girl's large hands held on to the reins in a way that showed she knew how to handle the team of oxen.

Valenko noted Gavin looking at the girl. He winked at the American lieutenant. "Is named Irena. Big chest, big butt, got thighs like tree trunks. So good for to roll in blankets vith. Keep a man varm on vinter night vith much rumpty-dump! Ha! Ha!"

Gavin's face reddened, but he smiled and tipped his hat. "How do you do, Miss Irena."

She grinned and replied, *"Kak dela?"*

Valenko stood up on the seat and looked back at the train over the canvas top of his wagon. *"Moi narod! Myeri kodi,"* he bellowed, then sat down and grabbed his whip, cracking it over the two teams of oxen that pulled the large vehicle. Irena snapped the reins, and they were in motion.

Gavin took the hint and shouted out, "For'd, *yo!*"

Immediately, settlers and soldiers alike began to move, following privates O'Hearn and Fenlay as they eased in the direction where the two rivers came together far out on the plains of the wild and unsettled Kansas Territory.

Gavin and the count chatted as they traveled along. Whenever he got the chance, Gavin would pull away and ride down one side of the fourteen-wagon caravan and up the other, seemingly to check things out and keep an eye on his soldiers. But he always slowed a bit when he reached the wagon where Basil Karshchov and Natalia Valenko rode. He enjoyed seeing her pretty smile until the realization that she and Karshchov slept together finally dawned on him. At that point, the young lieutenant ceased his inspections and stayed at the front where Valenko led the way, seated beside his peasant wench.

The day was warm, even approaching hot, and the wagon wheels stirred up the first insects of the season. Though not numerous, nor particularly irritating, the flying bugs still created a minor nuisance as the people swatted at them. The morning passed with little incident, as the low, hilly country was easily traversed through the expert scouting and trail blazing of O'Hearn and Fenlay, who made sure only the easiest portion of terrain was utilized.

A short midday break was held when the sun was directly overhead. As the Russians settled down for a quick meal, Sergeant Douglas set out some guards a short distance from the wagon train.

Gavin ate with Valenko and the girl Irena. She quickly whipped up some soup with hot water, vegetables and dried meat. Valenko, lounging against a wagon wheel, pointed to where one of the soldiers stood gazing out onto the empty prairie.

"Is Indians out there?" he asked.

"Could be," Gavin said. "We don't want to take any chances. They had a hard winter, so I doubt if any war parties are about looking for mischief. But some Cheyenne or Pawnee hunters might be tempted to raid us if they catch sight of the wagons and try to sneak in."

"I look around all morning and I see nothink of Indians," Valenko said with a shrug.

"You never see them until too late," Gavin remarked.

"Bah! Are sawages!" Valenko said.

"We are in their country, where they are the experts on everything," Gavin pointed out. "And that includes fighting."

Karshchov and Natalia Valenko joined them for the meal. Gavin was polite, but had decided to remain distant from the young woman. He replied to a couple of her questions in short words, making no attempt to be particularly pleasant. Thinking of her wrapped up in blankets with another man galled him, though he tried to tell himself it was absolutely none of his business. No matter how hard he tried, however, he couldn't make light of the situation.

Natalia sensed the coldness and turned her conversation to her father and fiancé. She also seemed to be quite friendly with Irena, obviously not disturbed by the fact that the peasant girl was carnally involved with the count.

The break from traveling only lasted a bit more than a half hour. By that time the travelers and soldiers had eaten and were ready to move on. Valenko's bellowing in Russian and Sergeant Douglas's shouted orders got the group on the move again.

They rolled on into the afternoon, now moving into flatter country as they eased south toward the river junctions. The Kansas sky was stretched wide from horizon to horizon, emphasizing the stark flatness of the prairie country. A couple of hours after the midday halt, Gavin gave a signal and brought the wagon train to a stop.

"Sergeant Douglas!"

The noncommissioned officer rode up and reported in with a salute. It seemed an unnatural gesture due to the lack of military attire.

"I want a reconnaissance made in all directions," Gavin said. "Once more we must use only the experienced men."

"I take it you want a look-see for Indian sign, sir," Douglas remarked.

"Exactly," Gavin said. "We stand out here like a fly on a white table cloth. I don't want any hostiles approaching us through the buffalo grass."

"I'll tend to it, sir," Douglas said.

Gavin rode over to Valenko's wagon while two scouting parties were organized. He nodded to the count. "We'll hold up here for an hour or so, Your Grace. I'm sending a couple of small patrols out."

"But vhy?" Valenko demanded to know.

"We'll all feel better if we know about any Indian activity around here," Gavin said.

Valenko's temper snapped. "Is crazy! Ve never get to Nadezhda if ve all time make the stop!"

"Count Valenko," Gavin said. "I have been detailed as your escort. I'll conduct that duty in the best possible manner to guarantee that you, indeed, will arrive at your destination."

Valenko snorted. "Maybe I go vithout you, Lieutenant."

"In that case, I would be forced to put you under arrest and return to Fort Leavenworth," Gavin said.

Valenko stood up in the wagon and roared, "I am Count Vladimir Aleksandrovich Valenko! I demand ve proceed in the name of czar!"

"With all due respect, Your Grace," Gavin said patiently. "The name of the czar doesn't get you much out here."

Valenko started to crack his whip over his oxen, but something about the young American officer's expression caused him to pause. "Now ve vait," he growled. "But ve talk of this later I am thinkink."

"I shall be most happy to, Your Grace," Gavin said. "Excuse me, I have to see to my men."

The lieutenant rode off, leaving the fuming Russian nobleman fidgeting on his wagon seat. Irena watched the handsome young officer ride off. She noted Valenko's anger and giggled.

"Molyeaie!" the count snapped at her.

Irena shut up, but turned away still smiling. It seemed this American adventure was going to be more interesting than she had imagined.

Chapter 4

Irena Yakubovski walked toward the creek carrying two wooden buckets to fill with water. The containers were large-sized, and the amount of water they could hold would tax the strength of most men. But Irena had no doubt she could carry the double load as she walked in the steady, almost swinging gait common to large young women.

Irena was nineteen years old, and her presence in the world was the result of countless generations of sturdy Russian serfs reproducing themselves into an environment of drudgery and hardships. She, like her ancestors, took life's hard knocks in stride, enduring the pain, the toil, and the grief with the belief that the hereafter would offer an eternity of reward for bearing such suffering.

Her round face, ringed by pale blond hair, was set above a sturdy neck that bespoke of the muscles in her shoulders. A bit dull-eyed, Irena was the type of woman who could give birth to a child, then, within a couple of hours of delivering, be back in the fields swinging a scythe at the thick, heavy wheat of the Russian steppes.

It was Irena and her people who were the backbone of the czar's peasant economy. They did the hard labor, provided the soldiers, and kept their rulers' country populated. In their serf society, it was not considered particularly bad for her to be bedding down with Count Valenko. In a way it was a bit of a compliment, though her father complained about it to his friends as a matter of keeping face. But they, like he, knew there was nothing that could be done about it. After all, since they were serfs, he owned them. They were part of the estate he had inherited when the elder count passed away. He, or any other nobleman who owned property and serfs, could claim any woman in his domain for his pleasure whether she liked it or not. It was not unknown for peasants to be trained as musicians or even acrobats and actors, in order that their master could provide entertainment for visiting friends.

At least Irena was pleased with the arrangement and would stay with the old man until he died or sent her away. Then she would settle down with some peasant lad and begin birthing yearly.

Now, after walking a ways from where the wagons were situated for the night, Irena went through some brush to the edge of the creek. She pulled up her skirt between her legs and secured it to the waistband around her middle. After kicking off her sandals, she waded out into the creek and submerged both buckets in the water.

It was late evening, and the setting sun had begun to redden the prairie prior to darkness. In a way, the place reminded her of Russia, except the mosquitos were not quite so bothersome. When the buckets were filled, she waded back to the bank, effortlessly holding on to the heavy containers. As she stepped back up onto the dry land, Irena was startled to see two soldiers watching her.

Jack McRyan and Dennis Costello gave her bold looks. Jack nudged his pal, saying, "Now, I'd like a taste o' that big ol' gal, wouldn't you, Dennis?"

Costello, his eyes half-closed and bloodshot, gazed at the Russian girl who was larger than they. He licked his lips. "That's all woman," he said under his breath. "Look at them legs."

"It'd be nice to have 'em locked around your middle, wouldn't it?" McRyan asked.

"I'll say!" Costello exclaimed.

Irena could smell the liquor on their breaths and knew they were both drunk. She scowled at them and said, *"Prastityi."*

"You speak English, girl?" McRyan asked with a leer. "How's about we roll in the grass here, huh? You give us two soldier boys a good time, huh?"

"Maybe she'll do it for some money, Jack," Costello suggested.

"Yeah!" McRyan said. He grinned. "Hey, I got a bunch o' them cigar coupons when I bought a box o' stogies in town a while back. This dumb bitch won't know the differ'nce 'tween them and real money." He pulled the near-worthless pieces of paper from his pocket and waved them in her face. "We'll pay you real good for a poke. How's that, big gal?"

Irena didn't understand the words, but she could read the meaning in the tone of their voices. She stepped around the two dragoons to continue on her way back to the wagon.

McRyan grabbed her from behind, pulling the girl in close to his own body. "How 'bout it, sweetie? Wanta give ol' Jack a little bit?"

Irena dropped the buckets and grabbed McRyan's hands, easily pulling them away from their grasp around her middle. She spun around and hit him square on the nose, throwing every ounce of strength she could muster in her one-hundred-and-sixty-pound body.

"Ow!" McRyan yelled. He stumbled backward, grabbing at his smashed organ, feeling the warm blood pour down past his mouth and onto his chin.

"Hey, you Russian bitch!" Costello snarled. He swung a fist at her, but missed.

Irena grabbed the small, thin man and hoisted him up, then threw him into the creek. With flailing arms and legs, Costello went into the waist-deep water with a holler and a splash. He struggled to his feet, sputtering in surprise.

The sound of people crashing through the brush startled Irena. She turned to see Basil Karshchov and a couple of other Russians along with two other soldiers suddenly appear.

Sergeant Douglas looked at McRyan's bloody face and the ludicrous sight of Costello wading out of the creek fully clothed and soaking wet.

"What the hell goes on here, then?" the sergeant angrily asked.

"We just asked this gal if'n we could help her with them buckets, and she hit us with 'em," McRyan said. "I reckon she didn't understand what we meant."

Karshchov and Irena spoke to each other in quick, urgent tones. Then the Russian said to Douglas. "This girl tells me those two grabbed her."

"That's what I figgered," Douglas said. "Costello, come over here and fall in beside McRyan." He looked at Karschchov. "I'll take care o' this, sir."

"Thank you," Karshchov said.

"I'm sure the lieutenant will want to talk to the count when it's convenient," Douglas said.

"I shall see His Grace at the first opportunity," Karshchov said.

Irena again hoisted her skirt and went back to refill the buckets. After leaving the water, she slipped into her sandals and followed Basil Karshchov through the brush toward the wagon train.

"Now you two are in for it," Douglas said to the two

41

dragoons. He sniffed at them. "And you've been drinking, too."

"Aw, c'mon, Sergeant, the bitch led us on," McRyan said. "Didn't you see how she lifted that skirt and showed her legs off."

"Shut up! You may end up with attempted rape charges against you" Douglas snapped. "Right face, for'd *ho!*"

The sergeant marched the two men up from the creek bank and around the wagons toward the dragoons' bivouac area. Lieutenant Gavin MacRoss had ordered Valenko to encircle the vehicles for protection against Indian attack. He and his soldiers would stay outside, keeping watch in teams when it got dark.

Gavin, enjoying an early evening cup of coffee, looked up when he saw the three approaching where he was relaxing next to the campfire. When he noted McRyan's bloody nose and the fact that Costello's uniform was dripping wet, he got to his feet to receive the report.

Sergeant Douglas quickly explained what had happened, summing up the report by saying, "The victim busted McRyan's beak and flung Costello in the creek."

Gavin's temper snapped, and it was all he could do to refrain from punching and kicking the two soldiers. "Was the girl hurt at all?" he asked Douglas.

"No, sir," the sergeant replied. He grinned. "She whipped 'em good, sir."

Gavin glared at McRyan and Costello. "How long have you two been in the army?"

"A few months," McRyan said.

"You'll use the word 'sir' when you speak to the lieutenant," Douglas growled, slapping the side of McRyan's face.

"A few months, sir," McRyan repeated.

"I don't believe either one of you has been in the field before, have you?" Gavin asked.

"No, sir," Dennis Costello mumbled. "We just got outta recruit training in the middle o' winter." Then he quickly added, "Sir."

"I could make this a very serious issue," Gavin said. "But since the girl seems to have come out of it victorious in dealing with you two ferocious soldiers, I'll not bring any charges that could lead to a general court-martial. Also, from the smell of you, I'd say you've been drinking. That is true, is it not?"

"Yes, sir," McRyan said. "But we ain't drunk, sir."

"No," Gavin agreed. "But you've still been imbibing while in the field." He was thoughtful for a few moments. "I'm going to turn this over to Sergeant Douglas and let him handle the situation. But let me warn you. One more slip and you two are going to be facing a damned good and long term at hard labor in the guard house. Do you understand?"

"Yes, sir," the pair said in unison.

"Take over, Sergeant," Gavin said.

"Yes, sir," Douglas replied. He saluted, then turned toward the dragoons, snapping his fingers at Corporal Murphy. "Take a look in these son of a bitches' gear and search out the liquor."

"You bet, Sergeant!" Murphy said brightly.

"When you find the rotgut, pour it out on the ground, goddamn it!" Douglas growled.

"Yes, Sergeant," Murphy said in a more subdued tone.

Douglas turned his attention to the other dragoons, who stood grinning at McRyan and Costello. "Corporal Steeple and Private O'Hearn. Grab the ropes off McRyan's and Costello's saddles and join this formation!"

Then he marched the malfeasant duo toward the

43

nearby woods that bordered the creek. The sergeant took the men into the trees just far enough to be out of sight of the camp. "Halt!"

Corporal Steeple and O'Hearn stepped aside to see what Douglas would want of them. Whatever it was, they knew it wouldn't be to the liking of either McRyan or Costello.

Douglas was a compactly built man, heavy-shouldered, and quick. It took but a fleeting instant for him to slam one fist into Costello's face, then pivot slightly and smash a wicked backhand blow onto McRyan's already damaged nose. Both men were slammed to the dirt.

"The lieutenant was too damned easy on you," Douglas said. "I'd have you flogged 'til your backs were cut up into ribbons. But army regulations don't give me that much authority."

McRyan wiped at the blood now flowing once again from his nose. He snuffed and scowled while Costello rolled over on his hands and knees.

Corporal Steeple fingered the rope he held. "What're we gonna do with 'em, Sergeant?"

"Throw them ropes over that tree limb there, then secure 'em to their wrists and pull 'em up 'til their toes is just barely touching the ground," Sergeant Douglas said.

Steeple and O'Hearn went to work. Within moments, McRyan and Costello were hanging by their wrists while the tips of their boots hardly reached the ground. Both were moaning in discomfort within short moments.

"How long're you gonna leave 'em here?" O'Hearn asked.

"Four hours," Douglas said.

"Jesus Almighty!" Steeple said. "Four hours?"

"Not a minute less," Douglas said. "If the Pawnees come calling between now and then, they'll find these two son of a bitches waiting for 'em."

44

The three returned to camp, leaving McRyan and Costello writhing at the ends of the ropes, the feelings in their hands already gone while deep within their shoulder joints a burning pain began to increase with each passing minute.

While Douglas was seeing to the punishment of the two misfits, Gavin MacRoss walked into the Russians' circle of wagons to visit with Valenko. He found the count noisily consuming a bowl of soup that Irena had just served him.

"Good evening," Gavin said. "I've come to see how Miss Irena is doing."

Irena, hearing her name, guessed why the American officer had come calling. She smiled a greeting at him and gestured to the soup.

"No thank you," Gavin said, shaking his head. "I've already eaten."

Valenko translated for the girl, then looked at Gavin. "Irena is fine. I think maybe she hurt the two soldiers, eh?"

Gavin smiled. "She got the best of them alright. But I would like to apologize for my men's conduct. I am very embarrassed."

"I am tellink you before, I vas lieutenant like you in Russian army," Valenko said with a shrug. "Best men not soldiers, eh? Sometimes, they bad. Don't have the vorry. Irena is not hurt; she not even scared."

"I am very happy for that," Gavin said.

Valenko finished off the soup and broke off a hunk of bread. "If the soldiers rape her, she not hurt. Is no wirgin. Strong girl. Could take many men if she vanted."

Gavin didn't appreciate Valenko's cavalier attitude,

but he kept his feelings to himself. "Tell her I am sorry about the incident, please."

Valenko laughed. "Vhy?"

"Because it is important to me," Gavin said.

Valenko shrugged and glanced up at the peasant girl. He spoke to her in Russian, pointing to Gavin.

Irena walked over and smiled. She took a deep breath, hesitated, then said in halting English. "Thank—you."

"You are most welcome, miss," Gavin said.

"Ha!" Valenko laughed. "You make this peasant girl think she is czarina. Ha!"

"That would be fine with me," Gavin said. He doffed his hat and bowed to her. "I wish you a good evening."

Gavin left the pair and walked across the perimeter between the wagons. It was dark, the light of the numerous fires offering a flickering illumination of the scene. In spite of himself, he glanced over at the wagon used by Natalia Valenko and Basil Karshchov. He saw a small bed outside on which Karshchov was reclining as he read a book. Glancing across the open tailgate of the vehicle, Gavin saw another narrow bed located inside. Obviously, the engaged pair did not sleep together.

One of the serfs played a quick and happy tune on a mandolin. Between the music and the sudden realization that Karshchov and Irena weren't living as man and wife, Gavin felt almost giddy. Smiling to himself, he picked up the pace and walked along in time to the music.

The camp settled into the evening routine. One by one, the fires were allowed to flicker down to dying coals that would be brought back to life in the morning to cook breakfasts and take the chill off the early risers. The sound of murmuring and occasional laughter went on for a while, but soon that, too, was gone. The only sound was the posting of the first relief as Corporal

Murphy took the sentries around the wagons and posted them on the perimeter designated by Sergeant Douglas.

The first two hours of guard duty were uneventful. When the second relief was taken out to replace the first, Sergeant Douglas left the dragoons' camp and walked into the woods where McRyan and Costello hung writhing in the cruel tightness of the ropes around their wrists.

Douglas snorted. "Well! It seems the Indians didn't get you bastards, did they?"

"For the love o' God," McRyan begged. "Cut us down, Sergeant."

"Are you uncomfortable?" Douglas asked, pulling the knife from the scabbard on his belt. "What about it, Costello?"

"Lemme loose," Costello pleaded in a husky voice.

Douglas made two quick swipes with his blade, cutting through the ropes. Both men dropped to their knees and bent over groaning. The sergeant felt no sympathy for them. "On your feet!"

Fearful of more punishment, McRyan and Costello stood up. They waited as the ropes were untied from their wrists. Then, without being told, they went to the proper position of attention as their shoulders pulsated with sharp pains. Douglas marched them back to the bivouac and halted them in front of their squad's bedrolls.

"You two can forget it if you think you're getting any rest tonight," the sergeant said. "Grab your carbines. You'll spend the rest of the night out on picket at the same place you was hung up. Get them weapons, hurry!"

McRyan and Costello did as they were told, then were paraded back to the woods. The weighty carbines added to their discomfort, but they held on out of fear

47

of dropping them and earning more of the sergeant's anger.

McRyan asked, "What're we supposed to do, Sergeant?"

"Stay on picket duty here all night," Douglas said. "You'll not return to the bivouac 'til I send for you."

"Yes, Sergeant," McRyan said.

"Do you understand that, Costello?" Douglas asked.

"Yes, Sergeant," Costello said. "How long're we gonna be out here."

"If I forget all about you, maybe 'til we come back this way," Douglas said. "Now, wouldn't that be a terrible thing?" Without waiting for a reply, he walked back to the camp.

"God!" Costello said. "I never want to go through that again."

"I'll tell you something," McRyan said in cold anger as he rubbed one of his sore shoulders. "Lieutenant MacRoss and Sergeant Douglas are gonna pay for this. I swear they will!"

"There ain't much you can do," Costello said.

McRyan snarled, "I may be a new recruit in this damn army, but that don't mean I've never killed nobody before." He sat down under a tree and leaned against it. "Or that I won't again."

Chapter 5

The wagon train was close to the junction of the Republican and Kansas rivers at just past high noon on the sixth day out of Fort Leavenworth.

At that point, Gavin MacRoss called another halt. Count Valenko angrily and vigorously protested the decision, but Gavin would accept no arguments on the subject. He made the protesting count and other Russian immigrants wait while he sent his men on a wide-sweeping reconnaissance of the immediate area.

The entire prairie around where the two rivers flowed together was a favorite camping site of the Cheyennes. The lieutenant did not want to blunder into any large groups of warriors going out on the tribe's first hunting or raiding parties of the warm season.

An hour's careful searching revealed no sign of Indians. When Sergeant Douglas returned, there was an undeniable tone of relief in his voice when he said, "We didn't see no sign of hostiles, sir. Fact is, it don't look like nobody's been through there since the last snows melted."

"That is good news," Gavin said. He smiled. "Though I fear the lack of Indians may prove a disappointment to Private Carlson."

Douglas grinned back. "He'll get his chance to fight Injuns afore his hitch is up, I'm sure."

After Sergeant Douglas and the dragoons assured their commanding officer it was safe to continue the journey, Count Valenko and his people were allowed to move on toward the site of their future settlement. When they arrived at the junction, they found a slightly wooded area along the banks that promised a scenic place to eat their midday meal.

Valenko, sitting on the wagon seat with Gavin riding beside him, pointed to the trees. "Is beautiful those, eh? And ve get from there fire vood."

"Good idea," Gavin said. "You'll find it useful to gather wood at every opportunity."

"Is not much out here, eh?" Valenko asked.

"Unfortunately, trees are at a premium in the plains country," Gavin said. "However, there happens to be another source of fuel."

"Ha!" Valenko laughed. "No trees. Vhat out here goink to burn but the grass?"

Gavin grinned. "You've been looking at it ever since we left Fort Leavenworth." He waved at Private Paddy O'Hearn. "O'Hearn! Please be kind enough to bring us a good, dry hunk of buffalo chip."

It didn't take long for the dragoon to find an excellent specimen. He rode up with it and handed it to the officer.

"Here you go, sir," O'Hearn said. "Ready to heat some coffee, ain't it?"

Gavin held out the dried feces and showed it to Valenko. "This is fuel."

Valenko made a face. "Is cow *navos!*"

Gavin shook his head. "It is from buffalo. A big animal like a cow, Your Grace, that runs wild on the prairie. You'll see plenty before you've been out here very long. I assure you that once the droppings are well-dried

50

by the sun, there is no unpleasantness involved in handling them." He tossed the chip back to O'Hearn. "A demonstration, if you please, O'Hearn."

O'Hearn slipped from his saddle and set the chip on the ground. After producing a box of store-bought matches, he struck one and held it to the dried dung. After a few moments, a low flame burned along the surface. The dragoon looked up. "It don't look like much, but it's hot and it'll burn a good while. We use this for cooking all the time. So do the folks that settle out here."

"That is just one of several good things we've learned from the Indians," Gavin said.

Valenko broke into laughter. Irena, beside him, also giggled. "Is good. I am in new country, so I learn new thinks, eh? Ve gather ever'body and show them how to do this." He shouted loudly, and the people left their wagons to obediently gather around. He pointed to the flaming object at O'Hearn's feet and spoke for a few minutes in Russian. The people were amazed, and several stepped forward to sniff. They expressed surprise that no smell issued from the flames.

"Don't forget to tell them this is an important lesson, because wooded areas will be scarce where you are going," Gavin said.

Count Valenko spoke to the group. When he had finished imparting the information, he turned back to Gavin. "Is good to learn this. Now ve eat, then go on until dark."

"I'm sorry, Your Grace," Gavin said. "We'll stay here until morning. I want to do some more scouting."

"Vhy?" Valenko roared. "Already you are holdink us back vith your lookink around."

"We gave this immediate area good examination, but we must go out much farther to make sure the rest of the trip will be safe," Gavin said. "I shall be going, too, and taking all the soldiers. You'll be all right here."

"But you don't find no Indians," Valenko argued. "So is safe, *nyet?*"

"Just because they aren't close here, doesn't mean they are not moving in this direction or already within striking distance," Gavin said. "Believe me, Your Grace, I only stop our travel when I think it is absolutely necessary."

"Bah! Is vaste of time!" Valenko insisted.

"I must do my duty," Gavin said.

"Maybe I send some men to look around," Valenko said. "They do a lot of hunting in Russia."

"Please don't, Your Grace," Gavin asked. "I'm certain they're excellent hunters and trackers in Russia, but things are different out here. I needn't remind you of Indians."

"Ve don't care about no Indians," Valenko said.

"You will before you've been in the territory too long," Gavin said. "Excuse me, please, I must get on with the reconnaissance."

The officer rode off to meet with Sergeant Ian Douglas to organize into scouting parties that would encompass at least two hours of riding. This was a common action on the prairie, and it didn't take the two experienced leaders long to break down their small detachment into teams for a detailed reconnaissance of the area in the direction to be traveled the next day. After allowing the dragoons time enough for a quick meal of coffee, hardtack, and salt pork, the lieutenant and sergeant each took a team and galloped out onto the trackless, endless prairie country of northeast Kansas Territory.

Gavin rode with Corporal Steeple's squad behind him. The one exception was Private O'Hearn, who, although remaining in sight, ranged out ahead in case of

52

a sudden and most unwanted appearance of hostile Indians. The lieutenant glanced back toward the wagon train, glad to finally be out of sight of the vehicles and Count Vladimir Valenko's constant questioning and complaining about stops.

Now, for the first time since leaving the fort, Gavin MacRoss really felt the freedom of the open plains country. No man-made objects broke the view of the wild, empty terrain that knew only the tread of buffalo and Indian tribes on the thick, grassy carpet of earth. With no hills or woods, the wide vista was unobstructed, giving an impression of unparalleled immensity and emptiness. It was like being on another world, where the sky was clear, the air crystal clean, and the smells that pleased the nostrils were those of fresh-growing vegetation.

Even the dragoons' horses, after months of confinement in stables with only limited exercise, were happy at the sense of freedom brought about by the open wilderness.

Gavin felt like breaking into a wild gallop, but he also well knew another aspect of the country where he now traveled. Those Indians who roamed the plains were warlike, restless, and most definitely unfriendly toward whites whom they regarded as interloping threats, not only to their hunting grounds, but to their very way of life.

"Ho!"

Private Paddy O'Hearn's voice drifted across the distance, the echoes winding down across the endless distance. Gavin looked ahead to see the dragoon signaling the others to hurry to him.

"Gallop, ho!" the lieutenant ordered.

When they reached the point man, he waved toward the northwest. "There's an abandoned Indian campground about a half mile ahead, sir."

53

"Let's have a look," Gavin said. "Corporal Steeple, put out three men on a perimeter. For the love of God, tell them to stay on the alert!"

"Yes, sir!" the corporal responded. "Rodgers! Carlson! Walker! Take up positions around the campground when we get there. O'Hearn! Anderson! Stick close to me and the lieutenant."

They rode into the area that O'Hearn had spotted. Bare, circular areas in the grass showed where numerous lodges had been pitched. In the center of the rings of dead grass were fire pits used by the tepees' inhabitants. It had not been a small village.

"Cheyenne," Steeple said.

"No doubt," Gavin agreed. "They weren't here all that long either. That means they're moving around looking for game."

"Or soldier boys," O'Hearn added.

"Right," Gavin agreed. "Well, while we're here, let's see how many made up this particular band of Indians."

The lieutenant rode through the area, counting the signs left of the individual lodges. It took him almost ten minutes to complete the task.

"There were a hundred lodges here," he announced when he had finished. "That means from four to five hundred people."

"Yes, sir," Steeple agreed. "From that, I'd say maybe a hundred and fifty warriors, give or take a few."

"Let's determine which direction they went," Gavin said. "Reform the patrol, Corporal."

"Yes, sir."

The group quickly moved out again, O'Hearn once more doing the honors as point man. The trail left by the Indians was easy to follow. Grooves in the ground from numerous travois, hoofprints, horse droppings, and other markings showed the village had moved off toward the northeast. The directness of the trail indicated the Indians were perhaps going to another favorite summer camping area to begin the season's first serious hunting of buffalo. A half-hour's ride confirmed it. Gavin was relieved.

"At least they're going away from our destination with the Russians," he said.

"Luck is with us, sir," Steeple agreed.

Gavin checked his pocket watch. "I'd say we'd better return to the wagon train. That'll give us plenty of time to settle in before dark."

"Yes, sir."

The patrol turned back in the opposite direction and, continuing to take no chances by keeping men out on the flanks and O'Hearn scouting ahead, rode back toward the place where Valenko and his people waited.

When they galloped back into camp, they found that Sergeant Douglas and his men had preceded them by a quarter of an hour. The sergeant, who had been waiting with the other squad, wasted no time in reporting to Gavin. He appeared worried.

Gavin swung out of his saddle. "Did you find something, Sergeant?"

"Not on our scout, sir," Douglas said. "The area showed some activity, but it was headed out toward the northeast."

"That's what we determined," Gavin said. "There was an old Cheyenne campground of about a hundred lodges, but the Indians seem to have cleared out a couple of days back."

"Prob'ly the same group we tracked," Douglas said. He took a deep breath. "We might have trouble yet, sir. When I got back, I found out that three of them Russians left the wagons to go hunting."

"Goddamn it!" Gavin swore. "Which way did they go?"

"That count told me he sent 'em off to the northeast,

55

sir," Douglas said. "Right toward them Injuns. I been waiting for you to come back."

"Prepare all the men to ride out together, Sergeant," Gavin said. "I'll join you directly."

"Yes, sir!"

Gavin strode over to Valenko's wagon, where the count and Irena relaxed in the shade of the vehicle. Natalia Valenko and her fiancé also lounged there on a couple of chairs set out for that purpose.

Although the sight of Natalia was pleasurable, the American officer still had to fight to control his temper. He gave the young woman a stiff bow and tip of his hat before speaking to her father.

"Sergeant Douglas tells me that you sent some men out hunting," he said in a strained voice.

"Yes," Valenko said. "I think, vhy sit around doink nothink, eh? I tell them to get fresh meat."

"That was most unwise, Your Grace," Gavin said. "This is very dangerous country that we are crossing right now."

"His Grace sent good men," Karshchov assured Gavin. "They are older fellows who were soldiers in Russia. They carried fine muskets. All three are excellent shots and are mounted."

Natalia smiled. "Please don't be concerned, Lieutenant MacRoss. Those men are avid hunters and used to spend weeks out in the forests back home while hunting deer and even bear."

"I appreciate that, really, Miss Valenko," Gavin said. "But things are a bit different here in America. Particularly in this part of the country."

Valenko snorted. "You vorryink too much, young man."

"I think we should speak of this later," Gavin said. "I specifically asked you not to send anybody out."

"Maybe so," Valenko said with a shrug. "Maybe no."

"I haven't time to argue with Your Grace," Gavin said. "My men and I will ride out and fetch them back."

Karshchov stood up. "I would like very much to go with you, Lieutenant," he announced. "I, too, can be well-armed. And I do not fear Indian savages." He spoke loudly, obviously trying to impress his lady love.

Gavin shrugged. "Suit yourself, Mister Karshchov. I only ask that you stick close to me."

Karshchov smiled. "Of course. If it makes you feel better, eh?"

Gavin didn't bother to answer the question. "Get a horse. I'll wait for you with my men. And hurry up."

"Of course," Karshchov said. He turned to Natalia, taking her hand and kissing it. *Do skoroe vstrechyi, lyubimeya.* Then he rushed off to prepare a mount.

The lieutenant returned to his horse and found the dragoons ready to leave. "We'll be waiting for Mister Karshchov," he told Sergeant Douglas. "He wants to accompany us."

"Maybe he'll learn something through observing," Douglas noted with a grin.

"Not that fellow," Gavin said. "He'll end up trying to tell us how to do our jobs."

Karshchov showed up within ten minutes. Armed with a military musket and sitting a bit clumsily in the saddle, he said, "I am ready to go with you."

Without wasting any more time, Gavin led his men and the Russian out of the wagon camp at a canter, moving directly northeast. He noted Natalia waving at Karshchov and secretly wished it were him she had come to bid goodbye.

The trail left by the trio of Russian hunters was easy to follow. The immigrants, not worrying about being tracked, had simply ridden straight out into the prairie. Within moments, Gavin could see why they had ridden in a northeasterly direction. A prominent rise in the ter-

57

rain was easily discernible on the far horizon. By riding directly at it, all they had to do would be to keep it at their backs for the return trip across the trackless prairie to the wagon train. Natalia Valenko had been right about one thing. The Russians were experienced outdoorsmen and soldiers.

O'Hearn, experienced and alert, was back on the point of the dragoon formation, following the trail. With the flanks and rear also covered, Gavin felt secure. Even if a large party of Cheyennes suddenly appeared, they wouldn't be able to pull a sneak attack or ambush. The disciplined fire power of the soldiers would be more than adequate to make a successful break-away gallop back to safety.

"Mister Karshchov, if we come under fire from hostiles, please stay close to me," Gavin advised him. "We will make an immediate run for the wagon train."

"Why don't we teach the beggars a good lesson?" Karshchov asked in a haughty tone. "Your Indians are stone-age people, are they not?"

"I suppose," Gavin said. "But you must remember that they've had firearms thrust into their culture. They have learned to use them expertly and effectively in a very short time. A sure sign of intelligence in anybody's estimation."

"Bah!" Karshchov scoffed.

"Please, just do as I say," Gavin said.

The group continued on for another half hour before O'Hearn suddenly reined up. Gavin, with Karshchov close by, galloped up to him as Sergeant Douglas organized an impromptu defense position.

"Cheyenne sign, sir," O'Hearn announced, pointing to the ground. "See there? They cut the trail. No doubt they're after them Russians."

"We'd best hurry," Gavin said. "But use caution, O'Hearn."

"Yes, sir," O'Hearn said. "Don't worry, Lieutenant. I ain't looking to give up my hair."

"What has happened?" Karshchov asked.

O'Hearn looked at him. "I'd say that about now or maybe a half hour ago, them pals o' yours was up to their asses in Cheyenne dog soldiers."

"I don't understand," Karshchov said. But he could easily see the soldiers were worried.

The column renewed their trek, this time with carbines primed, loaded, and carried in anticipation for a violent encounter. O'Hearn, relying on the others to keep him covered, pressed on as he gave his full attention to the track he followed. Less than a quarter of an hour later, he pointed in the distance.

"Crows!" he sang out. "And I don't mean Injuns."

"Oh, God!" Gavin said under his breath, knowing what the sight of the large, black birds meant.

Karshchov was thoroughly alarmed. He lapsed into Russian for a moment. *"Shto eto?* What is that?"

"The worst has happened," Gavin said in a low tone.

They pressed on a bit more, toward the source of the crows' attention. Sergeant Douglas sent Corporal Murphy and his men on a quick sweep around the area. When they found nothing, Gavin led the men forward, reaching the spot where they had to shoo the birds away.

Karshchov took one look and fainted, falling from his horse and hitting the ground before anyone could catch him.

Three bodies, stripped naked and filled with dozens of arrows, sprawled grotesquely in the grass. Slashed, dismembered, and violated, the Russian hunters had been scalped.

Karshchov groaned and rolled over onto his hands and knees. Gavin dismounted and grabbed him by the back of his shirt collar, hauling him to his feet. He pushed him over to the dead men. Now Karshchov vomited.

"Take a good look, Mister Karshchov," Gavin said in a calm voice. "Now you understand why I halted the wagon train and scouted the area, don't you?"

Karshchov nodded. *"Da!* I mean, yes!"

"You see what happens when hostiles catch whites out in the open," Gavin continued. "Not only are these men dead, but the Cheyennes now have three more muskets, powder, and ball."

Karshchov recovered, wiping at the tears in his eyes. "I will tell His Grace what has happened here." He forced himself to take another look. *"Strashanyi!"*

"Were they married?" Gavin asked.

"Yes," Karshchov said. "Now there are three widows. So sad." He took a deep breath, further steadying himself. "Are we going to take them back?"

Gavin shook his head. "You don't think their families should see this, do you?"

"No," Karshchov said.

O'Hearn had already pulled his spade from his saddlepack. He looked at the Russian and laid his hand on his shoulder. "This ain't the first time to see something like this for me, but I reckon it's always just as bad."

"Give me the shovel, please," Karshchov said. "I prefer to make the graves myself. These are my people— brothers of blood to me."

Gavin nodded to O'Hearn. "I think this is important to him."

"Yes, sir," O'Hearn said, handing over the tool.

Gavin watched the Russian begin to dig, suddenly having a new and growing respect for him.

Chapter 6

The wagon train had been rolling slowly and steadily for almost five hours in a continuous, monotonous, swaying trek. The journey, like the surrounding vista of flat, open country, now held no one's interest.

The travelers nodded and dozed with the gentle rocking caused by the flat, grassy prairie terrain. Others, walking alongside the wagons, were also lethargic on this journey which had now slipped into one of silence except for the occasional protesting squeaks from wheels that needed grease, a bit of murmuring between the people, or the thud of a dragoon mount's hoof onto the soft earth.

The Russians were all travel-weary. After long weeks of journeying out of Asia, into northern Europe, a sea voyage, then more overland trekking, the former subjects of the czar neared the point of exhaustion.

Lieutenant Gavin MacRoss, however, was wide awake and alert to his surroundings. The longer they rolled along, the more he looked at his map and studied the countryside through which they traveled. Finally, satisfied that he knew their exact location, the army officer stood in his stirrups and looked around in all directions for one final time.

"Halt!" the lieutenant hollered out in a loud voice.

The startled people, along with the dragoons, reined in. There was a bit of bumping inside the wagons as some of the loads shifted slightly. Suddenly everyone was wide awake and a bit fearful as they peered around half expecting to see a horde of shrieking Indians appear from nowhere.

Gavin cantered over to Count Valenko's wagon and gave him a cheerful salute. "We've arrived, Your Grace."

Valenko held a musket in his hands. "Vhere?"

Gavin gestured all around. "My calculations say this is where you chose to establish your settlement."

Valenko, now in a better mood, stood up on the seat and slowly turned as he took in the vast panorama around them.

"Are you sure, Lieutenant?" he asked.

"As sure as I can be without surveying instruments," Gavin said. "But don't worry. Even if you're not exactly on the spot, you and your people can still claim this area, and any government land office will recognize your ownership through first rights of possession."

"Then, ve are here, eh?" Valenko said. "This is Nadezhda."

"Nadezhda, Kansas Territory," Gavin reminded him. "A part of the United States of America." He pointed outward. "See that creek? That's the one shown on this map, and that curve there matches it exactly. For that reason I am absolutely positive we are in the exact location. This is where you chose to put down stakes."

"Stakes? Vhat is this here stakes?" Valenko asked.

"Never mind, Your Grace," Gavin replied with a grin. "You've no competition out here, so it won't be necessary."

Valenko jumped down from the wagon and kicked the blades of grass aside to reach down and grab a handful of dark earth. He crumbled it, letting the soil fall through his fingers.

"Is good this dirt," the count said. "Is somethink I learn from serfs. They know the land and if it is good or if it is bad."

"I'm no farmer," Gavin said. "But from the way the wild plants grow, I would venture to say you are in a most fertile area."

Valenko turned his attention to the Russians, shouting at them in their language and gesturing wildly. They cheered and waved back. He yelled again, and they began to drive their wagons into a protective circle. Valenko winked at Gavin. "Now you see, Lieutenant? I am learnink from you. Until ve got houses, ve keep vagons like this for protection."

"Excellent idea, Your Grace," Gavin said. "It looks like my job is done where you and your people are concerned."

"You are not to be leavink us soon, I hope," Valenko said. "I vould like if you vill spend some time vith us."

"I regret that we are only able to stay overnight, thank you," Gavin said. "I have some mapping to do between here and Fort Leavenworth. I must return to my duties."

"Of course," Valenko said. "You are a soldier, eh?"

"Yes," Gavin said. "Soldiers have duties to perform, do they not?"

The Russian smiled, saying, "I am hopink it is truly duty that calls you from us. You are not mad because I yell at you vhen ve stop so many times, are you?"

"Not at all, Your Grace," Gavin said. "Please let me assure you that no offense was taken."

"Then, I inwite you to have supper vith me this ewenink," Valenko said. "Irena vill cook good Russian food to send you off strong like ox."

"I accept your invitation with thanks," Gavin replied.

"*Udivitelnya!*" Valenko exclaimed. "I haf Russian wodka safed for special purpose. Tonight, ve drink some toasts to our friendship."

"Thank you very much," Gavin said. "I would be delighted to have drinks with you." He saluted again. "I know you are busy, Your Grace, and I must speak to my men. Please excuse me."

"Of course," Valenko said. "*Da skorogo!*"

Gavin rode his horse down the line of circling wagons to where Sergeant Douglas waited. He passed the vehicles belonging to the widows of the men killed by the Cheyennes. It had been a terrible experience to bring back the news of their deaths.

The wives had immediately gone into uncontrollable hysterics, shrieking and wailing. Other women had to physically hold them back from harming themselves. It reminded Gavin of the time he'd seen some widows of slain Indian warriors cut themselves in their frenzy of grief.

After the women had calmed down some and returned to their senses late in the afternoon of the next day, they had demanded to know why the bodies hadn't been brought back for burial by the group. Basil Karshchov tried to explain to them in the most delicate of terms that the cadavers had been mistreated by the Indians. When this didn't satisfy the widows, the sensitive Russian had been forced to describe in some detail—but not fully—the condition of the corpses. Their only consolation came when Gavin informed them the men had obviously already been killed when the mutilations took place. At least they hadn't been tortured to death.

The situation had also shaken Count Vladimir Aleksandrovich Valenko down to the core of his noble soul. In their private conversation about the killings, Karshchov had spared the old man nothing in his description of how the arrow-pierced and stripped bodies had been sliced and hacked into pieces until it was difficult to tell who was who among the trio of dead men.

After the conversation, an ashen-faced Valenko had sought out Gavin to apologize for giving him so much argument about all the worry concerning security from Indian attack.

Now, riding up to Sergeant Douglas, Gavin took the noncommissioned officer's salute. The lieutenant smiled and shrugged. "Well, this part of the mission is accomplished, Sergeant."

"Yes, sir," Douglas said. "We got 'em here safe and sound alright. When're we heading back, sir?"

"First thing in the morning," Gavin answered. "We can spend a final evening with our Russian friends, I suppose. Only God knows when we'll get a chance to see them again."

"Especially the lady, huh, sir?" Douglas boldly asked.

"What lady?" Gavin snapped.

"I've knowed you for some years now, sir," Douglas said. "I ain't never seen you look at a woman like you do that daughter of Count Valenko."

"The lady is engaged to marry Mister Karshchov," Gavin said. "There is nothing more to say about it."

"Yes, sir," Douglas said.

Gavin turned to ride away, but he stopped and looked back at the sergeant. "Was it that obvious?"

"Only to me, sir," Douglas assured him. He gave the younger man a paternal smile. "You'll get over her, Lieutenant."

Gavin nodded. "Of course."

"She's just one o' many you're gonna meet," Douglas said. "A perty gal captures the heart, but another'n frees it from the first."

"You're right," Gavin said.

"I'll see to settling the men in and organizing a guard for the night," Douglas said.

"Thank you, Sergeant." Gavin wanted to ride out in the country a bit to be by himself. He wasn't as flippant as he appeared when it came to leaving Natalia Valenko. Deep in his heart he knew his affection for her was a lost cause, and the ache would be a bit easier to bear with some solitude.

The lieutenant purposely went out of sight and sound of the wagon train. A lone cottonwood stood a few hundred yards away. He rode directly to it and dismounted. After hobbling his horse to allow the animal some calm grazing on the grass, Gavin sat down in the shade cast by the leafy branches and leaned against the thick trunk.

Natalia Valenko certainly wasn't the only pretty girl he'd known. But most of the others were obtainable. In fact, a couple had obviously set their caps for him, but he'd managed to avoid matrimony when army duties called him away for long absences. Gavin MacRoss admitted to himself that a couple of the young ladies could even be described as prettier than Natalia Valenko—though not much—and one had the added attraction of political connections through an uncle serving in the U.S. Senate. Such a situation had the potential of being very advantageous to an army-officer husband.

Yet, Natalia had a charm about her. Her voice was soothing and melodious in a nice way, and her smile warmed his heart. The way she walked and moved was pure feminine charm that could capture any man's admiring glances. Unfortunately for him, she didn't love Gavin MacRoss; she loved Basil Karshchov.

"Goddamn it!" Gavin cursed and got to his feet. "This is ridiculous! I can't sit here and brood, for God's sake! I'll forget her after a while anyhow." The he sadly added, "At least I hope so!"

The lieutenant quickly unhobbled the horse and

swung back into the saddle to ride back to the wagon train. He vowed that in the future when he began to think of Natalia Valenko, he would consciously smother the image and turn his mind to something else.

Gavin was glad to see the wagons were in a tight circle, arranged so that everybody could cover the neighbor on either side of them in the event of an Indian attack. Valenko and his people were fast learners. He was also sure that the terrible deaths suffered by three of their members had impressed them about the very real danger they faced out on the prairie.

As the lieutenant rode into the middle of the vehicles, he noticed the Russians all gathered at one end of the circle. A couple of off-duty dragoons, O'Hearn and Carlson, also stood there. Curious as to what had attracted their attention, Gavin turned his horse in that direction and cantered across the open space.

O'Hearn saw the lieutenant ride up. He grabbed the bridle of the officer's horse as Gavin dismounted. After rendering a salute, he announced, "Them Russians is flogging one o' their men."

Gavin pushed his way through the crowd to find a shirtless man tied by the wrists to a wagon wheel. Another Russian, large and muscular, held a short length of rope. From the look of the prisoner's back, he had already been given three or four good, blood-drawing blows.

"Hold on!" Gavin shouted. "What's going on here?"

Valenko stepped away from where he stood with Irena. "Ve got a man vhat talk vithout respect to me!" He glowered. "To me! Count Vladimir Aleksandrovich Valenko!"

"That's too bad, Your Grace," Gavin said. "But you have no right to have him beaten."

"Vhat? Vhat?" roared Valenko. "I am member of nobility!"

"That's true," Gavin agreed. "But you haven't the authority to order a civilian beaten for exercising his constitutional rights."

"Rights?" Valenko questioned. "He don't got no rights! He is serf! A peasant! My property!"

"Maybe in Russia, Your Grace," Gavin said. "But here, unless a person is black, he can't be owned by anybody. I might add that there's many an American working on changing that cruelty, too."

"But—but," sputtered Valenko. "He call me stupid; he says I am wrong about setting up town. Then he tell me to close my mouth!"

"That's the freedom of speech guaranteed everybody," Gavin said. "Besides, he wasn't given a choice of staying in Russia or coming out here, was he?"

"Of course not!" Valenko said. He glared at the man who dared to speak back to him. "Bah! I will have him beat!" Valenko turned back to the man with the rope whip. *"Besprerviya!"*

The man raised the device to strike as the prisoner braced himself for more painful hits to his back.

Gavin yanked his revolver free of its holster and fired the weapon straight into the air. Everyone jumped, including the whipper, who looked in alarm from Count Valenko back to Gavin.

"If you have the man struck again, I will arrest you and take you back to Fort Leavenworth for trial," Gavin declared. "That goes for the man carrying out the punishment, too. This is federal territory, and as an army officer I am charged with enforcing United States law out here."

"Vhat you talkink about?" Valenko asked. "I see your sergeant hang the two soldiers from tree by hands for bother Irena!"

"That is permitted by Army Regulations," Gavin

said. "Even in Russia, is not military law more severe than civil law?"

"A little," Valenko said. "But only a little. But not for serfs who don't got the respect for their masters."

"You are not his master," Gavin said. "If he chooses to follow you, then he may. If he chooses to leave you, then he may."

"Then, how do we punish wrongdoers?" Valenko demanded to know.

"First, make sure they are truly wrongdoers," Gavin admonished him. "Talking back to you is not a crime. I hope you will remember that, Your Grace."

"Then, vhat ve do vith criminals, eh?" Valenko asked. "Vhat ve do vith thiefs?"

"Banish them from your midst, if you will," Gavin said. "But any penalty must be according to law and the processes provided. If any of the people of Nadezhda commit a serious crime, you must bring them to Fort Leavenworth for trial and any punishment if they are found guilty."

Basil Karshchov stepped forward. He held a small pamphlet. "I have here a copy of the United States Constitution that I bought while we were in Boston. Must we go by this?"

"Yes," Gavin said. "Read it to everyone here, so they can understand the Bill of Rights and other provisions of the document. If you don't break the rules in the Constitution, then you'll be all right."

Valenko kicked at the ground in anger. He muttered in Russian, and the bound man was freed. Then the count turned and faced Gavin. "Do not forget! Dinner tonight! Ve drink wodka!"

"I'll be there," Gavin promised. "You're not angry with me, are you?"

Valenko thought a moment; then he smiled. "*Nyet*, my

young friend. I have no anger for you. Alvays you are teachink me somethink, are you not?"

"I'm certainly trying," Gavin said.

"Remember! Don't be late."

"I won't," Gavin said. He took his horse from O'Hearn and led the animal toward the dragoon camp where Sergeant Douglas lounged by the small cookfire. "I'd like to have a word with you in private, Sergeant Douglas."

"Yes, sir." The sergeant stood up and accompanied the officer on a short stroll out of earshot of the other dragoons.

"Did you hang McRyan and Costello by their wrists for attacking that young Russian woman?" Gavin asked.

"Yes, sir," Douglas answered in a flat voice.

"Some time ago, I ordered you to dispense with such harsh punishments," Gavin said.

"No, sir," Douglas said. "Begging your pardon, Lieutenant, but you told me to *consider* not giving out tough licks."

Gavin sighed. "I suppose I did, but you know I disapprove of discipline that is either extremely painful or humiliating. I don't care if Army Regulations permits it or not."

"They deserved what I done, sir," Douglas said stubbornly.

"It's all right to give men extra duty," Gavin argued. "Even hard labor such as digging deep holes or chopping down trees. There is at least a semblance of dignity in work."

"Are you ordering me not to apply ropes or kicks and punches no more, sir?" Douglas said.

"Yes, Sergeant Douglas, I am," Gavin said. "I respect you very much and consider you a friend, you know that."

"Yes, sir," Douglas said. "I'm happy to have your

friendship, sir. It don't always happen in the army between an enlisted man and an officer. We got a proper way between us, and we can speak plain and still keep military respect mixed with kindly feelings for each other."

"I hope you understand how I feel," Gavin said.

"No, sir, I don't," Douglas said. "I'm just an old-fashion soldier, and always will be."

"But an excellent one," Gavin interjected.

"Thank you, sir," Douglas said. "I reckon you know I won't do nothing behind your back."

"I do," Gavin said.

"Then, that's that," Douglas said.

"Is there any coffee back at the fire?" Gavin asked.

"You bet, sir," Douglas said. "Let's go have a cup. It'll perk us up some."

The two soldier-friends walked side by side together back to enjoy some strong army coffee and a bull session.

Chapter 7

Gavin MacRoss did not sleep well that last night with the wagon train.

The supper at Valenko's wagon was the cause of the restless, interrupted napping on his blankets that went on all through the hours of darkness. All in all, Gavin had to admit it was one of the most unpleasant evenings of his life.

The little social affair had started off nice enough. When Gavin presented himself at the wagon, Irena was cooking a kettle of soup. The smell coming from the pot was delicious, blending in nicely with the wonderful aroma of fresh-baked bread that the peasant girl had made through an ancient Russian method of baking in an earthen oven using rocks and hot coals to produce a large loaf.

Valenko greeted the guest in his usual warm, exuberant way, inviting Gavin to join him in a couple of drinks to begin the festivities. That had been rather friendly and pleasant. The lieutenant felt guilty about enjoying alcohol when it was forbidden to his men, but realized that his position as an army officer mandated his participation in the party. This was especially necessary when the host was a member of foreign royalty.

After the two men had enjoyed three stiff drinks

apiece, Natalia showed up arm in arm with Basil Karshchov. Gavin didn't know if it was the liquor or not, but never had the presence of Natalia bothered him so much. She was most lovely and charming, looking good enough to be the belle of any ball.

Gavin performed a compulsory, polite greeting to her and Karshchov, then tried to give the count most of his attention. He was determined to keep his eyes off the beautiful girl as much as possible.

It was a losing battle for the lovelorn young officer.

The engaged couple sat close together in a couple of chairs, with Karshchov constantly holding his fiancée's hand. Now and then they exchanged fond glances with each other. Gavin was just glad they didn't start kissing. He tried to cover his resentment and falling mood with a few more quick, strong drinks.

After an hour passed, Irena Yakubovski served a supper of soup that was hot, thick, and plentiful. Gavin, as always when in the field, ate well, though he could have done better if Natalia's presence weren't continuing to prove to be quite upsetting to him.

After the meal was consumed, a pair of musicians showed up. One played the mandolin and the other the violin. They performed and sang while Valenko took out a bottle of vodka and some small glasses. Gavin, the count, and Karshchov began to drink toasts. They toasted the United States, The Russian Empire, the czar, the president, Kansas Territory, the prairie, the wagons, and anything else they could think of. The strong liquor went to Gavin's head in spite of his experience of hard and fast drinking in the army. He began to get drunk enough that it was noticeable. His speech slurred, and he started laughing a lot and making jokes.

After a while, Karshchov, who had consumed twice as much as his American guest but showed no effects, stood up and requested a song of the musicians. They responded, and he danced a Russian folk dance. It wasn't long before the count joined him. Gavin, along with Irena and Natalia, clapped in time to the music. Then Valenko and Irena danced, Irena and Karshchov, and Irena and Gavin. Then Valenko got his daughter into the activity, and she danced with everyone, including Gavin as her last partner.

The closeness and touch of the girl was pure torture for Gavin. He immediately sobered up as he felt his arm around her waist and hers around his neck. She smiled and moved in closer, obviously enjoying the music more than her partner. But the heady smell of femininity and the press of her flesh caused yearnings that Gavin knew would never be fulfilled.

The young army officer, suddenly cold sober and melancholy as hell, was grateful when the evening finally came to a close.

After making the proper good nights, Gavin went back to his blankets and lay down. As hard as he tried he couldn't sleep. All his efforts to keep the Russian girl out of his mind failed, and the remembrance of the slight and feel of Natalia Valenko kept exploding and reexploding in his brain like a shower of shooting stars in a black prairie sky in summer.

Sometime toward dawn, Gavin began to drift into troubled naps that lasted ten or fifteen minutes. Finally, he sank into a regular sleep brought on by pure fatigue.

"Sir!" Sergeant Douglas's voice broke into Gavin's slumber.

"Huh?"

"Sir, get up!" Douglas urged him.

Instinct bred from years of frontier soldiering brought Gavin into an upright, sitting position.

"What the hell is going on?" the lieutenant asked, reaching for his weapon.

"We got some boys that went over the hill," Douglas said.

"Deserters?" Gavin asked. "How many?"

"Five, sir," Douglas said. "McRyan, Costello, Evans, Rodgers, and Walker. They lit out with their mounts and all equipment. Rodgers was on the last guard relief, so they left after he went on duty."

"That means they have at least a two-hour headstart on us," Gavin said.

"More'n that, sir," Douglas said. "Rodgers told Anderson he couldn't sleep and took his relief, too. They've been gone four hours."

Gavin got to his feet. Still dressed, all he had to do was grab his hat and field equipment. "Let's go get them, Sergeant Douglas."

The lieutenant was glad to see all the other dragoons were up and ready to go. His own horse was saddled and prepared. As he mounted up, Count Valenko appeared in the growing light. He waved at Gavin as he approached.

"Good mornink, my friend," the count said.

"You got up early, didn't you?" Gavin remarked.

"Got up?" Valenko laughed uproariously. "I have not been to bed yet! Basil and I still drinkink. I come out here to relief my bladder." He looked in puzzlement at the soldiers, who were obviously ready to ride out. "Vhat is goink on? You leaf so soon?"

"Some of the men deserted," Gavin said. "We must go catch them."

"Yes, ve haf that trouble in the Russian army," Valenko said. "You catch and you shoot, eh?"

"We have to find out where they went first," Gavin said. "But in our service, a man isn't legally considered a deserter until he's been gone at least thirty days."

"So! You catch and put in jail, then?" Valenko asked.

"I hope so," Gavin said. He leaned down and offered

75

his hand. "I must say goodbye, now, Your Grace. I'll not be able to return. By the time we catch up with the runaways, we will have to get to our mapping duties right away."

"I am wishink you good luck and hope to see you again before long," Count Valenko said.

"Thank you." Gavin turned and signaled to his men. "For'd, yo!"

They rode out in a double column, easily picking up the trail left by the deserters. Once more O'Hearn took the point as flankers were sent out on each side of their formation.

"Tell me what you know about the deserters," Gavin requested of Sergeant Douglas, who rode beside him. Like most officers in the army, his contact with enlisted men was brief and only happened when necessary. The sergeants and the corporals were the ones who personally saw to it that most orders were carried out.

"Well, sir, you're more'n familiar with McRyan and Costello," Douglas said. "Evans and Walker is just a coupla fellers that ended up in the army because they was no good in civilian life. They ain't much as soldiers either, I reckon, so they've decided civvie street is more pleasant than living in the barracks."

"That happens often enough," Gavin said. "What about Rodgers?"

"That's another story," Douglas said. "I think I know him from somewhere before."

"Maybe he's served previously and had to reenlist under another name," Gavin suggested.

"That's it, sir," Douglas said. "I think he must've been posted in the East, 'cause he don't act like he's got any experience on the frontier. I figger I seen him somewheres while I was back there to pick up recruit contingents."

"But you're convinced he's a former soldier, are you?" Gavin asked.

"Yes, sir," Douglas answered. "I was suspicious on account o' he looked familiar like I said, and he took to drill real quick like he already knowed it. Rodgers prob'ly got in trouble and was given a bad conduct or dishonorable discharge. After some tough times on the outside, he made up a new name for hisself and enlisted."

"It's hard to keep track of who's coming and going in a small army spread across a gigantic continent," Gavin said.

"Just the same, I wish the recruiting service was more careful about who they signed up," Douglas complained.

"It's hard to enlist youngsters for soldiers under any circumstances," Gavin said. "Maybe if the government raised the pay, better men would be attracted to enlist. There seems to be two types—those who are proud to serve and others who do so because of some problem in their lives. That makes it difficult for you noncommissioned officers."

"Yes, sir," Douglas agreed. "But don't forget them lads like Carlson back there. He's here looking for glory and adventure. He ain't a bad soldier either, let me tell you."

"Yes," Gavin said. "He seems eager enough."

"He won't reenlist, though, sir," Douglas said. "I know the type. He'll serve to the end of his hitch and get an honorable discharge." The sergeant chuckled. "Then he'll spend the rest of his life boring family, friends, and strangers with stories of his army days."

"Sergeant Douglas, we shall *all* do that," Gavin said with a laugh.

Up ahead O'Hearn let out a yell and pointed due east, indicating he was changing direction.

"That's what I figgered," Douglas said. "Those son of a bitches is making a beeline for Missouri. I'll bet a month's pay that Rodgers knows where they can sell the horses and equipment for a good price."

"Once they are in civilian clothing and scattered, then they'll never be found," Gavin said.

"If I ever see Rodgers—or whatever his real name is—back in uniform again, I'm gonna personally give his ass a damn good kicking," Douglas said. "The army's been too good to that bastard as far as I'm concerned."

The pursuers continued onward for another hour before Private Paddy O'Hearn signaled for a halt. He rode back and reported to Gavin.

"Sir, they're turning south a bit," O'Hearn said. "I don't think they mean to. They just ain't experienced in moving across open country."

"You're right," Gavin said. "They're starting to wander off in a circle. That's easy enough to do in flat country."

O'Hearn said, "Sir, I'd like to suggest that we keep heading due east. I'm sure they'll turn back toward that direction, and maybe we can cut 'em off."

"That's good thinking, O'Hearn," Gavin said. "Carry on."

O'Hearn saluted, then galloped back to his position at the front of the column.

Sergeant Douglas said, "There's a good steady soldier, sir. O'Hearn is into his second hitch and doing fine. I think he's ready for corporal."

"Very well, Sergeant," Gavin said. "If that's your recommendation, I'll turn it into Captain Hanover. We'll have chevrons on O'Hearn's sleeves as quick as we can."

The dragoons settled into a regular routine that went on for the next three hours. Flankers were changed off and positions alternated in the column to keep the monotony down for the men, in order that they might stay alert. Only Gavin, Douglas, and O'Hearn kept to the same positions as they pressed on across the deep sea of prairie grass after the five deserters.

Suddenly O'Hearn gestured and pointed south. All eyes turned in the direction to see the distant figures of five riders moving steadily in a northeasterly route.

"That's them!" Douglas exclaimed. "God damn their eyes!"

"Gallop, ho!" Gavin commanded.

The entire group, with the lieutenant leading, rapidly headed toward the other riders. Within five minutes, the deserters spotted them and made a frantic turn due south, breaking into a wild run for freedom.

O'Hearn, out farther, used his position to turn the escapees into a more westerly route. There would be nothing for them in that direction except wilderness and hostile Indians.

The pursuers drew in closer and closer through skillful herding of the inexperienced deserters. In less than a half hour, the fugitives headed down into a draw that slowed them considerably. Douglas, taking Corporal Murphy and two men, quickly skirted the gash in the ground and covered the only escape route out of it.

The chase was over.

Gavin, Sergeant Douglas, and their seven men quickly positioned themselves until the deserters were completely surrounded. The only advantage they had was good cover down in the gully.

"I want you to come out of there one man at a time," Gavin yelled to them.

McRyan's voice, defiant and angry, came back shouting, "Go to hell, you son of a bitch!"

"I know McRyan doesn't speak for all of you," Gavin hollered. "Just step into view with your hands raised. Leave your horses behind."

Another voice, that of Walker, could be heard. "What's to happen to us?"

"You'll be given a court-martial," Gavin replied loudly and truthfully. "You're still not deserters yet, only away from your posts without permission."

"Will we go to the guardhouse?" Walker asked in a yell.

"As sure as shit stinks!" Sergeant Douglas roared back at the fugitives.

A few moments of silence followed. Suddenly shooting erupted from the gully, and Gavin was forced to leap from his saddle and hit the grass as bullets whined around him. He knew they would have to go in after McRyan and his friends.

Sergeant Douglas, bent double, trotted over to Gavin and flopped down beside him. "Orders, sir?"

"Yeah," Gavin said thoughtfully. "Leave one man at the rear of the gully. Have another care for the horses right here. The rest of us will move in as skirmishers on foot and rout them out of there. It's going to be close in there, so we'll use pistols."

"Yes, sir!" Douglas made a quick exit. In less than five minutes he returned with six of the men. Their carbines were slung over their shoulders, and each held his pistol, loaded and primed, for the job ahead.

"I stationed Anderson to cover the rear," Douglas said.

"Form as skirmishers," Gavin ordered. "Move out!"

Advancing in one rank with as much space as possible between themselves, the dragoons followed their young lieutenant. He led them slowly and carefully into the dense brush of the draw. Cottonwood and redbud trees grew close together, branches intertwined. Thick vegetation filled the gully floor.

Gavin strained his eyes as his gaze darted back and forth, searching for a sight of the runaways.

A shot exploded from the right front, whipping the air ten feet above the skirmish line.

Sergeant Douglas and the two corporals immediately responded, sending three slugs whipping into the brush.

"Oh, God!"

Walker, the front of his buckskin shirt bloody, staggered sideways from cover. He fell down, then held up an imploring hand. "Say, boys, don't shoot me again, will you?" A moment later, he collapsed in death.

"Move on," Gavin ordered. "Take care now!" He stepped over Walker's body and led the men deeper into the draw.

Suddenly a fusillade of shots detonated from straight ahead. Belken, in the skirmish line, pitched forward onto his face. Now everyone returned fire.

The sounds of men crashing through the brush ahead showed the deserters were quickly withdrawing after firing their desperate volley.

Douglas knelt beside Belken. "Dead, Lieutenant."

"Poor old soldier," Corporal Steeple said.

"Follow me and keep your eyes open," Gavin said.

Another full five minutes of silence followed. Gavin signaled a couple of halts to listen; nothing but silence dominated the scene. Birds and insects had been frightened into flight or silence by the shooting.

Some shots farther down the gully could suddenly be heard. Gavin picked up the pace, but after going only ten yards, closer firing poured at the skirmish line.

This time the lieutenant spotted his quarry.

He gestured to Douglas and Steeple, who followed him over to the left side of the draw. Gavin pointed with his revolver and immediately fired three times. Douglas and Steeple did the same. The sound of bodies falling into bushes could be heard. Gavin and his men moved in with great care until they found the bodies of Evans and Rodgers lying close together when they had been ripped by bullets from the trio of revolvers.

"That leaves McRyan and Costello," Douglas said.

Gavin yelled, "McRyan! Costello! Give it up! Walker, Rodgers, and Evans are dead. There is no sense in you ending up the same way."

No insults or taunts answered the advice. Once more the skirmish line eased into the thick vegetation. Still stopping momentarily, it took almost twenty minutes to travel the length of the draw before reaching the exit. Gavin stepped back up on the level prairie and saw Anderson sprawled in the grass.

He rushed over and knelt beside the badly wounded may, the other skirmishers joining him. "When did this happen?" Gavin asked.

Anderson, pale and dying, had blood bubbling from his lips. "McRyan—Costello—shot me—sir," he stammered with his last breath.

Douglas stood up and looked outward. "That's that shooting we heard before we hit Evans and Rodgers. I'll bet them two set the others up, then snuck off to make a run for it."

"Yeah," Gavin agreed. "They caught poor Anderson here and shot him." He walked out a few yards and found the trail. "They're heading due south."

"That's Kiowa and Comanche country down there," Douglas said. "Are we going after 'em, sir?"

Gavin shook his head. "No, Sergeant. We have to keep to schedule. All we can do is report them and hope that they can be picked up before the Indians catch them or they make it to the East."

"Maybe they'll run into some patrols from Fort Scott or Fort Gibson," Douglas said.

"That will give them a quicker, easier death by firing squad or hanging," Gavin said. "If the Indians catch those two, they'll be a long time in going to their maker."

"They'll show up in hell still screaming," Douglas said.

"Yeah," Gavin said. "The thought of that bothers me not one bit!" He turned and looked back at the draw. "Well, Sergeant, we have some dead to bury, then some mapping duties before returning to Fort Leavenworth."

"The army's business goes on no matter what," Douglas said.

"As always," Gavin intoned.

They headed back to where Fenlay had the horses.

Chapter 8

Sergeant Ian Douglas gazed over Lieutenant Gavin MacRoss's shoulder as the officer carefully and fully drew a map of the immediate area where they stood.

"Damn! You got a good hand, sir," Douglas marveled. "I swear that's the most lifelike pencil work I ever seen in all my life."

Gavin smiled. "Sketching was one of the few classes in which I excelled at West Point."

"Maybe you ought to try painting pitchers like folks hang in their homes," Douglas suggested.

"I don't feel my artistic ability is quite that good," Gavin said.

"If I could draw, I'd do them naked ladies like is put up in saloons," Douglas said seriously.

"That's something to consider alright," Gavin replied in amusement.

The dragoon detachment, fulfilling its mapping duties, had worked its way to a point north of the junction of the Kansas and Republican rivers. They weren't far from where the wagon train had made its turn to the place destined to be known as Nadezhda.

Gavin glanced around at the area, appreciating the lay of the land. "I was just thinking that this would be an excellent place to establish an outpost," he remarked.

"Why is that, sir?" Douglas asked.

"A camp established here for the summer could well support patrols and other activities out of Fort Leavenworth and Fort Riley as well as keep a permanent surveillance on this area," Gavin said. "Another thing to consider is that the Santa Fe Trail is but a few miles south. If there was any trouble down there, units stationed here would be close enough for a quick response."

"Yes, sir," Douglas said. "It would make for a handier way to get to problems down that track."

Gavin continued to look around. "There is plenty of water here, and the open terrain could accommodate a small military outpost."

Douglas also gave the place a quick, professional appraisal, picturing where it would be best to locate barracks, latrines, the parade ground, and other features necessary for a proper army installation.

"I think you're right, sir."

"It would be rather nice for troops to have another good place to stop and rest up for extended patrols," Gavin added. "Such a situation would be much easier on them than having to face thousands of square miles of wild territory before finding another haven."

"Again, I got to say you're right, sir," Douglas said. "Are you gonna follow up on this idea?"

"Yes," Gavin said. "I believe I shall submit a report and suggest such an action."

"In that case, maybe they'll put an outpost here someday, sir, and call it Camp MacRoss, after you," the sergeant said with a wink.

"I doubt if such recognition would come from a simple suggestion in a report," Gavin said. He chuckled. "But perhaps if I led you and the other five men on a victorious raid against the Comanches down south, that would happen. What do you think of my doing that?"

"Not a hell of a lot, sir," Douglas said. He grinned. "I'd prefer if this patrol stuck to mapmaking. Let 'em name the post after somebody else. Especially if they have to take on the Comanche Nation to get official recognition."

"I agree," Gavin said. "Posthumous honors do not interest me in the slightest."

"Me either," Douglas said sincerely. He quieted down to let the lieutenant finish the task.

Gavin had already drawn a map showing distinct terrain features. To add to that effort, he now sketched a landscape showing certain important lays of the land. He paused and glanced at the men.

"How is young Carlson doing?" the officer inquired.

"Attending to his duties proper, sir," Douglas answered.

The aftermath of the fight with the deserters had left rookie trooper Carlson badly shaken. When the shootout's excitement died down and the realization that five of their number were dead sank in, he fell into a melancholy mood. The young man even came close to weeping. Only a superb amount of self-control kept his emotions from bursting forth. It was at that time that another aspect Sergeant Douglas's leadership qualities came to the fore. He took the lad aside and had a talk with him.

"Now, it's a tough thing to lose men from your company, Carlson," Douglas said. "That's something that all real soldiers must do. It's just part of the job."

"It ain't so much all the others as Benny Anderson," Carlson said.

"So you and Anderson was barracks and mess mates, was you?" Douglas asked.

"Yes, Sergeant. Anderson and me were good friends," Carlson said in a low voice. "Me and him come out here on the same contingent and went through recruit drill together and ever'thing."

"There's nothing I can say that's gonna make you feel better," Douglas said candidly. "You're gonna be grieving and that's a fact. I lost some close friends myself fighting Injuns and the like." He put a friendly hand on the boy's shoulder. "I'm leaving you alone for a bit, Carlson. If it makes you feel better to cry over Anderson, then have at it." He paused. "I've done it. The army, as far as us soldiers is concerned, revolves around our little comp'ny. We're A Comp'ny, and as long as we serve in this regiment, we'll be the A's afore anything else. Anderson was your friend, and them other fellers, even the deserters, was A's, too. Grieve proper, young soldier, your friend Anderson deserves it. He was a good lad."

"Thank you, Sergeant," Carlson said.

"Join us in a bit when you're feeling better," Douglas said. He turned and walked away.

By the time the graves had been dug, words spoken, and the dirt thrown in on the dead, Carlson had calmed down quite a bit. There was no doubt he was bound to be a good soldier and had the moral and inner fortitude to take whatever hardships and grief he might encounter.

Paddy O'Hearn, feeling a bit like a big brother, went out of his way to be especially friendly toward the younger man. As they rode together in the column, he told Carlson some amusing anecdotes about the army and allowed the lad to join his and Fenlay's mess team. That meant he would cook and eat his rations with the two veterans.

Now, under the warm spring sun of the Kansas prairie, Lieutenant Gavin MacRoss went on with his mapping duties. He had only a pocket compass as an instrument to gauge the azimuths he detailed on the sketches. Distances, when possible, were carefully paced off and written down in the notes that would be turned in with the cartographical efforts. It was not as precise as the Topographical Engineers could do with their surveying paraphernalia, but it offered anyone venturing forth over the trackless wilderness of grass a reasonably good idea where to find water, good camping areas, and a guide to judge distances to travel.

After completing a thorough job around the rivers, the dragoons moved to the northeast toward Fort Leavenworth. Gavin had been charged with map-sketching in a straight line back to the post. Most travelers followed a more southerly course to the Santa Fe Trail, so that particular part of the country farther east was well-known and documented. Gavin's efforts would offer an alternative westerly route in case of bad weather, Indians, or both.

Sergeant Ian Douglas, as usual, took extra pains with security so that no war parties of Pawnees or Cheyennes could sneak up on their group. Although their numbers were down because of the desertions and deaths, the dragoons still maintained an alert perimeter while their young commander went about his duties.

It was Private Olaf Carlson who sighted the two riders at the exact moment they appeared on the southern horizon. He gave out a yell and kept his eye on them as they approached. Sergeant Douglas and Corporal Steeple joined the young soldier in observing the horsemen.

"Them's white men," Steeple noticed after a short bit.

Douglas, whose eyesight didn't allow any accurate viewing in the distance, said nothing as he waited to see what would happen.

"Hey!" Carlson piped up. "Them's Russians! Look! See how they're dressed?"

"You're right!" Steeple said. "I wonder if they're running away from that count feller."

"There ain't no law against that," Carlson said. "Me and O'Hearn was there when the lieutenant told the count he couldn't whip nobody and didn't own 'em like in Russia. He told that ol' count that if any o' them people wanted to light out, he'd just have to let 'em."

Douglas didn't give a damn whether the count whipped all those peasants or not. He was curious as hell about what would bring two of them away from the settlement, especially after some of their friends had been killed by Indians for doing exactly the same thing. He nudged Steeple and Carlson.

"Give 'em a holler," Douglas ordered. "And show yourselves so's they'll know you ain't Injuns."

The pair whooped, whistled, and waved for a couple of minutes before the Russians noticed them. They gestured back at the dragoons and immediately broke into a wild gallop toward them. It took them a full ten minutes of hard riding before they reached the soldiers. From the appearance of the horsemen, they were exhausted and badly disturbed.

"Lieutenant!" one cried out to Douglas as they reined up.

"I'm *Sergeant* Douglas," he replied in some indignation. Sergeants did not like to be taken as officers.

"Lieutenant!" the other said frantically. "Lieutenant! Lieutenant!" He waved a piece of paper at the three American soldiers.

"I think he wants to give that note to Lieutenant MacRoss," Steeple said.

"Lieutenant! Lieutenant!" the Russians cried. "Lieutenant! Lieutenant!"

"That's all the English they know," Carlson observed. "I'll bet either the count or that Karshchov taught 'em that one word to use."

"Damn right," Steeple agreed. "They been sent to find us. Maybe they was hit by Injuns."

"Right," Douglas said. He nodded to the Russians. 'C'mon with me, then."

Douglas found Gavin on the other side of a stand of buffalo grass, using his compass to shoot an azimuth at a distant rise in the ground. The lieutenant turned at their approach and was surprised to see their two visitors.

The one with the note leaped from his saddle and, cap in hand, approached the American officer. He bowed and handed the missive over, saying, *"Pazhalusta!"*

Gavin unfolded the message and quickly scanned it. "Good God!" he exclaimed. "This was sent to me by Karshchov."

"I take it something bad has happened, sir," Douglas said.

Gavin nodded. "Indeed! The Russians have been attacked. Several killed and prisoners taken."

"Well, sir," Douglas said. "We can either go see what we can do, or head for Fort Leavenworth for help."

"Fort Leavenworth can't do much out here," Gavin said. Worrisome thoughts about Natalia Valenko leaped unbidden into his mind. "The hostiles will have headed either south, west, or north. We'll go back and get all the information we can on the attack, and see if there's any way we might help or ease the situation. Order the men to mount up!"

"Yes, sir!" Sergeant Douglas knew the lieutenant was worried about the Russian girl, but he was smart enough not to make any remarks about it.

Within moments the entire detachment of seven dragoons, along with their Russian companions, were on their way to Nadezhda.

"I reckon they can change the name o' that town from 'Hope' to 'Hell,' " Douglas shouted over the pounding of the horses' hooves.

"It won't be the first settlement to be done in," Gavin observed.

"Or the last," Douglas added.

The Russians, though near exhaustion, tried to push the pace, but Gavin knew better than to tire the horses unnecessarily or to risk riding into the war party that had hit the Russian settlement. Although he had begun to grow frantic about Natalia's safety, the lieutenant kept the group down to a canter. There was no way he could inquire about her from the two messengers since they didn't speak English.

With Private Paddy O'Hearn as always out in the front to guide them while flankers stayed on the alert to avoid ambush, the dragoons and their Russian companions continued to move as rapidly across the plains country as the lieutenant allowed.

It took the rest of the day to finally reach their destination. Wisps of smoke on the far horizon gave away the exact location of Nadezhda long before it was in sight. The first view of the newly established town eased out of the distant haze as the column drew closer.

Finally the burned wagons and the smoldering remnants of unfinished cabins were in perfect view as they finished the last leg of the journey and rode into what was left of Count Vladimir Aleksandrovich Valenko's dream.

"God have mercy!" Douglas exclaimed.

"Amen," Gavin agreed. He looked around hoping to catch sight of Natalia somewhere in the people hurrying toward them with expressions of panic and fear on their faces.

Valenko and Karshchov, with a forlorn crowd of the settlers following, greeted Gavin as he rode up and dismounted. The count cried out, "My heart is breakink!" He began to weep openly, tears trickling down his cheeks into his heavy beard. "It is a catastrophe! A tragedy!"

Karshchov, a bit more under control, wailed, "We were attacked in the early morning before all were awake. They were cowards! Wretches!"

The people, though not understanding the words spoken by the young intellectual, backed him up with mournful exclamations. Several of the women carried on like the widows of the three men killed by Indians had done. The difference this time was that there were so many, it was impossible to control them. The shrieking and yelling became so loud that the American officer could not carry on a normal conversation with Valenko and Karshchov.

"Shut up!" Douglas roared at them. "Quiet down so's we can sort this thing out!"

"I'm sorry," Gavin said. "You must tell me what happened so I can see what I can do." He glanced around and noted the dispirited sight of a newly established cemetery.

"Moya docha!" Valenko interrupted with a wild yell. He finally lost control of himself. The count fell to the ground on his knees and began beating at the dirt. *"Moya docha!"*

"He cries for Natalia," Karshchov said piteously. "How terrible for him and me both."

"Natalia!" Gavin exclaimed. "What happened to her?"

"The villains took her away!" Karshchov yelled. Now he started to cry, his sobbing uncontrollable for long moments. "They took her away with the others!"

Gavin, extremely upset, used the extra minutes to regain his own composure. When he spoke, he did it in controlled tones, holding down his feelings.

"Now please explain to me what the Indians looked

92

like. That way we can determine which tribe committed the outrage."

"Indians?" Karshchov said. "They were not Indians, Lieutenant MacRoss! They were white men and black men and brown men all dressed like you."

"Like us?" Gavin asked. "They were soldiers?"

"You are not dressed like soldiers," Karshchov said.

Douglas leaned toward Gavin. "Remember, sir. We ain't in uniform."

"Yes," Karshchov said. "They looked like you, but they had no sabers or army saddles. These were bandits and murderers. They showed no mercy. Even children and babies were killed by those knaves!"

Gavin looked back at Douglas. "Who the hell could they be? I know of no outlaw gangs operating out here. There are no trains or banks to rob."

"I can't figger it out either, sir," Douglas said. "What would such frontier riffraff be doing wandering around a wild, unsettled area peopled by hostile Indians?"

Suddenly Gavin's face went pale. He grabbed the sergeant's sleeve and looked into his eyes. "Wait a minute! I can't believe they've come this far north."

"What are you talking about, sir?" Douglas asked. "Do you know who those son of a bitches might be?"

"I know exactly who they are," Gavin said. "They are the worst! The very worst! God damn their souls to hell!"

Douglas, knowing the lieutenant's distress was something to take seriously, almost shouted when he asked, "Who the hell are they?"

Gavin took a deep breath. "Comancheros!"

Chapter 9

The shocked and frightened prisoners endured rough treatment as their captors prodded them along. Although curses and insults were bellowed at them to pick up the pace, none understood the words. Even Natalia Valenko, closely attended to by Irena Yakubovski, could not understand the vulgarities in the shouts. The young noblewoman's education in English did not include swear words. But the physical abuse crossed any language barriers between the two groups.

The captives were a mixed lot of men, women and even a few older children. A couple of the males limped from wounds suffered in the raid against their new settlement while others displayed slight injuries that needed tended to.

The prisoners were closely guarded and surrounded by a large crowd of motley men who kept them stumbling toward the south. Although wild-looking, these sentries had an organization that seemed to be held together by a loose, but strictly enforced discipline. Each individual was nearly fanatic in attending to the duty of making sure none of the unfortunate Russians were able to escape. Constant vigilance, punctuated with shoves and kicks, appeared to be the order of the day.

Behind this strange and noisy group were several

wagons loaded with loot. Off to one side, but well within sight, was a small herd of oxen being attended to with a bit more care and consideration than the prisoners. All of this had been part of the loot taken during the raid on Nadezhda.

The man in charge of this conglomerate was a short and very muscular individual named Guido Lazardo. The two-days' growth of beard on his swarthy jowls was of a quantity that most men would require two weeks to raise. A large, black moustache, carefully waxed and curled completely on the edges, dominated the area between his thick lips and large nose. Heavy eyebrows, formed into a perpetual frown, ran together to form a bushy roof over his small, beady eyes. A greasy, leather wide-brimmed hat covered his bald head, and large gold earrings decorated ears that sprouted so much hair it seemed a wonder he could hear any of the clamor going on around him. More hair showed all around his collar, giving evidence of the thick mat of fur that covered his body.

Lazardo was very energetic like his men. Excited and tense, he rode back and forth along the group, shouting and gesturing at everyone in a strange mixture of languages. He cursed the guards with as much fervor as he did the prisoners.

"*Presto*, by God!" he yelled. "I going to kill the *bastardo!* Keep going! Pronto!"

He rode a rapid circle completely around the moving crowd, pausing to look into the wagons filled with loot, then inspecting the oxen.

"Pretty damn good!" he said to the herdsmen. "We'll make 'em fatter and have big feast!"

Next he galloped up to where the prisoners stumbled along. The man in charge there was named Monroe Lockwood. He was a heavily bearded individual whose large amount of body fat hid tremendous physical strength and agility.

He nodded a greeting to Lazardo. "How's it all look to you, Mister Lazardo? he asked.

"Pretty damn good, I say," Lazardo said. "Look at them men. Big, hardworking fellows, eh? We get a good price from the mines in Mexico. It would take nearly half a year to work them to death, eh?"

"You bet!" Lockwood said. "Some o' them gals is gonna fetch a fancy price, too. Take a gander at that one there, see?"

Lazardo looked into the group of prisoners and spotted the one pointed out. "She is big."

"That gal could take on a whole mining camp and not blink an eye," Lockwood said. "She's gonna make some whoremaster a lot o' money."

"She is too big, make better sense to sell to Indians for worker," Lazardo said.

"Maybe you're right," Lockwood allowed. "I bet some squaw'd be glad to have her to boss around during buffalo-skinning time. That big ol' gal could take a buffalo apart faster'n you could blink your eye."

"Maybe she wouldn't need a knife," Lazardo suggested. "She could pull the buffalo apart like a roasted chicken."

Both men laughed at his humor. The woman they talked about, Irena Yakubovski, walked in a bold, defiant way, keeping her head high. The only time she turned her eyes was to give Natalia a visible inspection to make sure she was able to keep up.

"Wait!" Lazardo said. "See the small blonde on the other side of the big one?"

"That li'l ol' thing?" Lockwood said. "What about her?"

"Bring her to me," Lazardo commanded. "I want to look at her close."

Lockwood slipped his bulk from the saddle and quickly darted in, grabbing Natalia Valenko by the arm. Irena followed, cursing and threatening in her native tongue while the Comanchero dragged the struggling girl over to where Lazardo waited.

"Here she is, Mister Lazardo," Lockwood said. He gave Natalia a gaze of measurement. "She ain't much." He glanced at Irena, who glared at him in bold hatred. He grinned and stuck out his tongue at her, wiggling it back and forth.

Irena spat and cursed him, his mother, and all his ancestors in fine Russian swear words.

Lockwood laughed. "I think she's taking care of the littler one, Mister Lazardo."

"That is fine," Lazardo said as he leered openly at Natalia with such intensity that she turned her eyes away from him. He smiled. "Don't let nobody else touch this one. She is mine."

"Suit yourself, Mister Lazardo," Lockwood said.

"Make sure nobody don't put no marks on her," Guido warned him. "I don't like bruises and scrapes."

"I'll see to it personal," Lockwood promised. "You want this big'n to go with her?"

"Sure!" Lazardo said. He laughed loudly. "She can probably protect her better than any of you."

"You could be right," Lockwood allowed. He turned and hollered over at another Comanchero. "Big Joe!"

A black man kicked his horse into a trot and rode up. "What?"

"This here is Mister Lazardo's woman," Lockwood said. "The other'n is looking after her. You make sure nothing happens to either of 'em."

"I gone put the wimmen in one o' them wagons, then," Big Joe said. "Is that all right wit' you, Mister Lazardo?"

"What you need to do to keep the small one clean and nice for me, you just do it," Lazardo said.

"Yes, sir!" Big Joe said. He dismounted and took Natalia from Lockwood. "Now looky here, missy. If'n you do what I say, I won't get riled at you. Now c'mon!" He frowned at Irena. "You come, too, you big ol' gal."

Lazardo watched Big Joe take the women over to one of the wagons. He laughed, saying, "I'll have a nice time when we get back to camp, eh?"

"I prefer the big'n," Lockwood said.

"Then, she is yours until we sell or trade her to Indians," Lazardo promised. "Now I go look around again!" He kicked his horse's flanks to begin another circuit of the column.

Guido Lazardo had been born thirty-five years earlier in the highlands of his native Sicily. His birthplace was in the upper reaches of craggy canyons in a small mountain range known as the Montagni Roccicio. This was wild country where outsiders dared not venture. The people there were an inbred but clever lot of yokels who lived by a fierce code in which honor and acts of valor were everything while personal wealth and possessions—outside of weaponry—meant nothing.

The history of Lazardo's homeland was one of foreign colonization and conquest. The Sicilians had been ruled over the centuries by Phoenicians, Greeks, Romans, Vandals, Ostrogoths, Byzantines, Arabs, Normans, and Bourbons. Rather than be cowed by such manipulation and oppression, the wily people had learned to adapt and be servile on the outside while fighting back the best way they could in subtle but deadly ways. Bandit raids, thievery, vandalism, and other small, brief violent acts were the only way the Sicilians could strike at their rulers. It was impossible to fight a grand revolution against a foe that could completely and ruthlessly crush any rebellion against its authority. Therefore, unable to attack like lions moving in for the kill, the Sicilians made hit-and-run attacks like swift wolves.

The people of the Montagni Roccicio were on different. Isolated for the most part, their contacts with others in the lower regions generally meant trouble for all concerned. Soldiers bullied them and made them obey the laws, other Sicilians were openly insulting, and with no money or means to purchase much, they were not welcome in the towns that dotted the island nation. Known contemptuously as Rocceri, they were considered only slightly better than Gypsies.

The Rocceri fought back, giving and taking their lumps. Finally, it dawned on them that as long as they were bashing heads they might as well do it in a manner that guaranteed success for the most part, such as sneaking up behind some other fellow and slamming him good and hard when he wasn't expecting it. After that, the Rocceri noticed that when that victim was lying still and unconscious, he was helpless to stop anyone from stealing whatever possessions he had on his person.

This led to violent robberies in which several Rocceri banded together to guarantee success. It wasn't long before a gradual ascension into criminal activity and outright banditry of travelers turned to raids on towns and isolated farms. When the frightened citizenry of one small village made an arrangement to pay in silver coins for the Rocceri's promise to leave them in peace, the enterprising mountain men began to tribute from other areas in exchange for not attacking and robbing the people living there.

The authorities tried to put an end to the crimes, but whenever the law showed up in any force, the Rocceri simply ascended into the craggy shelter of their mountains and waited out the inconvenience. As soon as the forces of order withdrew, they went back to their old ways. Unknown to the Rocceri, in the thirteenth century another group, better organized and located, emerged to do exactly the same thing, but on a grander scale. This was the Mafia, who could commit crimes on a level unimaginable in the Montagni Roccicio, but perhaps not with the same zeal when compared individual by individual.

By the time Guido Lazardo's mother writhed and groaned on a crude pallet in a mountain hut to push him from her belly in 1811, the Rocceri were well-established in their own area, earning their daily bread from extortion mostly and outright robbery when either necessity or boredom dictated it. Guido grew up unschooled in anything except hunting and crime, and by the time he reached his nineteenth year, he had established himself as a solid citizen of the Rocceri from having participated in all manners of criminal activities in which he had managed to murder no less that five people in the lower regions.

It seemed that Guido Lazardo was destined to become a leader in his family's group, but the temptations posed to him by a fourteen-year-old girl of another Rocceri clan proved his downfall. Her name was Liliana Bonabella. At her age, she was ripe to get married and begin birthing other little Rocceri to grow up and make the world a bit more miserable for other people. Lazardo saw her on a festival day in early summer. He felt a wild and passionate attraction to her, and was determined to have the girl as his wife.

One balmy evening, when the sun hung high for a bit longer than usual in the Sicilian sky, Lazardo slicked down his hair and waxed his moustache to a shiny pair of curls. Even at that age, his beard and body hair could nearly match the pilosity of a bear. After dressing in his best suit and putting on a pair of boots recently pulled from the feet of a frightened traveler on the road between San Cipirello and Camporeale, Lazardo stuck his stiletto in the bright-colored sash around his waist and strode off to make his honorable intentions known to Liliana's father.

What was supposed to be a fine evening turned into an embarrassing ordeal for the young man. Not only did Liliana Bonabella loudly express her dislike of him, she compared his appearance to that of a monkey and shrieked to her father that before she would marry Guido Lazardo she would hurl herself off the highest peak in the Montagni Roccicio. Like most men of the Montagni Roccicio, Signore Bonabella didn't give a damn whether his daughter wanted to marry any particular individual or not. Her opinion did not matter. However, in this case, the father most especially did not care to have grandchildren who resembled Lazardo. For that reason, he gave in to his daughter's wishes and told the young man to give up any plans for courting her.

Lazardo went home to sulk and have a fine outburst of temper. He kicked his dog, threw the family cat against the wall of the hut, broke up the kitchen table, and would have done more had not his mother begun beating him with her broom until the handle broke. Sicilian men respected their mothers, and he made a quick exit to sit in the dark of the mountain forest and ponder his humiliation.

Lazardo decided that the only answer to having Liliana Bonabella as his wife was to use the time-honored tradition of *ratto della donna*. This was the custom in which a young man, spurned by his ladylove or her family, would kidnap her and take the girl away to rape her. Since she would be violated and impure, no self-respecting swain in the Montagni Roccicio would deign to marry her. Even though the act was against her will and forced on her, the young woman in question was humiliated and shamed by the affair. Therefore, she would have to marry her rapist to avoid any blemish on

101

her reputation. To refuse him would put her outside normal society, and she would be considered a common whore. Her marriage would restore her as a decent woman, and her family's honor would be upheld.

It took Lazardo several long weeks of careful stalking before he managed to find Liliana in an isolated place where she was alone. She had gone to pick berries and had wandered a couple of kilometers from her family's home. Lazardo skillfully crept up on her to pounce and drag the struggling, screaming girl to a place he had prepared in a cave.

Liliana fought back fiercely, screaming insults and scratching until Lazardo was forced to beat her into unconsciousness. It was then that he ripped off her long skirt and deflowered her as she lay in a moaning swoon with one eye swollen shut and her nose broken. When he finished, he slapped her face to bring her around.

Liliana's discovery of her condition brought her out of her state of insensibility into another fit of rage. She hit, kicked, and even bit his hand. Lazardo's hysterical anger took him beyond rationality as he fought back. The muscular youngster punched and booted the girl until she fell to the floor of the cave once again. But he didn't stop. In his fury, he continued to kick her until only physical exhaustion calmed him down.

By then Liliana Bonabella was dead.

Now Guido Lazardo was in serious trouble. If her family discovered he had murdered her, they would do more than take it out on him. His relatives would also suffer. The Bonabella clan was an extremely large and powerful one. There wasn't a single area in the Montagni Roccicio where a member of their numerous group didn't live.

Guido decided he had two choices. He could hide the body and carry on as if he knew nothing about her disappearance. That stood a slim chance, because her people probably already figured she was a victim of *ratto della donna*. That would make him a prime suspect, and any interrogation from them would be thorough and unpleasant. That left only the alternative of his fleeing the scene and getting not only out of the Montagni Roccicio, but off the island of Sicily. Either way, some of his family's blood was going to be spilled. Therefore, Lazardo reasoned, there was no real reason not to save himself.

The rapist-murderer waited for night to settle in; then he began a rapid but careful descent down the far side of the mountains. His plan was to reach the port of Marsala and get aboard a ship.

When he finally reached the base of the mountains and found himself on the main road, the young Sicilian didn't bother to rest. He started out toward his destination with worried glances behind him, concerned that some of the Bonabella clan were already trying to find him.

When Lazardo reached Marsala, he found it easy to get a berth aboard a ship. A sailor's life was one of drudgery and isolation, and most crews were short at least a dozen men. The first ship the fugitive approached was merchantman, and the first mate was more than glad to accept Lazardo's request for work to fill out the understrength crew that sailed the vessel.

At first Lazardo worked as a simple deckhand. He knew nothing of ships and had no skills required of an able seaman. But, with a quick mind, he soon mastered such things as knot tying and other rope work. Strong and agile, he could respond with vigor once he learned what was expected of him. But where the new sailor really shined was high in the masts, where the sails were furled and unfurled. Used to scampering thin mountain trails, the heights held no fear for him, and he soon became a permanent part of that team that toiled in the upper regions far above the decks.

Lazardo spent almost two solid years aboard the ship, going ashore to squander his meager earnings on port city whores and cheap liquor all over the Mediterranean and northern Atlantic. His fall from grace came when one of the crewmen commented on the Sicilian's hairiness while toiling under a hot sun, voyaging between Corsica and France. All the sailors were stripped to the waist, and one, noting the heavy cover of fur on Lazardo's body, made a joke that sent the other members of the crew into spasms of laughter.

"Why don't you take off your shirt like the rest of us, Lazardo?" the man asked. "That wool one you're wearing must be hot as hell."

Liliana Bonabella had spurned him because of his body hair, and Lazardo wanted no reminder of his physical repulsiveness. Rather than go at the man at that moment, however, the Sicilian waited his chance. It came during a late-night watch when he snuck up on the unfortunate joker, slicing him across the throat with his knife and dumping the man overboard.

One hell of a row was raised by the ship's officers, and an investigation was launched. Although no proof of the murder could be found, Lazardo was invited to leave the ship when it docked in Marseille a week later. Paid off and willing to get on another ship, Lazardo went to a cheap waterfront bar to have a few drinks. In that piss-soaked saloon, he met some people who changed his life. They were Italian-speaking Corsicans who operated a crude crime syndicate involved in prostitution, gambling, robbery, and murders for hire. They immediately made an approving judgment of the muscular Sicilian and invited him to join their group. Thus, Guido Lazardo's education in the world continued.

Lazardo adapted as easily to Marseille's underworld

as he had shipboard life. Utterly without a conscience, there was no act he would not commit for money. He beat up rebellious whores, pulled burglaries in the city's well-guarded residential areas of the wealthy, killed three men on an agreement worked out with the gang's boss, and worked his way up to the exalted position of managing one of his crime union's better saloons and gambling houses.

The latter position brought about the third downfall of his life.

Temptation proved too great for Guido's growing ambitions. At first he crudely embezzled funds from the establishment and also began to run his own string of whores in a bordello he set up smack in the middle of the waterfront. It took his bosses less than a month to find out about the whorehouse. A bit of further investigation on their part revealed the theft from the saloon. An immediate assassination was ordered, but the wily Roccero was already aware they were after him from the attention they were showing the books of the saloon. He didn't bother to pack, only concentrating on being able to get away in time. With plenty of cash, he headed for Italy and lived in a high, wild style before finally running out of money in Napoli. This reverse in his fortunes took him to the sea once again.

This time a British ship gave him a home. His past experience helped him back into the top masts, and he added to his skills as a seaman while acquiring a good knowledge of English. In fact, after three years he was fluent in the language. When they docked in Galveston, Texas, Lazardo jumped ship and headed inland to see what the New World had to offer to an enterprising and ambitious Roccero who could speak the local lingo.

Lazardo was gleeful when he discovered the hinterlands of Texas. The mountain man had been too long aboard ships and in cities—places where he didn't belong. His natural and most comfortable environment was a wilderness like the untamed Montagni Roccicio in Sicily. His first job was on a rancho owned by a wealthy Texican. As usual, when in a new profession, Lazardo started off at the bottom. But he learned quickly, becoming an expert cowboy who could ride a horse with the best vaqueros in Mexico or Texas. He also learned to use firearms, holding back his faithful blades as backups when he was out of ammunition. Saloon brawls, bunkhouse fights, and running battles with Kiowa and Comanche Indians rounded out his training as a frontiersman.

After five years of hard ranch life, Guido Lazardo returned to his favorite occupation. Once more he became a professional criminal.

Lazardo became a cattle rustler, whiskey and gun smuggler, and bank robber. His activities eventually led to a meeting with a diverse group of outlaws called Comancheros.

These men, of every conceivable race and creed, had but one thing in common—the morals and ambition of starving lions. They took frontier lawlessness to new lows, adding slavery to their crimes as they dealt with unscrupulous clients in the wild lands of the West. They raided Indians, Mexicans, and whites alike, taking captives to be sold and bartered to work as slaves in mines, large ranchos, or even in various tribes of Plains Indians. Guido Lazardo rode with this loose-knit group for a couple of years before recruiting his own Comanchero gang to move into the central and north prairies where untapped sources of wealth and slaves had yet to be visited. He heard tales of the Santa Fe Trail, in which raw goods went in one direction to be traded for gold and silver that was brought back along long stretches of desolate prairie.

The first strike was the settlement found in Kansas

Territory. Lazardo and his men could not believe their good fortune as they swept down on the unsuspecting Russians, who, thinking all they had to fear were Indians, at first greeted them as friends. The slaughter had not been complete, but enough prisoners were taken to guarantee great profits when the sales and trades were made with Indians and Mexicans.

Now, smiling in anticipation, Guido Lazardo rode up to the rear of the wagon where Natalia Valenko sat hunched in fear, trying to fight back the tears. Irena Yakubovski, defiant as ever, kept a protecting arm around her charge.

As Lazardo looked into the interior of the vehicle, the sight of the frightened young woman reminded him of Liliana Bonabella in that cave so long ago in Sicily. The memory fanned his passions. He couldn't wait to get the blond beauty back to his lodge in the Comanchero town. He blew her a kiss, then rode off to keep an eye on the column.

Natalia began to weep piteously, praying and crossing herself as she begged God for deliverance from the evil into which she had been cast. But a glance out of the wagon showed only empty prairie country.

Chapter 10

Private Paddy O'Hearn pulled on the reins of his horse and came to a halt. He could see the trail left by the Comancheros plainly laid out in the grass across the prairie. The veteran soldier fully realized that this was not careless behavior on the outlaws' part. The lack of any attempt to hide their trail gave stark evidence of the strength of the criminal group.

All of that made O'Hearn an extremely nervous and cautious dragoon.

After a few moments of contemplation, O'Hearn kicked his mount's flanks and galloped back to where Lieutenant Gavin MacRoss and Sergeant Ian Douglas rode with Basil Karshchov. The Russian fidgeted in his saddle, glancing about in the hopes of seeing something. The emotional man could not hide the anxiety that tortured him.

O'Hearn saluted. "Sir, them Comancheros is leaving a trail a blind man could foller. They ain't worried none about anybody catching up with 'em. They're either spoiling for a fight, or just don't give a damn if they get into one or not."

"I have to agree," Gavin said. "That means they're strong enough to have no fear of anyone. That would include any Indian war parties that might be in the area."

"I'd say you're right about that, sir," Douglas said. "Just take a look at us. We ain't much of a threat since we're only seven strong. Eight if you count Mister Karshchov."

"I definitely count him," Gavin said. He took another look at the tracks he had been studying since leaving Nadezhda the day before. "I figure there are about two to three dozen of them along with their captives."

"Yes, sir," O'Hearn said. "They also got a herd o' oxen and two wagons."

"We must press on," Karshchov insisted.

The Russian intellectual rode the horse that had belonged to the now-dead deserter Rodgers. None of the horses belonging to the settlement were worth much in mounting a pursuit. They were more useful in pulling plows. That was the reason the Comancheros had not bothered to steal them. Oxen could be eaten, and used in trade with the Indians.

The remaining dragoon horses had been left in the care of Count Valenko back at Nadezhda. Besides having Rodger's mount, Karshchov was also armed with the dead dragoon's carbine. After a few quick lessons, he showed he'd learned to effectively us the weapon. That made him worth something to Gavin.

"We are moving against a very strong force," Gavin explained to the distraught Russian. "They are well armed, as you should know, and have no reason to fear us."

"They have my lady love," Karshchov said. "I am willing to die for her."

Gavin, forced to keep his personal feelings for Natalia to himself, fought down his desire to shout out his own misgivings and worries. Instead, he spoke in a controlled voice, saying, "I appreciate your concern, Mister Karshchov. Believe me, we shall do all we can do. Getting us all killed will not rescue Miss Valenko. It will not only mean uselessly spending our lives, but the losses would only add to her anguish."

"But I think of what they will do to her!" Karshchov cried. "She is like a lost kitten!"

"You must believe that we are all very concerned about Miss Valenko's safety," Gavin said. "I promise to choose the best course of action."

"You are right, of course," Karshchov said. "I appreciate very much your kindness and consideration to allow me to accompany you and your brave men. Forgive me, Lieutenant MacRoss, if I sound like Count Valenko urging you to hurry against your better judgment."

"It is perfectly understandable," Gavin said. "Believe me, Mister Karshchov, I do appreciate your feelings."

More Russians had wanted to travel with the dragoons, but Gavin would not permit it. Stripping the town of its now severely limited manpower while Pawnees and Cheyennes still roamed the locale would have been foolish. Even though the extra guns would come in handy during confrontation with the Comancheros, taking men out of Nadezhda could very well mean a complete massacre and destruction of the settlement.

Karshchov was only allowed to accompany the soldiers because of a special request from Count Valenko. Since Karshchov had also threatened to go on foot if not allowed to ride with the dragoons, Gavin thought it best to bring him along.

"I will walk into hell itself to rescue my Natalia!" he had tearfully sworn.

Gavin had no doubt the Russian meant what he said, and the lieutenant really didn't blame him. Losing Natalia would be more than the temperamental man could bear. It was at that time that he'd ordered the horse and weapon turned over to the Russian.

After leaving Nadezhda, Gavin did not have his men arranged in a column because of the threat of attack from all sides to his small force. Instead, they moved slowly and steadily across the prairie in a diamond-shaped formation that gave them all-around security. In case of attack from any or all sides by a surrounding enemy, they would pull into a tight group that would afford them the opportunity to blast out coordinated, disciplined, and carefully spaced volley fire from their percussion carbines.

Now, after nearly a full day of travel, it was apparent that an all-out assault on the Comancheros was doomed to a quick and bloody failure. At that point, had anybody asked him, Lieutenant Gavin MacRoss would have been forced to admit that he didn't have the slightest idea of what he was going to do about rescuing the prisoners.

"Keep up at the front, O'Hearn," Gavin said. "But concentrate on the horizon more than the trail. Those tracks are easy enough to follow, but we don't want to suddenly find ourselves facing a surprise attack by a couple of dozen Comancheros."

"I understand, sir," O'Hearn said. He saluted, then rode back to his position.

Gavin kept his men moving until a deep dusk settled down over the prairie country. At that point he knew it was much too dangerous to continue on against such an overwhelming force. If the Comancheros had outriders or posted guards a good distance from their main camp, the dragoons were sure to be discovered. Comancheros, though despicable villains, were expert plainsmen and would be no easy enemy to deal with in the wilderness.

The pursuers settled into a cold camp in a shallow valley along a narrow creek. For refreshments, they drank water from their canteens and gnawed on salt pork. They were spared from grinding their teeth on the bricklike hardtack army crackers because the Russians had supplied them each with several huge loaves of freshly baked bread. The outside crust was firm and hard, but under that was a soft, delicious example of the baker's art.

The hobbled horses, not too tired because of the day's slow pace, contentedly grazed on patches of the sweet grass that stretched out from the creek while their human companions maintained strict noise discipline.

The horse soldiers lolled in silence or napped with their heads on their saddles. Karshchov, worried sick, sat up and fidgeted while clasping and unclasping his hands as nervous energy kept him charged up. Among the dragoons, only the men on guard stayed alert as the evening blended into night and a bright moon rose to glow in the cloudless sky.

The night was quiet except for occasional breezes that made sudden and brief appearances out of the rolling emptiness of the Kansas countryside. These gentle winds brought in the smells from afar that told of distant plants and flowers and the rich, dark virgin earth that had never known a plow or any other disturbance except for wildlife or the tracks of travois dragged by wandering Indian tribes.

The regularity of the sleeping men's breathing and an occasional snort or snore were the only other sounds in the grove of trees. Gavin MacRoss was the only army man who could not slip into the blessed comfort offered by the arms of Morpheus. He and Karshchov slept only in short fits, as worrisome thoughts of Natalia Valenko's fate danced through their troubled minds.

Gavin pondered on the amount of sleep he'd lost during the past weeks because of the Russian girl. He wondered if she was worth it. After all, he really didn't know her, and she was in love with another man. But logic would not win out over emotion, and he spent as disturbed a night as Karshchov, the man who possessed her heart.

The last stint of guard was taken by Sergeant Douglas. With their numbers down, the noncommissioned officer wanted to make sure the men got as much rest as possible. Although he could have posted the last guard and spent the entire night in dreamy comfort with his head resting on his Ringgold combination dragoon-and-light-artillery saddle, he had enough concern for the well-being of the men serving under him to forget his rank, and do a trooper's job.

The sergeant, manning his post behind a tree and looking out onto the open country around their camp, waited for the dawn to pinken the sky before he set about waking up the men. His first call was the lieutenant. He reached down to shake the young officer and stopped.

"Are you already awake, sir?" Douglas asked.

"Yes, Sergeant Douglas," Gavin said. He stretched and sat up, then got to his feet. "Have the men eat a quick meal of a hunk of bread. Then saddle the horses. We'll be moving out shortly."

"Yes, sir."

Karshchov, like Gavin, was already awake. He quickly got to his feet. After some impatient bites out of his loaf of bread, he washed it down by scooping up water from the creek into his cupped hands. Then he saddled his horse as the dragoons had taught him the day before. When he finished, he looked at his companions and was irritated to see they had only then finished eating and were beginning to roll up their blankets.

"Please, my friends!" he pleaded. "Many lives depend on us. They have stolen children, too, and a young lady is in grave danger. Please, hurry, my friends!"

Private Paddy O'Hearn took pity on the Russian. "Sure we will, Mister Karshchov. Don't you fret yourself

113

a'tall." He turned to his soldier friends. "Come on, lads. Wouldn't you want to shake a leg if yer own true love was in the hands o' them Comancheros?"

"Think about them kids, too," Fenlay added.

The dragoons silently complied as they gobbled down their bread, then threw saddles across the horses' backs. Within short minutes, the group was ready to ride. Paddy O'Hearn, knowing where he had to be, led the way from the little prairie creek and took them back to the trail they had been following so diligently.

The previous day's routine was picked up once again. Great care was taken to watch the far horizons. This was one advantage to moving across the plains country with its wide skies and rolling expanse of land. No mountain ranges, forests, or other natural obstacles obscured the view. The vista was only limited by distance or heat haze.

But even that dancing pseudo mist did not hide the sight of the six riders traveling perpendicular to the dragoons' direction.

O'Hearn stood in his saddle and signaled, pointing in the direction of the horsemen he had just spotted. Then he held up his fingers to indicate the number of riders he had spotted.

Gavin waved back at the point man to let him know he had seen him. Then the lieutenant pulled his field glasses from his saddlebags and studied the unsuspecting subjects of his attention.

"Those are Comancheros, by God!" he exclaimed.

"What'll we do, sir?" Douglas asked.

Gavin grinned viciously. "Let's get 'em!"

"I'm for that," Douglas said.

The lieutenant waved O'Hearn and the rest of the men in close. When they gathered around him, Gavin said, "We're going after those fellows. They are not following the trail of the larger group, so I figure they are

114

scouts or outriders. We'll intercept them, and see what they can tell us. Everyone stick close to me."

The six Comancheros headed in a westerly direction. Gavin led his men at a quick canter toward them until they were once again within sight. At that time, he moved slightly more to the south until they were just out of sight over the horizon. If the dragoons couldn't see the riders, then they couldn't see the dragoons.

Gavin continued the pace and direction for a few moments, then turned westerly. When the lieutenant caught a glimpse of the Comancheros, he once again dropped back to a southerly direction. A few moments later he took another look. The pursued men, unaware of the attention they received from the dragoons, continued at a slow, steady pace.

At one point Gavin couldn't see the riders, but turning farther north brought him back into eye contact. He and his men were gaining on the unconcerned Comancheros. The army officer once again dropped back out of sight over the horizon.

Gavin and his dragoons pressed on for ten more minutes. Then, kicking into a fast gallop, the experienced lieutenant judged it to be the right moment to bring the pursuit to a climax.

He swung his men inward to cut down the angle of travel between themselves and the Comancheros. When they thundered over the skyline into view, the outlaws were a mere hundred yards away. Gavin pressed on, making no effort to conceal his small command.

Within moments, one of the Comancheros made a casual glance to the rear and caught sight of the dragoons bearing down on him and his companions. His shout was audible, though the exact words were inconceivable. Whatever he said, however, was enough to set the group off into a frantic run for safety. They turned south, then east, obviously heading back toward the main group of Comancheros.

Gavin pulled his pistol, holding the .36 caliber Colt in his right hand while his left grasped the reins. The other, with the exception of Karshchov, who carried only a carbine, did the same as the distance between themselves and the outlaws halved, then halved again, and once again until they were right on top of them.

Gavin knew a shouted command to halt would mean nothing in the situation. He kicked his horse into a faster run and pointed the muzzle of the Colt at the nearest Comanchero. He fired, the bullet hitting the man in the right shoulder. The impact knocked the outlaw forward around his horse's head as he slipped and bounced to the ground, dead.

The five surviving Comancheros split up. A pair turned farther east while the remaining three continued back toward the main group of their friends. Douglas waved at Corporal Steeple and Fenlay to follow him, and the trio rode hard after the two-man team of escapees.

Gavin, Karshchov, and the remaining three dragoons pounded in hot pursuit of the other Comancheros. O'Hearn, an expert shot in the saddle, aimed at the foremost outlaw. Giving enough lead and keeping the barrel of the Colt level, the veteran horse soldier fired two quick shots.

The man's horse tumbled to the ground, and the one immediately behind collided with it. Both riders rolled forward in the grass from the momentum of their spills.

Gavin pointed to them and shouted. "O'Hearn! Carlson!"

The two dragoons wheeled around to capture the fallen duo. Meanwhile, the lieutenant, Corporal Murphy, and Basil Karshchov kept a stubborn pursuit of the remaining Comanchero. The Russian, knowing he was far from expert in using the carbine at a dead-gallop, wisely held back as he allowed the two military men to close in on their quarry. The Comanchero suddenly wheeled to the east, then reined in hard. He leaped from his horse, dragging his long gun from its saddle boot. Immediately dropping to a stable, kneeling position, he took quick but skillful aim before firing at the nearest dragoon who charged down on him.

Gavin felt the ball whip close to his head as he rode past the outlaw. Murphy also streaked by, and made a quick turn with the lieutenant for another charge, Karshchov, fifteen yards behind, looked in terror as the Comanchero pulled his pistol for a shot at him.

Once more the snarling outlaw aimed carefully. But before he could fire, another shot sounded from the near distance. The Comanchero threw up his arms and pitched forward.

Gavin rode up, the third bullet from his pistol in the man's skull. The sight of bloody brains spread around the cadaver showed there was no sense in checking out the man's condition.

"Let's go back to O'Hearn and Carlson," Gavin said.

The pair, dismounted, stood by two Comancheros sprawled on the ground. "Both goners, sir," O'Hearn said.

"One's shot, and the other must've broke his neck when he fell," Carlson added.

"At least they won't be going back to the main group and reporting our presence out here," Gavin said. He looked toward the east where Sergeant Douglas, Corporal Steeple, and Fenlay had ridden off. The horizon remained empty for a few minutes; then four horsemen appeared. One, sitting awkwardly in his saddle, had his arms tied behind his back.

Ten minutes later, the three dragoons dismounted

and reported in with a prisoner. "His pal is dead, but we got this one," Douglas said.

"He didn't want to take any chances by staying on the run," Steeple said.

"Well!" Gavin said, glad to see the captive. "This means that none of the Comancheros escaped to warn the main group. So let's settle down for a session of question-and-answer with this fellow."

The prisoner was a half-breed. His choice of clothing, similar to his bloodlines, was a mix of civilized and Indian attire. He wore a wool shirt and beaded, antelope-hide trousers. His hat sported an eagle feather, and he wore his light brown hair in Plains Indian style braids. His skin was fair, but his features could have been those of any average Kiowa or Comanche. He was quite a handsome man, but several scars across his face spoiled his looks.

"How're you called, fellow?" Gavin asked.

The man spat. "My name is Michael."

"Michael what?" Gavin inquired. "What is your family name."

"That is my white name," Michael answered. "That is all you need to know."

Douglas hit the half-breed so hard that he spun around. But the Comanchero didn't fall. He spat again; this time it was blood.

"That's enough, Sergeant!" Gavin snapped.

"Yes, sir," Douglas said, glaring at the prisoner.

"We know you are from the Comanchero band that raided the settlement up north," Gavin said. "So don't bother to deny it."

Michael remained silent, looking off in the distance.

"Where is you gang headed?" Gavin asked.

Michael shrugged. "To the south."

"Where in the south?" Gavin asked.

"To the south," the Comanchero repeated.

Karshchov could no longer contain himself. He leaped forward and grabbed the prisoner, shaking him. "Tell me about the pretty blond girl!" he yelled. "Where is she?"

Sergeant Douglas grabbed the Russian and pulled him away. "Take it easy, Mister Karshchov." He looked at Gavin. "Why don't you and him take a walk, Lieutenant? You both need some cooling down. We can wait to talk to this fellow for a few minutes." He turned his attention to the prisoner. "I'll have to convince him he should open up some more."

"I won't have that man tormented, Sergeant," Gavin said. "I mean it."

"Yes, sir," Douglas said. "You can trust me, but can you trust yourself?" He gave Gavin a meaningful glance. "I'm talking to you as both a friend and your second in command, sir."

"I could lose my self-control," Gavin admitted. "You're right, Sergeant. I need a stroll to calm down." He took Karshchov's arm. "I think a short walk would serve you well, too, Mister Karshchov. Let's go off for a bit and collect ourselves."

"Yes, Lieutenant," the Russian said. "Are you fearful you will do some cruelty to this man?"

"I am," Gavin said. "I can make him talk, but I need to be in complete control of myself."

The pair left the others and slowly ambled away. The Russian was worried. "Will the man tell us what we need to know?"

"I hope so," Gavin said. "There is much information I require before I can make any intelligent or meaningful decisions about what we must do."

They walked a few more minutes before Karshchov said, "I would like to be your friend."

Gavin was thoughtful for a few moments. Then he replied, "And I would like to be yours, Mister Karsh-chov."

"My Christian name is Basil," Karshchov said. "If you wish to call me that, I would be honored."

"I am Gavin," the lieutenant said.

The two men shook hands, then continued their stroll. "If something happens to Natalia, I do not wish to live," Karshchov said. "If I decide to stay and die even if it is useless, you must allow that. Surely you understand."

"Yes, Basil," Gavin said. "I believe I do."

"Have you ever loved a woman?" Karshchov asked. "I mean in a sincere manner in which you go beyond lust. A woman for whom you really care?"

Gavin didn't answer for a minute. Then he said, "No."

"I hope someday that you do," Karshchov said. "Only then will you know your true emotional and intellectual capacity as a human being."

Gavin's respect for Basil Karshchov took another step upward. He made a silent vow to reunite him with the woman he loved. The Russian deserved that, and so did Natalia. Gavin would have to push his personal feelings aside. The girl's happiness was all that mattered.

A shot sounded from the place they had left the dragoons and prisoner.

Gavin, with Karshchov following, raced back. When he arrived he found the half-breed lying dead on the ground. "What the hell happened?" Gavin demanded to know.

"He tried to escape, sir," Sergeant Douglas said.

The other dragoons looked impassively at their commanding officer as if to indicate they had nothing to do with the situation one way or the other.

"With his goddamned hands still tied behind his

back?" Gavin asked. "Now how are we supposed to interrogate him?"

"The Comanchero band is headed where the Little Arkansas and the Big Arkansas come together, sir," Douglas said. "That's where they've set up a town. After checking out this prairie country and the Santa Fe Trail in particular for another month or so, they'll take their loot and prisoners down into Mexico to sell and barter."

Gavin looked at the dead Comanchero, now noting that he had been given a good beating. Both eyes were black, and his nose was freshly broken and bleeding.

"Sergeant!"

"Am I relieved of my rank, sir?" Douglas asked.

Gavin sputtered, "No! But—"

"Will I be facing charges when we return to Fort Leavenworth, sir?" Douglas inquired further.

"No, Sergeant Douglas, I will not press any court-martial where you are concerned," Gavin said.

"It's the sergeants in the army that get things done," Douglas reminded him.

"Thank you for telling me," Gavin said. "But with you around, I shall never forget that fact." He walked toward his horse. "Let's mount up. We've a ways to go before we reach that Comanchero camp."

O'Hearn, grinning, swung up into his saddle. As a professional soldier, he liked to see things done quickly and effectively. It was much more efficient, many times, when Army Regulations were bent until they broke. He waited for the others, then headed out to his usual position at the head of the formation.

Chapter 11

The Comancheros laid out their camp in a specially selected area where the Little Arkansas and Big Arkansas rivers came together in south central Kansas Territory.

The outlaws had an excellent reason for choosing that site to locate the band's headquarters. River junctions, prominent bends in tributaries, and other features of waterways were used by everyone as landmarks in the flat, undistinguishable terrain of the prairie. With no outstanding land features such as valleys, peaks, or canyons, the only way to identify a certain place was by its proximity to either a watercourse or a prominent spot near it.

Since Guido Lazardo planned on sending plenty of scouting parties out, their quick and accurate returns with information and possible targets would be easier if they were able to find one of those rivers and follow it south toward the camp. Since none were familiar with that part of the country, they had no knowledge of the proximity or number of soldiers on those vast plains. Lazardo wanted to learn of all possible opportunities offered to him in the relatively unexplored wilderness of the Kansas Territory, but he didn't want to lose any men in the effort.

Another consideration of the choice was that of defense. In the rare case some force strong enough showed up to attack, the rivers would hinder any outright assault.

The Comanchero camp—or town—was a hodgepodge of shelters that gave ample display of the ethnic divergence of the band. Store-bought canvas tents, Indian lodges, quickly constructed log cabins, crude lean-tos, and sod habitations had been located in a haphazard pattern that spread itself across the open area between the rivers. The woods there had been raided for trees to obtain building materials.

Certain areas were allotted for tending to nature's calls, while the corral to keep horses and stolen cattle was on the south end to keep the animals from defiling the living area. On the north of the camp stood an imposing and sinister structure. Made of a double row of logs, this was the stockade where prisoners would be confined prior to removal to the south for sale to Mexican mines, Indian tribes, or others who had use for captive workers.

The inhabitants of Lazardo's nomadic and murderous kingdom were the worst criminals of a lawless, wide-open frontier who knew law enforcement only as a sporadic, ineffective show of force that gave them little to fear. Naturally wild and troublesome, their conduct in the camp, though barbarous at times, was mostly kept under control. This was done out of stark fear of the leader, Lazardo. He knew from his own youth in his bandit culture that it was necessary to have some set of rules or complete chaos would break out in the form of murder, vengeance killings, thievery, and woman stealing. He also knew that he faced the constant threat of rebellion from some ambitious or disenchanted faction. This called for aggressive vigilance on the leader's part.

Any habitual troublemaker was dealt with swiftly and

without mercy. Lazardo's favorite form of execution was to hang the condemned head-down until death. If the chief was particularly upset with the offender, a small fire would be set under the unfortunate to slowly roast his head.

The Sicilian had one idiosyncrasy he forced on his people. Lazardo made sure everyone called him *Mister* Lazardo. During the time he had served aboard the British ship, he'd noted the way seaman addressed ship's officers as "mister." The captain, of course, was always addressed by that title. At first Lazardo wanted to be called captain—or one of the various foreign versions of that rank: *capitan, captaine, capitano*. But he found out there were higher ranks than that, such as admirals in navies and colonels or generals in armies. For that reason, he settled for the more sweeping title of "mister"— not *señor, monsieur,* or *signore*—but mister.

Somehow the English word carried more weight because it reminded him of the cadre of stern officers aboard British ships. Therefore, everyone regardless of nationality was required to address him as Mister Lazardo, or suffer some very unpleasant consequences.

Lazardo's quarters were located in the very center of the settlement, and consisted of several structures. A fine tent stolen from a Mexican army garrison was his dining room, complete with looted furniture of mismatched table and chairs. Some fine silver taken from a large Texas ranch house served as eating utensils.

He slept and took females for his pleasure in a sod-and-log structure that was thick enough to stop anything fired at it. Cannonballs could eventually bring it down, but only after several direct hits. Like his dining tent, the small house was furnished with fine but diverse chairs, beds, nightstands, and commodes.

The Comanchero chief conducted his business from an open-sided lean-to, where a large, thronelike padded chair of heavy mahogany was located for his august person to sit in while making command decisions. That hefty hunk of furniture had come from a Mexican hacienda in which an entire family of patricians was massacred.

Located away from Lazardo's lodging, where it was out of sight and smell of the headman, was that crude but strong stockade for the prisoners. It was a hideous, open place, where the wretched prisoners suffered many indignities during their confinement. The sun baked them during the hot afternoons, and the notorious prairie cloudbursts and thunderstorms tormented the people who had no shelter. Sanitary conditions did not exist within the area, nor was modesty taken into consideration. The prisoners had to relieve themselves in full view of the guards and their fellow sufferers.

Following the return from the raid on the Russian settlement, Lazardo took a hot bath, soaking his hairy body in sudsy water, then drying off and applying liberal splashes of cologne. After changing into his best clothes, which consisted of a silk shirt, fine wool pants and jacket, thick velvet cravat complete with diamond stickpin, and a tall beaver fur hat, he summoned his second in command, Monroe Lockwood.

The portly man promptly presented himself at the master's quarters when he received the word he was wanted. Like other members of the band, he felt a stab of fear when called by Lazardo. Monroe Lockwood was an expert gunman, strong as a bear, and quick as a rattlesnake, but he was as nervous as a beaten dog around the Comanchero chief.

Lockwood smiled and nodded respectfully. "What can I do for you, Mister Lazardo?"

Lazardo stood in his tent, checking his reflection in a small mirror mounted on the center pole. He carefully curled the tips of his moustache. "Fetch me the young blond woman."

"Yes, sir, Mister Lazardo," Lockwood said. "I reckon I'll get Big Joe to help me out." He chuckled nervously. "That big ol' gal looking after her is gonna throw a fit."

"Do it any way you wish, Lockwood," Lazardo said. "Just get the beauty over here. I am anxious to enjoy her charms after I break her to my will."

Lockwood hurried away, grabbing Big Joe by the arm as he walked past his cookfire. "C'mon, we got something to do," he said.

The black man shook himself free. "Hey! I'm fixing to eat. It'll have to wait."

"Mister Lazardo's orders," Lockwood said.

"I'm with you, Monroe," Big Joe said. "What're we gonna do?"

"We got to fetch that little blonde," Monroe Lockwood said. "That big friend o' hers is gonna raise some hell, you bet."

"That's a big, strong woman," Big Joe said. He stood six-and-a-half feet high and weighed a solid, no-fat, muscular two hundred and fifty pounds. "She's gonna be a load!"

"I'm just glad we're both big fellers," Lockwood said.

The pair of giants hurried through the camp until they reached the stockade. The guard in front waited for them to walk up to see what they wanted.

"We got to fetch a pris'ner for Mister Lazardo," Lockwood said.

The guard, a short, wiry Mexican, grinned. "I know which one. *La huera*—the blonde, eh?"

"That's her," Big Joe said. "She's really caught Mister Lazardo's eye. Hurry on up and open the gate. We figger we'll be fighting the large gal taking care of her."

The guard pulled out a key and slipped it into the huge padlock that held a restraining chain in place.

"You'll fight more than her, *amigos*. All them men in there has gathered around the blonde to protect her."

"What the hell are you talking about?" Lockwood demanded to know.

"You'll see when you get in there," the guard said. He finished his unlocking chore and held open the gate. *"Pasan, caballeros,"* he invited.

When Lockwood and Big Joe stepped inside the stockade, they noticed all the prisoners were gathered together at the far end. They were quiet, but stared at him and Big Joe with suspicious looks. In the middle of the group sat the blonde and her large companion.

"Clear the way, damn you!" Lockwood shouted. "We want that blonde there."

Immediately everyone leaped to their feet. The women and children drew off to one side while the men closed ranks, glaring at the two Comancheros.

"We said for y'all to move your butts!" Big Joe warned them. "Now, we ain't playing. Somebody's gonna get they heads busted up good!"

The Russians, glaring in anger, held their ground. Some muttered in their language in a manner that showed they were giving their own warnings to the pair of Comancheros.

Lockwood sighted Natalia among several of the larger men. "You just come on with us, honey lamb," he said in a futile attempt to sound soothing. "Mister Lazardo just wants to give you some loving. Why, you'll plumb like it. All the women is crazy over him."

Natalia spoke up in a loud voice filled with angry defiance. "I will not go with you, sir!" she exclaimed. "I have ordered this man standing next to me that if it appears I am to be taken away, he is to kill me."

Big Joe looked at Lockwood. "What's all this shit?"

Lockwood shrugged. "I ain't never heard nothing so crazy."

"She says them fellers is gonna kill 'er!" Big Joe exclaimed.

Lockwood only shrugged. "Aw! C'mon, let's go get her."

The two Comancheros surged forward but were met by an onrush of the prisoners. Lockwood picked out the nearest man and swung a heavy fist, knocking him back. Another Russian leaped over his fallen friend and drove an elbow into Lockwood's jaw, staggering him. The American punched out with rapid blows to drive his tormentor away.

Big Joe was having trouble of his own as he got an ear boxed and took a straight jab to the nose. He, too, fought back but was overwhelmed by the organized resistance.

The large Russian men now worked together as they pummeled and kicked the Comancheros, driving them back all the way to the gate.

The guard observed the altercation with a wide grin across his face. "I told you two *pandejos* that them men was protecting her."

Lockwood and Big Joe charged again in savage fury. The two were no easy pushovers for anybody. Using their combined physical courage, expertise, and strength, they attacked with fists and boots, but the desperate anger of the captives again forced them to withdraw with additional scrapes and bruises.

Big Joe snuffed and wiped at his bleeding nose. "Them fellers is crazy, Monroe."

Lockwood gingerly laid a hand on his bruised jaw. "I ain't never seen nothing like this. Why, you'd think she was a queen or something."

"We got to get her, though," Big Joe warned him. "Or Mister Lazardo is gonna have us hanging headdown from that big ol' cottonwood near his digs." Then he added, "Over a fire!"

"Let's go!" Lockwood said.

The pair waded in again, alternating their fisticuffs with wrestling holds. A couple of the Russians went down, but they came back up fast, damning the pain as they joined the others in the punch-for-punch and kick-for-kick contest.

Once again, Lockwood and Big Joe were manhandled by the big men and pounded back to the gate. The damage to Big Joe's nose had now grown to a fracture. Blood streamed from it and dripped heavily down on his shirt. He pulled his revolver form its holster, but Lockwood grabbed his arm.

"Hang on, Big Joe!" he said. "Them fellers is worth a lot of money. We'll really be in the soup if a couple get shot. Dead men don't fetch no prices from Mexican mines."

"Then, what the hell are you gonna do?" Big Joe demanded to know.

"I got to tell Mister Lazardo," Lockwood said. He snapped his fingers at the guard. "Get your butt over to Mister Lazardo and tell him we got special trouble down here."

"*Ay, chingado!*" the guard exclaimed. "I don't want to. He might get mad about what's going on."

"Goddamn you!" Lockwood said. "You'd best do as I say, or I'll see that you're hung from a tree by your balls instead o' your feet!"

The guard reluctantly turned, then walked toward the center of camp to fetch the Comanchero chief.

"Them foreigners is crazy," Lockwood complained. "They didn't fight this hard at the settlement. I wonder what's got 'em suicidal all of a sudden."

"They didn't have no real leadership when we jumped 'em out there, remember?" Big Joe said. "We hit 'em when they wasn't expecting it. I think the shock unnerved 'em, and they been organizing or something."

A few moments later an angrily curious Lazardo showed up with the guard. "What is the trouble here?" he asked. "Can't you two get your hands on that woman? Is the big one even more than large men can handle?"

"Something's crazy as hell, Mister Lazardo," Lockwood said. "Not only does that li'l blond gal refuse to come out, she said she told some o' them fellers to kill her if it looks like we're gonna take her."

"It don't make a lick o' sense, Mister Lazardo," Big Joe added.

Lazardo stepped through the gate and approached the prisoners. Once again they formed up for a fight. "Where is that blond girl?" he yelled.

The Russians, not understanding him, maintained their silence as they glared at him and the other two Comancheros. Their silence was mute defiance and determination.

"You'll not have me!" Natalia's voice, coming from the back of the crowd, had a ring of bravado in it. "I have ordered these men to kill me before allowing me to be taken by you."

Lazardo, being a European, instantly recognized the facts in the situation. He asked, "Who are you?"

"I am Lady Natalia Valenko, daughter of His Grace Count Vladimir Aleksandrovich Valenko. We are a noble family of the Czarist Empire of all the Russias!"

Lazardo had known she was a noblewoman before he asked. It was a situation that no American could possibly fathom.

"Where is your father and what are you doing in the American wilderness, Lady Natalia?" the outlaw leader asked.

"The settlement you blackguards attacked is owned by my father," Natalia said. "He has come here to set up an estate." In spite of her spirited showing, Natalia had been frightened almost beyond sanity. She was sincere about having herself killed rather than suffer the shame of being ravished. Now she realized she was safe, and the relief was mixed with shame as she stood in the midst of her people.

"Thank you, Lady Natalia," Lazardo said. "I assure you that you will not be harmed." He knew full well that a raped noblewoman was not a good bargaining tool. The threat of her outrage would mean more money and a quicker reaction from her family than if a commoner had already had his way with her.

"What the hell's this all about?" Monroe Lockwood asked.

"It is something you do not understand," Lazardo said. He gave his full attention to Natalia, suddenly becoming polite. He bowed, saying, "I am Guido Lazardo. I wish for you to look upon me as your protector until arrangements can be made to have you safely returned to your father."

Natalia pushed her way through the crowd and stood face-to-face with Lazardo. "I know what you mean. You are going to ask ransom for me, are you not?"

"Of course," Lazardo said.

Natalia put aside the horrible fear she had been hiding. Now was the time for her to conduct herself by the philosophy of *noblesse oblige*.

"You must return my people with me," the young woman demanded.

Lazardo shook his head. "These are peasants. I know, for I am a peasant, too. But a very smart one. I will sell these strapping fellows and lusty wenches along with the children down in Mexico or to Indians in Texas."

"I will not permit it," Natalia said. "I demand their release in the name of the czar!"

"The czar be damned," Guido said. "But I will grant

131

you one consideration. The big woman can return with you." He indicated Irena Yakubovski, who stood nearby.

"That is not enough," Natalia argued.

"I am in charge here," Lazardo reminded her. "That is my only concession, Lady Natalia."

"I command you to release us all!" Natalia cried out. "Do you hear? I command you!"

"Save your mandates for your miserable peasants," Lazardo said. "Meanwhile, as your protector, I will have you put in more comfortable quarters where you can wait for your release in dignity and grace."

"I will stay here with my people," Natalia said.

"As you wish, my lady," Lazardo said. "However, I will instruct the guards that if you desire to see me or seek more luxurious arrangements, you may send them to me."

"That will not happen!" Natalia vowed.

"You speak English in the manner of the British," Lazardo said. "I am a great admirer of those northern people. They are conquerors."

"Our conversation is at an end," Natalia announced. She turned and walked back into the crowd of Russians.

Lazardo bowed and said, "As you wish, my lady." He turned and went back to the gate with Lockwood and Big Joe following.

Lockwood was curious. "Just what the hell happened, Mister Lazardo?"

"Yes, sir," Big Joe said, echoing his own confusion. "I can't figger nothing about this."

"Europe has come to the American prairie," Lazardo said. He sneered. "It is something bumpkins would not understand."

Lockwood and Big Joe stopped and watched their chief return to his quarters. "I'll tell you something," Lockwood said. "That little gal may talk high and mighty, but she ain't gonna pull nothing on Mister Lazardo."

Big Joe grinned. "I think the fun is just starting."

Chapter 12

Gavin MacRoss sat in the comfortable crook of two large branches in the heights of a cottonwood tree growing along the Little Arkansas River. The foliage, thick for early spring, gave him plenty of cover as he peered through his field glasses at the Comanchero camp on the other bank. If it hadn't been for the danger he faced, he would have enjoyed his perch. The weather was beautiful, birds chirped, and the sound of the flowing water was very soothing.

He had climbed into the lofty regions of the tree just before dawn while it was light enough to allow a safe ascent, yet too dark to be spotted by any alert outlaws who might be early risers.

The lieutenant was well-prepared for a day-long stay in the tree. A haversack across his shoulder held the food he would consume until it was dark enough in the evening to climb back to the ground without danger of observation from the Comanchero camp. His canteen, hanging by its strap on a branch near him, was filled with water from a creek a couple of miles away where the rest of the dragoon detachment, along with Basil Karshchov, waited for his return with whatever information he could garner.

The lieutenant's time was not wasted. He had spotted

the stockade where the prisoners were held on the north end of the encampment, and the large corral for the Comancheros' horses in the exact opposite direction at the southern extreme. The young officer estimated the size of the settlement to be approximately a half-mile long with a width that ranged from a few feet where the two rivers joined, expanding out to a couple of hundred yards up to the stockade. He was surprised to see numerous women and children, obviously belonging to Comancheros, living in the primitive village. The outlaw band, like other similar ones, was a culture unto itself that stayed outside the bounds of normal society.

Between visual sweeps with the binoculars, Gavin sketched the layout of the camp, noting easy accesses and areas where the population was the heaviest. After he'd completed his drawing, he studied it at odd intervals. Several plans of entering and exiting the settlement for a rescue mission made tentative appearances in his alert mind.

Various-sized bands of Comanchero horsemen kept busy all day, riding in and out of the place. Gavin wondered how long it would be before they noted the absence of the group he and his men had intercepted two days before. As a professional military man, he surmised that the riders were scouting and exploring the countryside to gather information for any future forays of murder and kidnapping they might wish to conduct. Eventually, he realized, some of those Comanchero riders would discover the bodies of their dead compatriots.

By mid-afternoon, Gavin had gathered all the information he needed. In order to keep from getting bored until it was safe to withdraw, he kept a sharp eye on everything that went on. As far as he could determine, there wasn't a race of man, outside of Orientals possibly, that wasn't represented in the band. Whites, Mexicans, Indians, Blacks and various mixtures thereof were in great evidence among the population.

As the day progressed, the army officer also noted a couple of fights, camp chores by the women, loud games enjoyed by the children, and other activities that hardly betrayed the evil of the participants. He wondered how many of the small boys running and laughing would end up as cold-blooded killers and slavers.

The day drifted by slowly, but eventually the sun eased into its westerly slide toward the horizon, growing redder as it continued its eternal journey. When the shadows grew long enough and the evening's gloom settled in, Gavin slowly and carefully descended from his perch and stepped down on the thick grass of the patch of woods. After a few moments of careful waiting and listening, he withdrew into the deeper interior of the copse where his horse was hobbled. He led the animal to the other side of the trees and, when clear of the woods, mounted up for the ride back to the dragoon camp.

Private Olaf Carlson was on guard duty when Gavin returned. The young trooper stood up and waved the lieutenant on in to the bivouac. He smartly presented arms as his commanding officer rode past.

"Glad to see you back, sir," Carlson cheerfully greeted him.

"I'm real happy to be back, believe me," Gavin said as he returned the salute and went into the trees alongside the creek to dismount. The others waited eagerly for him, especially Basil Karshchov, who wasted no time in approaching him.

The Russian asked, "What did you see? Was Natalia there? Is she all right? What about the others? Are they all dead or alive?"

"Hold on," Gavin said. "One question at a time. But to answer the most important for you: no, I didn't see

Miss Valenko. But I did spot where she and the others are being kept."

"I pray she is not harmed," Karshchov said.

"I saw no mistreatment of the prisoners," Gavin remarked. "They seemed to be simply kept in confinement without having to bear any undue torment. But their circumstances are most unpleasant."

"The suffering people!" Karshchov said. "My poor darling!"

Sergeant Douglas, curious as to what would be going on for the next several days, joined them. He carried a cup of coffee that he handed over to Gavin. "I figger anybody that's spent the day in a tree should at least have a cup o' java."

The lieutenant smiled his thanks. "This is just what I need."

"Sorry I ain't got any brandy or whiskey to lace it with," Douglas said.

"That would be most appreciated, Sergeant Douglas," Gavin said, grinning. "Believe me!"

"Have a good day, sir?"

"A very good day, Sergeant," Gavin said. "Let's sit down and talk over some very important subjects."

Karshchov, too nervous to relax, remained standing as the two dragoons settled in for a professional consultation between themselves.

Douglas knew there was more work to be done before they would settle in their blankets that night. "I'm all ears, Lieutenant."

Gavin pulled his sketch-map from his pocket and handed it over. "That's the layout of the Comanchero camp. It's as accurate as I could make it from peering out of a tree across the river."

"Christ!" Douglas exclaimed. "There's enough shelters there for a hundred and fifty or two hundred people."

"My count exactly," Gavin said. "There are even women and children living with the Comancheros. Whole families of the sons of bitches."

"The dogs are breeding future generations," Karshchov said in anger.

"It appears so," Gavin said. He turned his attention back to the map. "At any rate, here's the layout."

"It's a good map, sir," Douglas said. "But you still ain't completely happy with what you've learned, are you?"

"There's nothing like a personal reconnaissance to take care of any unanswered questions or to gain knowledge of the unknown," Gavin said. "That camp is going to have to be visited in order to fill in any missing information I couldn't get from looking and sketching."

"Sounds like a job for an experienced officer and his sergeant," Douglas said.

"That is exactly what I was thinking, Sergeant," Gavin said. "If we enter the place in the dark, our field dress should make us inconspicuous as long as we leave our military accouterments behind."

"Except for belts and holsters, right, sir?" Douglas asked.

"Exactly," Gavin said. He smiled, saying, "I don't think we should take our sabers along."

Douglas chuckled at the idea of lugging the bladed weapons with them. "Alright, sir, if you insist. It's a shame we can't go over there in all our martial glory."

"We would need blaring bugle calls to add to our appearance," Gavin joked back.

Douglas laughed. "Say! Don't forget that O'Hearn has his old bugle with him. As I recall he was pretty damned good with the thing."

"He is going to wish he remained a field musician before this is over," Gavin said.

"He gave up his bugle for a carbine because he wanted to do real soldiering," Douglas replied.

"I admire him for that," Gavin said. He changed the subject, asking, "When can you be ready to go?"

"I'm ready right now," Douglas said. "You're the one drinking coffee."

Gavin quickly drained the cup. "Let's be on our way. By the time we get there, it will be dark enough for us to enter the place."

Karshchov grabbed Gavin's sleeve. "I shall go, too, Gavin."

"I'm sorry, Basil," Gavin said. "This is a very ticklish job. I don't believe you've the experience needed if we have to go low and sneaky to get in and out of the place."

"I must go for the sake of my ladylove!" Karshchov exclaimed.

Douglas put a friendly hand on Karshchov's shoulder. "We're working out a plan to rescue the lady and all your friends. You don't want to queer it, do you?"

"Of course not," Karshchov said.

"Then, let us do our job, please, Mister Karshchov," Douglas asked of him.

"Yes. I am sorry," Karshchov said. He turned to Gavin. "Please, then, you try to find out if Natalia is all right or not, will you?"

"Of course," Gavin said.

"Tell me the truth when you find out," Karshchov pleaded. "I must know, no matter how horrible!"

"I'll not lie to you, Basil," Gavin promised. "You can count on that."

"Let's go, sir," Douglas urged him. "It'll be completely dark in another fifteen or twenty minutes."

The pair of senior-ranking men turned the detachment over to Corporal Steeple, then mounted up for a slow, careful ride across the dark prairie to the grove of trees across from the Comanchero camp.

They reined up, and Gavin said, "I suggest we leave our mounts here and enter the place on foot. We'll attract less attention than if we are riding." He pointed to the left. "That's a shallow area where I noticed some kids playing," Gavin explained. "We can wade across it without any trouble."

The two dragoons dismounted and secured their horses. Gavin led the way as they walked slowly and carefully through the dense brush. The sound of the river lapping against its banks drowned out any noise they made. When the pair of dragoons reached the shallows, they halted and gave the immediate area to their front a careful scrutiny.

"I wish the moon wasn't so bright," Douglas said.

Gavin shrugged. "That won't make any difference. We'll be strolling past campfires anyhow. As long as we don't attract any undue attention to ourselves we should be fine."

"We should be, huh?" Douglas asked.

"Come on," Gavin said.

"Hell, yes, sir," Douglas said. "I never planned on living forever anyhow."

Gavin pulled off his boots and socks and began to roll up his trouser legs as Douglas did the same. Within moments they were in the water that came up to mid-calf on the two men. The river bottom was rocky, causing some discomfort before they finally reached the other side.

"Those Comanchero kids were running barefoot through this stuff," Gavin said, stepping gingerly onto the sandy bank.

"That shows how tough the little bastards are," Douglas remarked as they quickly pulled on their footgear.

"I want to check out the corral first," Gavin said. "It's closer."

The two skirted the camp in a southerly direction, trying to keep to the shadows as much as possible.

"Hey!" a voice called out. "What the hell're you two up to?" An armed Comanchero stepped out into the light. "I seen you two wading across the river. Just what the hell's going on?"

Gavin tried to think of something to say, so Douglas quickly stepped in. "We'll tell you if you keep it to yourself."

The Comanchero sneered. "Keep what to myself?"

"We got some kegs o' liquor outta that raid a few days ago, and we stashed 'em over there in the woods," Douglas said. "We don't aim to share none of it, but if'n you promise not to tell nobody else, we'll let you in on one."

"How'd you bring any liquor outta there?" the man asked.

"We put 'em on a wagon and throwed some stuff over it, that's how," Douglas said in an angry tone. "Now, do you want one or not?"

"Maybe I want two, by God!" the outlaw insisted.

Douglas looked at Gavin. "What 'a'ya think?"

Gavin feigned reluctance. "He'll just want more."

"We gotta give him something," Douglas said. He turned back to the Comanchero. "Two will be fine. But we got to go get 'em now. We don't want to be messing around with it in the daylight. Somebody's bound to see us. Are you coming with us?"

"Damn right!" the man said eagerly.

Douglas took Gavin's arm to steer him as he headed back toward the river. The outlaw hurried up to join them. As he stepped between the two dragoons, Douglas's knife came out, and he slashed deep into the man's throat. Unable to yell, the victim choked and staggered

141

as blood filled his mouth. The sergeant struck hard three more times with swift stabs to the abdomen. The Comanchero's knees collapsed, and he went to the ground. Douglas wasted no time in dragging him to the river and rolling him in. The current immediately pulled the corpse out into midstream and carried it south.

"If there ain't no more shallows, he'll be in Injun territory by morning," Douglas said.

"Good work," Gavin said. "I was caught flat-footed by that fellow."

"I'm a natural-born liar, sir," Douglas said. "It comes in handy now and again."

"I prefer to think of you as a most creative teller of tales," Gavin said.

"Let's get this job over with," Douglas urged. He looked at the camp. "I don't feel good about this a'tall, sir."

They were a bit more careful as they resumed their errand toward the corral. It was so noisy from the running rivers when they reached the place, all they had to worry about was avoiding being seen. The two waterways merged, swirling over rocks to create plenty of splashing, while the horses in the corral stomped their hooves and whinnied now and again. If there were any guards, they were out of sight and not too attentive. As far as the Comancheros seemed to be concerned, the corral was not a place to expect a serious attack.

Gavin put to work the engineering skills he'd learned at West Point. He walked around the corral, grabbing posts and shaking them to judge the effect the movement had on the structure. Finally the dragoon officer found what he was looking for. It was the farthest one, and when he shook it, all the rails in the barricade rattled.

Douglas was puzzled. "What are you doing, sir?"

"If this particular post gets pulled down, the whole

142

thing will go with it," Gavin said. "The better to turn horses loose fast and simultaneously."

"I'll take your word for it, sir," Douglas said.

"Now let's give that stockade a study," Gavin said. "But I fear it will be constructed three or four times sturdier than this corral."

They walked in a northerly direction, keeping to the edge of the camp on the inner side of the foliage that grew along the riverbank. Although it was well past midnight numerous campfires still burned in front of the crude dwellings, giving the place an eerily weak, dancing sort of illumination that suited both Gavin and Douglas. It was difficult to accurately judge another person's features in the poor light.

They hadn't gone far when a drunken Mexican staggered up to them. He shoved a bottle of clear liquid at them, saying, *"Ya, agarran un traigito!"*

"What the hell is that?" Douglas asked angrily.

"I got tequila," the Comanchero said. *"Soy papa!* My woman have baby. *Fiesta grande*—big celebration. Take a drink! *Un traigito,* eh?"

Douglas took a sip from the bottle and passed it over to Gavin, who also swallowed some of the fiery liquor.

"Good luck to you," Douglas said. He patted the man on the shoulder, then turned him and sent him staggering away.

"At least we got a free drink out of this, huh?" Gavin remarked with a chuckle.

"I needed it, sir," Douglas said sincerely.

They went on for a few more yards before they were once again interrupted. This time it was a shrill, complaining voice.

"Say, fellers!" A woman's voice called to them.

Douglas glanced over at a lean-to made of buffalo hide. He spotted the female who had called to them.

"Yeah?" he responded in a husky voice.

143

"Have either o' you seen Michael?" she asked.

Gavin quickly whispered, "Isn't that the name of the half-breed fellow we captured?"

"I think so, sir," Douglas said.

"You know him, don't you?" the woman asked. "A 'breed. He wears his hair like an Injun, but it's brown not black."

"Didn't he go north with some other fellers?" Douglas asked.

"Yeah," she said. "They got sent out some days ago. Me and the kids is waiting."

"Well, him and his pals ain't back yet," Douglas said. Then he added under his breath, "And not likely to be either!"

"God! This Comanchero life causes suffering for everybody, doesn't it?" Gavin said.

"Better them than other folks, sir," Douglas said.

When they drew close to the stockade, Gavin led them into the shadows of the nearby trees. "They'll have alert guards on duty there, so it's not going to be quite as easy as the corral."

"Maybe we should each check a side," Douglas suggested. "We can meet back here and compare notes."

"Good idea," Gavin said.

"I'll take the front area there," Douglas said. "Since we'll probably pull 'em out of the back, you'd best check that part out, sir."

"Let's get to it, Sergeant," Gavin said.

Both army men pulled the brims of their hats down over their faces and affected nonchalant attitudes as they parted. Gavin walked away from the gate guards, making it appear as if he were on his way to some destination near the river. When the lieutenant entered the shadows of the trees, he made a sharp turn to skirt the perimeter of the stockade. He continued walking until he was on the far side before testing the structure.

The Comancheros had constructed their prison with the idea of keeping people inside it. The fact that someone might want to break *into* it had never occurred to them. Gavin saw that the outside logs were loosely placed and tied together. A couple of swipes with a sharp knife would cut through the ropes that laced the restraints together. It would only take a bit of pushing and tugging to make a hole wide enough for someone to squeeze through. If the escape was made on that far side, it would go virtually unnoticed. Without outside help, the only practical way out would be over the wall.

Gavin knew exactly how he would pull off the escape of all the Russian captives. The problem would be keeping it going once they were out on the open prairie. But that was a problem he would deal with later. He figured it time to find Douglas and get the hell out of the place.

Gavin, staying in the shadows, retraced his route toward the front of the prison. When he reached the trees, he could see Douglas engaged in quiet conversation with the sentries. Gavin smiled, knowing his sergeant would be gaining valuable information about changes in the guard, routine of the prisoners, and other bits of intelligence that might make the escape attempt even more effective.

Suddenly the sound of men approaching sounded from the front. Gavin instinctively ducked back but was glad to see that Douglas put on an appearance of being completely unconcerned. When the oncoming Comancheros walked into the weak lantern light, it was easy to tell they were the guards who would be taking over from those currently on duty. Douglas still played his role, acting as if he belonged there, too.

Suddenly Gavin gasped.

Two of the men in the group were the deserters Jack McRyan and Dennis Costello.

Chapter 13

Sergeant Ian Douglas may have felt an angry, almost fearful shock at seeing Jack McRyan and Dennis Costello, but he covered it with bravado.

The veteran soldier displayed an expression of complete contempt, even striding toward them, stopping and emitting a loud laugh when he reached a spot directly in front of the two deserters.

"Now here's a pair o' useless bastards if I ever saw any!" he roared in what appeared to be genuine hilarity. "I thought the Injuns musta got you. Maybe the redskins decided you wasn't worth much just like the army did."

"You son of a bitch!" McRyan hollered. "Grab him! He's a goddamned soldier—a sergeant!"

The Comancheros immediately leveled their long guns on the sergeant. Their leader was Monroe Lockwood. The big man stepped forward and gave Douglas a long look.

"What the hell are they talking about, stranger?" the Comanchero asked.

"They're just happy to see their old sergeant," Douglas said.

"You ain't dressed like no damn soldier," Lockwood

said. "But that's sure enough a army belt and holster you're wearing."

"Look at us," McRyan said. "We ain't wearing no uniforms neither. All of them fancy duds was left behind in the barracks when we come out into the field. Ever'body in the army does that."

"I ain't calling those two dumb bastards liars, am I?" Douglas said. "Hell, yeah, I'm in the army. Carried on in the job of line sergeant, if you really want to know."

"Well, I really want to know," Lockwood said.

Costello sneered at the sergeant. "We'll be seeing you hanging by your heels afore tomorrow's sun sets, you asshole! If'n you think stringing me and Jack up by our wrists was rough, wait'll you get a taste o' that."

"Shut your Bowery boy mouth!" Douglas snapped in disgust. He took one more step forward, this time coupling the move with a swift swing of his right fist. It collided with Costello, slamming him to the ground.

The sergeant made an instantaneous spin toward McRyan, kicking out and hitting his carbine. The weapon detonated as it whirled through the air and landed a few feet away. Douglas didn't let an instant pass before he held the deserter's collar with his left hand and punched him rapidly in the face with his right.

"These boys ain't real tough," Douglas said, letting McRyan drop beside Costello. "Fact o' the matter, one o' them Russian gals throwed that'n in a creek."

"Hey!" Lockwood exclaimed. "What do you know about them Russians?"

"Plenty," Douglas said. "I was second in command o' the escort that brung 'em out here."

Lockwood motioned with his musket. "There's something about you that's getting me riled up. I'm taking you to see Mister Lazardo. These two may be a coupla the silliest bastards that rode across the Missouri River,

147

but they're right about you hanging by your damn heels. Now move! Don't try no shit with me, or I'll blow a hole in you wide enough to drive a team o' mules through."

"Now, that'd just about ruin my whole day," Douglas said.

"There ain't a hell of a lot that rattles you, is there?" Lockwood asked.

"I just try to get along," Douglas said in a calm voice.

Gavin watched the scene with worried attention. As Douglas moved in the direction indicated, the lieutenant realized there was nothing he could do for him at that moment. Gavin quickly moved back into the shadows and headed for the river. This time he would chance a swim across to get back to his horse.

None of the Comancheros caught the slight movement when the lieutenant withdrew. They were too busy following after Douglas and Lockwood in the light of a lantern held by one of the guards. Even McRyan and Costello, a bit stunned from being punched, tagged along on the short trek to the center of the camp where Guido Lazardo's quarters were located. They couldn't wait to see what was going to happen to the sergeant. Both hoped they would have a chance to participate in his miserable death.

It didn't take but five minutes to reach Lazardo's area. Although the hour was late, Lockwood didn't hesitate in the slightest to call out to the band's leader.

"Mister Lazardo!" the burly Comanchero yelled. "We got to see you! It's important!"

Lazardo, snuggled under his blankets with an Indian woman, knew that no one would disturb him unless it was extremely important. He immediately awoke and pulled on a pair of trousers, leaving the female companion with whom he had chosen to spend the night.

"What is it, Lockwood?" Lazardo asked, stepping

148

through the cabin door. He squinted his eyes at the sight of Douglas. "Who is this?"

"He's a sergeant in the army," Lockwood said. "Says he was one of 'em that brung them Russians out here."

Lazardo glared at Douglas. "Is that so?"

"Sure is," Douglas said.

Lazardo exhibited a wry smile. "You have come to rescue them?" He glanced around at the darkness beyond the settlement. "Are there more soldiers out there?"

Douglas shook his head. "I didn't come to help them Russians. Anyhow, there ain't enough soldiers left to do the job. Ask them two dipshits."

McRyan and Costello shuffled their feet. McRyan spoke up, saying, "He's right about that. They're could be no more'n—" he thought a moment as he remembered the names of the men in the section he had so recently deserted, counting them off on his fingers— "seven or eight of 'em left after us and others run off."

"Unless they went back to Fort Leavenworth to get more," Costello interjected.

"There ain't been time for that," Douglas said. "We killed the others, but these two got away after leaving their pals to cover their asses."

"There's still only seven or eight of 'em left in the detachment," McRyan insisted.

Lazardo was most interested in McRyan's estimate of the military's numbers. "You are sure of this?" he asked. "They are really that small a group?"

"Yes, sir, Mister Lazardo," McRyan said.

"Are these two members of our band?" Lazardo asked, indicating McRyan and Costello.

"That's right, Mister Lazardo," Lockwood answered.

Lazardo gave them a long, appraising look. "When did this happen?"

"It wasn't but about three or four days ago," the Comanchero answered. "They met up with Morales and Crazy Fox along with a coupla more o' the boys. That was a day or so after we raided the Russians. They brung 'em to me. Since they was soldiers on the run, I give 'em a chance to join up. When they found out we'd raided the Russians, they damn near went crazy. After they come here, they laid eyes on that big ol' gal in the stockade. They really wanted me to give her to 'em. But you'd already made her the blond lady's maid or whatever you call it, and I got first call on her."

Lazardo pointed a finger at McRyan and Costello. "You forget that big woman."

Douglas laughed aloud. "They'd better or she'll beat the shit out of 'em."

"You're interesting to me," Lazardo said, looking at Douglas. "How did you end up in here?"

"Kinda like them two," Douglas said. "I deserted, too."

"That's a damn lie!" McRyan yelled out.

"He's a sergeant for God's sake!" Costello echoed. "The meanest son of bitch in the U.S. of A. Army!"

"That's a right nice thing to say," Douglas said. "It pleases me that you two was so unhappy serving under my command. But I went over the hill just the same."

"He'd never run away from the army," McRyan said. "Hell! He's been in it for a lot o' years."

Lazardo gave Douglas an inquiring look. "How long have you been a soldier?"

"Oh, I reckon about fifteen years," Douglas said. "But I been thinking of getting out."

"That's a damn lie!" McRyan yelled out. "Anyhow, where's his carbine? If he deserted, how come he didn't take it with him? Ever' dragoon has one, and we're taught to keep it handy. This old bastard would never go nowhere without it."

"I had to leave my weapon behind," Douglas said.

150

"We stacked arms, and there wasn't no way I could get it without getting seen."

"Liar!" McRyan bellowed. "Dirty damn rotten liar!"

Lockwood cuffed him. "Shut up and let Mister Lazardo do the talking."

Lazardo said, "It seems strange a man who is second in command would run away."

"I was in trouble," Douglas said. "The lieutenant got mad on account o' I hung these two shitheads by their wrists for a little while."

"A little while, eh?" Lazardo remarked with a smile. He pointed to Costello. "How long did this man hang you by your wrists?"

"Four hours," Costello said.

Lazardo liked that. "I find it hard to believe doing such a thing would get you in trouble."

"The lieutenant don't like that kind o' discipline," Douglas said. "I'd been warned about it before, so he said he was gonna put me up on charges for disobeying orders. I'd lose my rank and pay, and have to go back to being a private."

It made sense to Lazardo. He had known of boatswains on ships being broken back to the rank of common sailors for infractions. But he was still suspicious. He asked Douglas, "How did you get here?"

"I walked most o' yesterday," Douglas said. "My horse busted his leg in a prairie dog hole, and I had to shoot him. I seen your camp and walked in."

"Did you know we were here?" Lazardo asked.

"Nope. I found y'all accidental," Douglas replied. "I was heading south to avoid the army, then was going to turn east and cross the Missouri River near the Arkansas line. But I seen this place and figgered it was a town."

"Well, mister, you walked into a Comanchero camp," Lockwood said.

"No shit?" Douglas remarked. "Maybe you could use me in your line o' work. I guarantee you that I'm better out here than them two strawfeet."

McRyan's hatred flared up. "By God, Douglas, I swore I'd kill you and I will!"

This time it was Lazardo who hit him. "I decide who dies here!" he yelled in a rage.

Douglas grinned at McRyan. "You sure been taking your licks in the past quarter hour, ain't you?"

Lazardo calmed down and became thoughtful. Finally, he said, "What is your name? Douglas, did you say?"

"That's it," the sergeant said.

"As you suggested, maybe we could use a man like you," Lazardo said.

Douglas indicated the stockade with a tilt of his head. "What're you gonna do with them Russians."

"Sell them for slaves in Mexico or to Indians," Lazardo replied. "All except for the pretty, young blonde. She says her father is a count."

"He is," Douglas said. "Count Valenko is his name."

"McRyan and Costello told us that, too," Lockwood said.

"We will ransom her to him," Lazardo said.

"He's real rich," Douglas said. "So you should get a good potful o' gold or greenbacks or whatever you want. I learned that he paid for all them folks to get over here and even bought the tools and wagons and other stuff."

By that time the new day's sun radiated a reddish light through the trees on the riverbank. The camp had begun to stir as the people emerged from their dwelling places to relieve themselves first, then build up the fires that had ebbed into coals during the hours of darkness.

By then Douglas was certain that Gavin had managed an escape. He felt relief with the realization and also because it seemed he would be able to move into

152

the Comanchero gang. The important thing, once he was accepted, was to make contact with the dragoon detachment to take advantage of the situation.

Lockwood had been thoughtful for the past several minutes. He finally spoke: "Maybe Douglas here ought to join me and Big Joe, Mister Lazardo. We can use an extry hand, particular one that's got experience in this part o' the country."

"Good idea," Lazardo said.

"Sounds fine to me," Douglas said agreeably.

"While you were riding about, did you see any more of my men?" Lazardo asked. "I have sent various groups numbering three to six strong to scout out targets. A couple have yet to return."

Douglas shook his head. "Nope. I ain't seen hide nor hair o' Comancheros 'til I come in here last night. Y'know there's plenty o' Pawnees and Cheyennes in these parts with Comanches and Kiowas showing up now and then."

"My Comancheros have plenty of experience with Indians," Lazardo said. "Most of the tribes now know us. My men carry gifts for them."

McRyan and Costello continued to glare in helpless fury at the man they considered their arch enemy. When they first sighted him in the camp, thoughts of him dangling head-down over a fire had danced through their minds. McRyan especially wanted to kill the sergeant.

Costello, dull-witted and slow, carried his hatred in the same manner. It waxed and waned with his attention to what was going on around him. Usually, his mind turned off anything lasting over five or ten minutes, and his gaze would wander about for a bit. It was during one of these almost unconscious glances about that his brain suddenly snapped back into action.

153

"What the hell is that over there?" he asked, pointing toward the river.

A couple of Comancheros waded across the shallows leading a horse. The animal was saddled and equipped, appearing to be well-cared for.

Suddenly McRyan crowed, "That's the sergeant's horse, by God! The lying son of a bitch said it busted its leg!"

Even Costello figured out what was going on. "It's been hid over there all night just waiting for him to come back!"

Douglas dropped his hand to his holster in an instant decision to go down fighting, but a heavy fist slammed into his jaw, spinning him around before he could clear leather with the Colt.

Douglas was barely aware it was Monroe Lockwood who had attacked him, but the dragoon fought back gamely. He struck out blindly, feeling a pudgy nose crunch under the impact of his knuckles. Another desperate punch hit Lockwood's gigantic belly, and Douglas connected with the hard muscle under the fat.

Jack McRyan moved in to take advantage of the dazed sergeant. He hit him with a whiplike motion that rocked Douglas's head back. Although small, McRyan could pack a wallop when he wanted to. Where Sergeant Ian Douglas was concerned, he most certainly desired to inflict physical pain. He smacked him around more.

Douglas rolled and dodged the best he could, barely able to make out his attacker as a haze of semiconsciousness settled over him. Dizzy, but game, he moved in to attack.

But Costello was not simply standing by. He rushed Douglas, delivering a vicious kick to the side of his leg that propelled him sideways.

"Take that, you bastard!" Costello yelled.

McRyan didn't let up. He was able to move in and out at will, peppering Douglas's face without sustaining any injury. Finally, able to plant his feet and punch deliberately, the deserter's blows broke the sergeant's nose, sending a spray of blood outward.

Costello worked the back of Douglas's head and neck with hammering punches that finally brought the victim down to his knees. Douglas was unaware of what was happening to him by then. His hands dropped to his sides, and he took the blows without feeling them for another full minute before finally passing out and falling face-first to the dirt.

"That's enough!" Lazardo roared.

Lockwood stepped in and grabbed the two assailants, easily pulling them away. "We ain't gonna get a dime outta him down in Mexico if you kill him, assholes!"

McRyan was giddy with happiness. "How much you want for him, huh? Me and Dennis'll buy the son of a bitch from you. How's that?"

Lazardo laughed. "He is worth at least ten thousand pesos. Where are you going to get that kind of money?"

"Can't we make some sort o' deal?" McRyan pleaded.

"You must really hate that man," Lazardo said.

"I never wanted to kill nobody so much in my life," McRyan said.

"Me either," Costello added.

"Maybe we can work something out," Lazardo said. "When he has come back to his senses, we will want some information about what the rest of those soldiers are doing. Meantime, throw him in the stockade with his Russian friends."

Lockwood nudged the pair. "You heard Mister Lazardo. Each o' you grab a leg."

The two deserters quickly obeyed. They dragged the unconscious sergeant as Lockwood followed along to see that they did no more damage to him. When they reached the stockade gate, the guards opened it.

McRyan looked at Lockwood. "Can we throw him in?"

"Sure," Lockwood answered. "Just don't let him land on his head."

Costello grabbed Douglas's feet, and McRyan his hands. They swung back and forth, counting:

"One!"

"Two"

"Three!"

"Heave!"

Douglas, limp and insensible, hurtled through the air and hit the ground hard. As the gate slammed shut, a couple of the Russian men came forward. Recognizing the new prisoner, they carefully picked him up and carried him to the spot where the others had gathered.

Irena Yakubovski called out to Natalia, telling her of the new arrival. The young noblewoman, tending to some of the children, left her task and walked over. She knelt down beside the sergeant.

"Is he hurt bad?" she asked in Russian. "Will he die?"

One of the men checked Douglas, who now moaned. "I think not, Lady Natalia," he answered. "But he has been given a severe beating."

Douglas began to awaken, his eyelids fluttering. Finally, a vision of Natalia Valenko swam into his sight. Still dazed and confused, he asked, "Are you an angel?"

Natalia smiled. "Not at all, Sergeant Douglas. You are locked up with the Russians."

Douglas groaned and, as his mind eased to wakefulness, sat up holding his battered face. "God!"

"How did you get here?" Natalia asked. "Where are the other soldiers?"

"If they're smart, they're halfway back to Fort Leavenworth now," he answered. Then he remembered

156

Gavin's feelings for the young lady. "On the other hand, Lieutenant MacRoss ain't always real smart."

"Will they rescue us?" Natalia asked.

"They'll either do it or die trying," Douglas replied. He tried to get up, but the effort brought on a bad spell of dizziness that took him back into unconsciousness.

Chapter 14

When Gavin emerged from his swim across the Little Arkansas River, he rushed to his horse and grabbed his carbine. Worried sick about Ian Douglas, he returned to the waterway's shore to slip into the brush. After loosening the Colt revolver in its holster, he waited to see if the sergeant would be making an escape bid. Gavin planned on giving his friend some covering fire in case he needed it, and the determined lieutenant didn't care if it meant sacrificing his own life.

But as the dawn began to lighten the area, Gavin knew it was useless. It had become time to employ cold logic rather than irrational bravado to the situation. Now he stood a good chance of being discovered himself. There was nothing to be gained by staying in the area, and a hell of a lot to lose.

Gavin decided to leave Douglas's horse in case the sergeant would need it if he managed to break loose. Reluctantly and sadly, the officer returned the two miles to the concealed dragoon camp.

His arrival without Douglas caused looks of concern from the dragoons and Basil Karshchov in particular. The Russian kept his curiosity to himself. He had become sensitive about bothering Gavin during that difficult time. Corporal Steeple had no such reservations.

"Where's the sergeant, sir?" the dragoon asked.

"They've got him," Gavin said. "McRyan and Costello are in the camp. They betrayed Sergeant Douglas. From the appearance of things, I am certain those two deserters are members of the Comanchero gang."

"God damn those bastards!" Steeple cursed. "How did they link up with Comancheros?"

"Beats the hell out of me," Gavin admitted. "But there they were, and they didn't waste a second in pointing out Sergeant Douglas to the others."

Basil Karshchov slumped noticeably as he sat down at the campfire. "All is lost!"

"It doesn't look good," Gavin admitted.

"Gavin," he said. "I think it is time for me to remind you of your promise."

Gavin turned his horse over to Fenlay and O'Hearn before joining Karshchov. "What promise is that, Basil?"

"That I be allowed to die for my Natalia," Karshchov said. "I could not leave without her and still want to live."

"I'll keep my promise," Gavin said. "But only when the situation is hopeless. Right now, we've work to do."

Basil sat up straighter. "Do we still have a chance?"

"Yeah," Gavin said. "Not a good one, I'm afraid, but it's better than nothing."

"Let's give her a try, sir," Corporal Steeple said.

"We certainly shall," Gavin said. "Fetch Corporal Murphy and make sure the rest of the men are out on guard. Comancheros are wandering around all over the place."

"Yes, sir," Steeple said. "I'll be back right quick."

Karshchov was miserable. "I feel so helpless!"

"Don't worry, my friend," Gavin assured him. "We are going into action soon, and you'll be right there in the middle of things."

159

"I will do my best," Karshchov promised.

"I'm sure you will," Gavin said.

Steeple and Murphy joined them, the veteran corporals calm and professional as they sat down to hear what orders their commanding officer was about to issue.

Gavin pulled his sketch map from his pocket and spread it out for all to see. "This is the Comanchero camp," he explained. "To the north is where the prisoners are kept within a log stockade. I have found and prepared a place where we can break inside in order to lead our friends out."

Murphy looked at the map. "What's that on the south end, sir? Another stockade?"

"No," Gavin answered. "It's the corral where the Comancheros keep their mounts. None are stabled or hobbled within the living area."

Murphy spat into the hot coals. "Even a gang o' miserable son of a bitches like Comancheros don't want to walk around in a bunch o' horseshit, do they?"

"I guess not," Gavin said. "That's going to be to our advantage. As a matter of fact, Corporal Murphy, that corral is going to be your responsibility."

"I'm ready, sir," Murphy said in a determined tone. "You just say, 'For'd ho!' and I'm on my way."

"The structure is held up by poles on which large saplings have been lashed," Gavin explained. "The pole that is closest to the place where the rivers converge is the key to the corral's stability. When it goes, the whole thing falls."

"Yes, sir," Murphy said. "If a rope is dropped over it and pulled, then down comes the saplings, and with some help from me and Fenlay, them horses take off."

"Exactly," Gavin said. "But don't make a lot of noise. The river will cover up any sounds of the corral's collapse, but we mustn't have the horses going into the camp. That would alert every Comanchero in the place.

My plan hinges on them being completely ignorant of what's going on. Therefore, you must very deliberately head the horses into the river."

"I understand, sir," Murphy said. "When that's done, should we join you?"

"No," Gavin answered. "You and Fenlay come straight back here and wait."

"Yes, sir!"

Gavin turned to Steeple. "You and the rest, along with Mister Karshchov, will go with me. We've got to time our activities to take place a little after the horses are turned loose."

"Is that to give the Comancheros a chance to figger out their mounts is freed up and swimming away?" Steeple asked.

"It sure is," Gavin said, pleased that the two noncommissioned officers grasped what he was going to attempt. "That is important because it will draw them away from the stockade. That's one reason I want Corporal Murphy and Private Fenlay to get the hell out of there as quickly as they can without getting spotted."

"We will, sir," Murphy remarked with a grin. "Don't fret none on that. I don't much hanker for an invitation from them outlaws."

Gavin smiled. "Can't say that I blame you."

"Go on, sir," Steeple urged him.

"With all the Comancheros' attention to the south, particularly when faced with the difficulty of retrieving their herd from the river, we can make a smoother escape from the stockade," Gavin said.

"What's our actions gonna be there, sir?" Steeple said.

"I want you, Carlson, and O'Hearn to stand watch outside while Mister Karshchov and I go inside to escort the prisoners out," Gavin instructed. "But before that, you and I are going to have some deadly business to take care of."

"Yes, sir," Steeple said. "Knife work, is it?"

"Exactly," Gavin answered. "There're two guards at the front gate. If they happen to notice what's going on inside the stockade instead of worrying about their horses, our mission will fail. So, you and I have to bring our blades into this. That means stab and slice the throats of those sons of bitches."

"You and me can do it, sir," Steeple said.

"They must die," Gavin said in all seriousness. "We can't have any unnecessary struggling and yelling."

"The bastards'll go quietly to hell," Steeple assured him.

"After that, I'm taking Mister Karshchov inside with me," Gavin said. "You others stand by and wait outside the walls."

By then Basil Karshchov was positively giddy with happiness and excitement. "You and me? We go inside, Gavin?"

"I'll need you to explain to your friends what to do," Gavin said.

Karshchov's mood suddenly fell. "That will be important if my beautiful Natalia is not there. Somebody must be able to speak Russian."

"Yes, Basil, I'm afraid so," Gavin said in a frank tone. "It is an unpleasant possibility."

"If that is the case, I will help you get my friends across the river," Karshchov said, "but after that I am going back."

"I understand, Basil," Gavin assured him. "That's when I'll keep my promise to you."

Murphy laid a hand on Karshchov's shoulder. "You're a brave man, Mister Karshchov. I admire that."

"We'll all hope for the best," Steeple told the Russian.

"All you dragoons are good friends," Karshchov said with great emotion in his voice. "That is the truth!"

"When do we do all this, sir?" Steeple asked.

"Tonight after midnight," Gavin said. "It would be impossible any earlier. That's something I've learned from both observing and entering the Comanchero camp. They're a lively bunch, but fatigue and the results of liquor settle in at that hour."

"We'd best rest up, then," Steeple suggested. "I got a feeling that we ain't gonna get much sleep this coming week."

"Yeah," Murphy agreed. "Especially if we're gonna get chased across half o' Kansas Territory by a bunch o' riled Comancheros while we're herding along civilians on foot."

"We'll be busy alright," Gavin said in understatement. "Now I want you two corporals to inform your men of the what, when, where, and how of this rescue. Make sure at least one guard is posted at all times. All the remaining hours of daylight should be spent in resting up for the ordeal ahead."

"Yes, sir," the corporals said in unison. They stood up, saluted, then moved out to gather up the men.

Gavin stretched out, leaning his head against his saddle put down by Carlson and O'Hearn. He closed his eyes, quickly drifting off as the exhaustion of more than twenty-four hours without sleep finally caught up with him.

Karshchov, long an atheistic intellectual, suddenly clasped his hands together and muttered a prayer he had learned in the Russian Orthodox Church as a youngster. He even murmured a fervent, "Amen!" before crossing himself for the first time in many years. Then, imitating his American friend, he lay down to get some sleep.

The hours eased by on a wonderful spring day. The

sky, deep blue with scattered mountains of cumulus clouds high above, haloed the Kansas countryside whose own horizons seemed to stretch into infinity. It was quiet within the grove of trees, and the sound of the creek's gentle current lulled the inhabitants of the temporary camp.

Evening came like a silent shadow without notice. Dusk moved across the flat terrain, dragging the night behind it, making shadows lengthen. The color of the sky followed along, the legions of stars and blackness pushing the blue down into the redness of sunset. By the time the moon made its appearance, the dragoons were wide awake and ready in spite of the hours of waiting still ahead of them.

Basil Karshchov, on the other hand, seemed almost at peace. The Russian was ready to face what he must, willing to accept the fate ordained for him. If he had any particular concern at that point, it was to be brave and honorable whether in life or death. Life without Natalia Valenko was not worth living as far as he was concerned.

The first time that Gavin stepped from the trees into the moonlight to check his pocketwatch, it was ten o'clock. He made his way back to his companions, taking care not to make any noise that might attract any wandering Comancheros.

With no fire, it was pitch-black within the grove, and only occasional reflections off the metal of equipment and bridles gave away anyone's presence within the silent group.

Gavin made three more trips out into the moonlight before it was after midnight. The final glance at the timepiece showed it to be a quarter to one. He emitted a low whistle to signal the others. Within moments a slight crackling of brush and the soft thud of hooves on prairie dirt announced the exit from the stand of trees.

The men swung up into their saddles and, barely able to see the man ahead, followed after Gavin MacRoss as he led them back toward the Comanchero camp that shared the banks of both the Little and Big Arkansas rivers two miles away.

When they reached the river, Gavin signaled to Murphy, then pointed to the direction of the corral. The corporal and Fenlay rode slowly into the shallows, fording the river and coming out in the deep shadows at the edge of the camp, where Murphy turned south with Fenlay close behind. Within a few moments the two dragoons reached the corral.

Murphy whispered to his companion. "Let's do it!"

"I'm ready," Fenlay assured him.

While Fenlay waited on the north side, Murphy went slowly around to the back of the corral until reaching the post described by Gavin. The corporal pulled his picket rope from the saddle and looped it first around the pole, then around his saddle horn. He kicked his horse's flanks, and the animal pulled hard, working against the resistance. Within moments the support pulled out of the sandy soil. Immediately the structure gave way, falling to the ground.

Fenlay moved forward toward the milling horses. They instinctively gave way, allowing him to herd them toward the river. Murphy pulled out and got into position to help. Within a very short five minutes, the entire herd was in the river, moving toward the deeper water until forced to swim.

"There they go," Murphy whispered with a grin. "Heading south."

"Let's get the hell out of here," Fenlay urged him. "I already heard some moving around back there."

The two dragoons, smug as hell with the self-satisfaction of doing a damn good job, went back into the river and took a slight northerly course as they headed back to camp.

Up at the stockade, in the heavy brush north of the structure, Gavin and his men bided their time. It seemed like an entire hour had dragged by before they noted a disturbance in the camp. It was hard to distinguish what was going on, but loud, angry talk convinced the dragoon officer that the Comancheros had discovered their horses' unscheduled swim.

"Now's our time, Corporal Steeple," Gavin said.

"Right, sir," the corporal replied.

They moved quickly around to the other side of the stockade, glad to hear the commotion building up. All the attention in the Comanchero camp was toward the river junction. The two guards had stepped out to peer into the settlement as fires quickly flared up and people moved around.

"I wonder what the hell's going on?" one guard mused aloud.

"Maybe something's riled Mister Lazardo," his companion said. "I sure as hell wouldn't—"

Gavin's arm went around his neck, and he drove his knife deep into the man's back, pushing the blade up high where it could do the most damage.

The first guard turned at the sound. The last thing he saw in his life was the distorted face of Steeple and the flash of the cutting weapon that bit deep into his throat, giving him another mouth. This was followed by two quick slashes across the belly.

The two attackers dragged the bodies into the darkness, then returned to the others waiting on the other side of the crude prison.

"Let's go, Basil!" Gavin said.

They went up to the loosened logs and Gavin pushed them farther apart. Then he and his Russian friend slipped in. They stumbled across someone in the dark who muttered angrily:

"Shto eto?"

"Ya Karshchov," the Russian said. He began to speak rapidly under his breath.

Within moments there was scurrying around. Now and then a child made a whimper or some adult had to be shushed, but within moments the entire group moved toward the opening, going through one at a time where Steeple, Carlson, and O'Hearn gathered them up.

Gavin felt a rough grip on his shoulder. "Who's that?"

"Sergeant Douglas reporting for duty, sir," came a gruff voice. "I hope you ain't taking the time I spent in here off my next furlough."

"I sure as hell am," Gavin said. He almost hugged his old friend. "How are you?"

"A bit scuffed up, but I can move around now," Douglas replied. He lowered his voice and put his mouth close to Gavin's ear. "The young lady's here, sir. She's the one what took care o' me."

"Glad to hear it," Gavin said.

More people moved past them until Basil came into view. "My Natalia is with me!" he said happily.

"Good," Gavin said. "Let's get out of here. We can talk later."

The two dragoons stepped through the opening. Gavin tapped Steeple on the shoulder, saying, "Take O'Hearn and scout out those shallows. Make sure nobody's there. If they are, do what you must to clear the way."

"Yes, sir," Murphy said. He winked at Douglas in the moonlight. "Glad to see you, Sergeant."

"Move out on your mission, Corporal!" Douglas snapped. "We ain't got time to blabber at each other."

Steeple grabbed O'Hearn, and the two disappeared

167

into the dark. Basil, with Natalia's help, organized the prisoners. They made sure the children stayed together with the women while the men formed around them.

Steeple made a quick return. "Let's go! It's clear!"

The group, moving as fast as possible, went to the river where O'Hearn waited. He stepped into the shallows, and the entire bunch followed him across to the other side. The dragoons retrieved their horses; then the escape continued until they reached the camp by the creek.

"Listen up!" Gavin said. "I want all the dragoons, with the exception of Sergeant Douglas and O'Hearn, to lead the Russian men straight out east. Then double back on your trail and return here to the creek. I want it to appear to the Comancheros that the whole group of us has taken off in that direction."

"Yes, sir," Steeple replied. Being the senior corporal, he would be in charge of that job.

"While you're gone, the rest of us are going to be walking in the water as far north as possible," Gavin explained. "When you get back here, follow after us. Stay in the creek to cover your tracks."

"Why go north, sir?" Douglas asked. "Fort Scott is due east."

"I know," Gavin said. "So do McRyan and Costello. They'll tell the Comancheros about the post, and they'll figure we've headed that way. The trail that Steeple's group leaves will help convince them we are making our way to Fort Scott."

Douglas moved close to the lieutenant. "May I speak with you, sir? In private?"

"Sure," Gavin replied. "Let's step over here."

They walked a few paces back into the darkness out of earshot of the others.

"Begging your pardon, sir, but we'll never make it to Fort Leavenworth," Douglas said under his breath.

"We're not going to Fort Leavenworth," Gavin said. "That would be impossible."

"No disrespect, Lieutenant," Douglas said. "But just where in hell are we going?"

"To Nadezhda," Gavin answered.

"The Russian settlement?" Douglas exclaimed. "That's impossible, too, sir."

"It certainly is," Gavin agreed. "But it's not as big an impossibility as Fort Leavenworth or Fort Scott."

"I counted them pris'ners while I was in the stockade," Douglas said. "There's twelve men, eight women, and six kids. That comes to about twenty-six folks, out of which fourteen ain't combatants."

Gavin chuckled. "You forgot to count Irena Yakubovski."

"Fine, sir," Douglas said. "Then, thirteen of 'em can't fight. Do you really expect to move 'em all the way back to that town and get 'em there safe and sound."

"Probably not," Gavin said. "Care to leave? You could mount up now and ride the hell out of here."

"Not me," Douglas said. He grinned. "Why should I have to miss all the fun that's gonna happen in the next few days?"

"You're always thinking of yourself, Sergeant," Gavin said, glad to have the full support of the noncommissioned officer.

"Well, Lieutenant, we'd best stop jawing," Douglas said. "We got a hell of a job to try to do."

The two returned to the group to find that Steeple and the others had already headed out to lay the false trail.

"O'Hearn!" Gavin called out. "Take the point!"

Chapter 15

The discovery of the horses' disappearance set the Comanchero camp into action. However, because of the darkness and the shortage of available mounts, there was little they could do except to send a few men on foot down the river in the hopes of catching any animal that might leave the water and come up on the bank. Most of the action taken was little more than cursing, shouting, and useless running around. This was particularly true because several of the participants were drunk from interrupted binges.

Guido Lazardo, though mad as hell at what he judged to be stupid carelessness on the part of his men, considered the situation beneath him. The leader of a large outlaw band did not act as a common herdsman no matter what the situation. For that reason, he dispatched Monroe Lockwood and Big Joe to supervise the roundup, then went back to his woman of that particular night. Waking up had roused his spent passions, and he treated himself to another taste of his companion's charms before sinking back into a deep sleep.

The first thing Lockwood and Big Joe did was to go to each shelter to make sure the inhabitant was up to participate in the recovery of the horses. It didn't matter if the Comanchero resident was still drunk from the previous evening or not. Those still in their cups were pulled from the warmth of their crude homes and yanked upright. A few sharp slaps in the face and kicks from the large men were enough to send the drunkards lurching and weaving after their fellow outlaws to see about regaining the wandering horses.

After getting all available hands to work, Lockwood and Big Joe headed for the river below the junction. One took the east side of the river and the other the west. The two large men bullied and kicked their charges along, threatening beatings, and even death, for slackness.

Running around in the predawn darkness was not something either one of the men enjoyed. They took their irritation out on any unfortunate who came within reach.

Meanwhile, the animals that had gotten out of the water were quickly rounded up and led back to the camp, where they could be properly saddled and bridled for a chase to catch the horses that had managed to get farther south. Within a couple of hours, ten mounted men galloped down both riverbanks to head loose horses back where the men on foot could manage them.

The sun was up by then, making the chore much easier. Mounts, cold from their time in the water, had gotten ashore to warm up and munch on the fresh sweet grass of the prairie. A few scattered when approached by the Comancheros, but most allowed themselves to be herded back to the now-repaired corral at the camp.

The job wasn't completed until midday. The final horses found were driven across the shallows and up to the gate to be slapped and yelled at until they were once again in confinement. At that late hour, the entire population, including Guido Lazardo, was present. The band's chief, already bored with the woman who had spent the night with him, had sent the trollop back to her own dwelling to wait for her man to return from the horse-recovery operation.

A small Mexican boy, who had been scampering about since the camp's arousal, now stood at the very front of the crowd, enjoying the spectacle. He stood near Lazardo watching the activity. The Sicilian had a genuine affection for children, even those he planned to sell into slavery. He always carried sugar candy and loved to toss it out to the youngsters. When he noticed the boy, he reached in his pocket and handed him a hunk of the sweets.

"Do you like watching all the excitement?" Lazardo asked him in Spanish.

The boy, who knew his mother but wasn't quite sure which Mexican Comanchero was his father, laughed. He answered, "Oh, yes! *Qué diversión!*" He took a bite of the candy. "But who are the dead men on the other side of the camp?"

Lazardo's smile froze. "What dead men, *muchacho?*"

Dead people were nothing new for the boy to see. He was only surprised to note they were lying unattended. "The two by the *estacada*—the stockade," the boy said. "They are *de nosotros*. They belong to us."

Now Lazardo frowned. "You mean where the prisoners are kept?"

"*Se fueron todos los prisioneros,*" the boy said. "They are gone."

"*Qué?* What?" Lazardo asked, stunned.

"There are no prisoners," the boy repeated. "I think they must have gone away."

Lazardo roughly grabbed the boy and shook him. "You're not joking with me, are you, *muchacho?*"

The lad started to sob. "N-no, I am t-telling what is true."

"Lockwood! Big Joe!" Lazardo roared, letting the boy go. "Come with me!"

172

The two men responded immediately, leaving the corral fence and trotting after Lazardo, who raced through the camp. Within moments other Comancheros, intrigued by the sight of a very furious Guido Lazardo heading north through the dwellings, followed the trio, though they hadn't the slightest idea what had disturbed their leader and his two chief lieutenants.

They found the slain guards, sliced and covered with dried blood, sprawled a few yards from the gate. Lazardo rushed over to peer through the logs that made up the enclosure.

"Gone!" he bellowed. "Everyone is gone!"

Big Joe pulled the keys from the belt on one of the cadavers and hurried over to unlock the gate. He kicked it open and allowed Lazardo to proceed him into the interior.

The place was completely empty except for the flies buzzing around the feces in the area the Russians had used to relieve themselves. Lazardo checked the walls, going around the perimeter until he reached the back.

"Here!" he yelled. "They went out here!"

He forced himself through the opening and noted that the outer logs had been parted, making it easy to manipulate the inner barriers. He realized that outside help had been employed in the escape. He reentered the stockade.

"Bring me those two army deserters," he said to Lockwood.

It didn't take long before Jack McRyan and Dennis Costello were muscled out of the crowd and pushed in front of the Comanchero chief.

"The prisoners have escaped," Lazardo said.

"We didn't do it!" Costello shrieked as pictures of himself and McRyan dangling over a fire danced through his head.

McRyan added his own protests, saying, "We hadn't

even been over here since we was on guard last. Honest, Mister Lazardo!"

"You are not being accused of anything," Lazardo snapped. "I am certain you are incapable of such a clever plan. It had to be the soldiers."

McRyan was relieved he was not going to be blamed for anything. He sneered. "I told you, you should have let me kill that son of a bitch Douglas."

Lazardo hit him hard, knocking him sideways. Lockwood cuffed him the other way, and Big Joe hit him in the back of the head.

Dennis Costello, not wanting the same rough treatment, cringed. "I didn't say nothing!"

McRyan did not even groan at the unexpected pain. He decided to avoid further abuse by staying silent and to simply reply to whatever was said to him.

"That sergeant did not lead the prisoners out," Lazardo said. "Someone broke in first to show them the way. I can tell from the way the logs on the outside row have been parted. Now you tell me about the rest of those soldiers, and what sort of man leads them."

"Yes, sir," McRyan said. "There's this lieutenant by the name o' MacRoss that's the commanding officer. He's got that sergeant, a coupla corporals, and three troopers. Remember? I told you about how many they was, Mister Lazardo."

Lazardo thought a moment as he recalled what McRyan had previously told him. "That is only seven men. Actually, six with the sergeant in the stockade." He paced back and forth. "But that would be enough to let the horses loose to divert us, then kill these two stupid guards and lead the prisoners out."

"He prob'ly done it all about the same time," Lockwood suggested. "That's the way I'd do it."

"You are right," Lazardo said. "A daring plan that

174

called for careful thought and risk. Perhaps that officer was in love with the beautiful blonde, eh?"

Costello piped up. "I don't think so, Mister Lazardo. She was 'fianced to a Russian."

Lazardo shook his head. "I don't think either of you would recognize true affection for a woman. I am sure the American officer came for her."

"We got to get 'em all back, that's for sure," Lockwood said.

"Yeah," Big Joe said. "That's a hell of a lot o' money that went through that wall."

"It is a great amount when one considers the ransom for the noblewoman," Lazardo said. He was also concerned about his reputation if the deed went unavenged. In the Comanchero world, that would be perceived as a weakness on his part. Numerous, serious challenges to his leadership were certain to be made if he didn't round up the escapees and punish whoever had freed them.

Big Joe asked, "Where do you think he'd take 'em?"

Lazardo glared at McRyan and Costello. "Well! You idiots! Where would the army officer take them?"

"There's a post called Fort Scott that's about a hundred miles away," McRyan said. "I never been there, but I know it's due east o' here. I heard the others talking about it. My pal Costello went there once."

"That's right," Costello said. "I was on a supply detail that took some stuff there from Fort Leavenworth between blizzards last winter."

"What sort of a place is this Fort Scott?" **Lazardo** asked.

"There's a lot o' soldiers posted there that could help the lieutenant," Costello said. "I'd say a coupla comp'nies o' dragoons and one o' infantry. They even got a cannon."

"It's a hundred miles, is it?" Lazardo asked.

"Yes, sir," Costello assured him.

That pleased Lazardo. "We should be able to catch them since most are on foot."

"If I know that lieutenant, he won't leave them prisoners behind neither," McRyan said. "He'll stick with 'em to the bitter end."

"So much the better," Lazardo said.

"There ain't gonna be no trouble catching 'em, Mister Lazardo," Big Joe remarked.

"That's right. I'll pull out a bunch o' the boys," Lockwood said.

"Do it now," Lazardo said. "I am personally going to lead this chase."

"The first'uns is gonna be these two soldier boys," Lockwood said.

McRyan and Costello nodded their mutual agreement. "I hope I can kill that sergeant and lieutenant," McRyan said with a hopeful tone in his voice.

"I think I'll let you do that to the sergeant," Lazardo said. "But that lieutenant is mine to deal with. Believe me, he will be begging me to end his life before I am done."

Lockwood turned and gazed into the Comancheros who had gathered around. He began to holler names, "Crazy Fox! Morales! Lop-Head! Marais! Cordova! Tarheel! Runs Fast! Lefty Dan! Faro."

Each man responded with an upraised hand as his name was called, then shouldered his way to the front of the crowd.

After handpicking good men, Lockwood and Big Joe began choosing others they didn't know too well by grabbing the Comancheros and pushing them to the front. At that point, they just wanted some extra guns to go along. They picked ten for a total of twenty-one. With the two of them and Lazardo, that would mean twenty-four total going after seven dragoons and some unarmed prisoners that included women and children.

Those chosen waited expectantly for whatever Lazardo would have to say to them. The leader quickly got down to business.

"We might be gone two or three days," Lazardo said. "There's gonna be some killing and prisoners taken. Other soldiers might come in on this, so be ready for that, too. I'll meet you on the east side of the river in one hour. Don't be late."

The chosen men wasted no time in rushing off to their dwellings to prepare for the mission. Guido Lazardo did not appreciate tardiness. Slow or careless conduct had led to a lingering execution on more than one occasion within the band of Comancheros.

By the time Lazardo had prepared himself and his horse for the mission and ridden over to the river, he found Monroe Lockwood, Big Joe, and the other twenty-one Comancheros already waiting. Without hesitating, the chief motioned them to follow as he galloped across the shallows of the river and came out on the other side.

"Find their tracks!" he shouted.

This set about a flurry of activity as the men spread out, heads bent low as they studied the ground. It was the one called Tarheel who found the trail.

"Over here!" he called out in his North Carolina accent. "They're a-headed dead east like McRyan and Costello said they would."

"Lead on, Tarheel," Lockwood commanded. "The sooner we catch 'em, the better."

The trail continued out of the trees along the bank and led the Comancheros across open country to another grove of trees that grew along a small creek. The soldiers and their Russian friends seemed to have waded across the creek and kept to their eastern course. That satisfied Lazardo as a good sign that they were trying to make it to the safety of Fort Scott.

"Ever'body keep your eyes open!" Big Joe called out. "Soldiers ain't stupid. They might set up an ambush to hit us."

"Yes," Lazardo yelled. "Remember! The prisoners are on foot. They won't be moving as fast as we will."

The Comancheros, though not acting under formal field orders, spread out instinctively to provide security for themselves as they followed the trail laid out through the prairie grass. For over an hour, the determined pursuers kept moving along, expecting to see their quarry at almost any moment.

Then the trail abruptly stopped.

"What the hell is going on?" Lazardo demanded to know.

Both Lockwood and Big Joe slipped out of their saddles and squatted down to study the strange situation. Big Joe slowly shook his head back and forth as he pointed to some grass blades bent the other way.

"They doubled back," he said. "See?"

"I sure do," Lockwood said. He stood up and waved over at Lazardo. "This is a false trail to lead us off, Mister Lazardo. We got to go back to that creek and start all over again."

Lazardo was furious. "*Tontos!* Fools! *Bouffons! Sciocci!*"

Big Joe whispered, "Let's get moving quick before he decides to shoot somebody."

"Amen!" Lockwood agreed.

They quickly mounted up and turned back, heading out at a gallop. The other Comancheros wisely followed their lead as Lazardo followed, his temper boiling over.

"You better not do this again, any of you!" he threatened.

When they reached the creek, Lockwood and Big Joe once more dismounted. They walked up and down the

178

waterway several times, but could find no tracks. Lazardo rode up and stayed in the saddle, watching his two chief lieutenants try to figure out what had happened.

"They obviously walked in the creek," Lazardo said. "It is not deep."

"Yes, sir, Mister Lazardo," Lockwood said. "But we can't figger out which direction."

Lazardo was thoughtful for several moments. "This lieutenant fellow is clever and brave. I am trying to put myself in his place to think what he must have done."

"He prob'ly went south a ways, then turned east toward Fort Scott," Lockwood said.

"That is exactly what he wants us to think after you fell for the false trail he laid out," Lazardo said. "But I don't believe he did that. In my opinion, our lieutenant has headed north."

"North!" Big Joe exclaimed. "It's way too far to Fort Leavenworth to try to get there, even if he did fool us."

"I did not say he went to Fort Leavenworth," Lazardo said. "I don't think that is his destination at all."

"Then, where in hell would he go?" Lockwood asked.

"Back to that Russian town we raided," Lazardo said. "The very least thing we would expect."

Lockwood slowly smiled. "By God, Mister Lazardo, you're right!"

"We will ride alongside this creek to the north until we find where our prisoners have been led out onto the open prairie," Lazardo said.

"The sooner we start, the sooner we get our hands on 'em," Big Joe said. He climbed back into the saddle. Catching sight of McRyan and Costello, he yelled over at them, "Hey! You two are gonna have a chance to kill that sergeant before tomorrow's sun sets."

"Don't forget the lieutenant," McRyan reminded

him. "We want to watch Mister Lazardo do a job on him."

Lazardo laughed. He was now in a good mood. "That is fine! I will make sure I put on a good show. Afterward, when Lockwood tires of the big woman, she will be yours."

"Yeah!" Lockwood yelled out. "I got first dibs on her!"

The Comancheros all laughed and hollered at each other as Lockwood and Big Joe began leading them northward along the creek.

It looked like there would be a lot of fun in the next couple of days.

Chapter 16

The day had been brutal for the Russians, who had weakened much since the attack on Nadezhda.

After the hard trek down from the settlement to the Comanchero camp, they had endured indifferent feeding and bullying by their captors. Now, after being led through the stockade walls to freedom, their physical conditions were not much better. The dragoons had nothing much to offer them outside of true friendship and concern, but that extra care and consideration seemed to help them along after the mistreatment from the Comancheros.

All the troopers, with the exception of Paddy O'Hearn on the point, walked. Their horses were used mostly by the six children, but now and again one of the four boys switched off to allow the women a chance to sit in the saddle. The soldiers also shared their field rations with the Russians, but that food was growing scarce now that they had been away from Fort Leavenworth for much more time than originally planned.

The one thing that worked in the Russians' favor was the fact they were peasant stock. Even the children had known at least a couple of years of famine or drought, so going long periods without proper nourishment was nothing new to them. No one born in a serf's *kizhina* survived past infancy unless they had a naturally strong constitution. The nice and warm spring weather helped them along, conserving the extra calories that would have been needed to keep warm in the Russian wilderness. This made the food shortage less of a problem.

The peasant men, stoic and seemingly unable to feel the sensations of pain or fatigue, simply moved along, dull-eyed but cheerfully obedient to the motions and hand gestures of the dragoons. They responded to the soldiers' encouragement of kind words and friendly grins with smiles of gratitude.

Basil Karshchov and Natalia Valenko, walking hand in hand most of the time, demonstrated the same care and concern for the others. But Natalia fast began to show the physical and emotional strain she had been under, and seemed to be fading. Basil saw to it that she spent a lot of time in the saddle in spite of her protests. He was helped somewhat by Irena Yakubovski, who physically grabbed the smaller woman and set her upon a horse on several occasions when she protested traveling the easy way.

Lieutenant Gavin MacRoss and Sergeant Ian Douglas walked together, casting glances all around as they watched the flanks, O'Hearn up ahead, and the Russians. The two shared a hell of a lot of responsibility which years of frontier soldiering made them take seriously.

"We been damn lucky, sir," Douglas said.

"Are you trying to make a point?" Gavin asked.

"Just that we ain't gonna keep this up much longer," Douglas said.

Gavin felt a flash of temper. "Goddamn it! I know we can't, Sergeant. Like I asked—what is your point?"

"I'm just saying that we're gonna have to get ready for the worst," Douglas said without being ruffled. "Our situation calls for some real planning and action."

"All we can do is try our damndest," Gavin said. "Sorry about snapping at you."

"Oh? Did you snap at me, sir?" Douglas asked.

Gavin winked at the sergeant as he checked his watch. "It'll be evening soon, and we're going to have to stop."

"Yes, sir," Douglas said. "Them kids is sturdy little shits, but we can't put 'em on a forced march. The women is doing fine if'n they can ride now and then."

"The men seem to be doing quite well," Gavin said. "At least they seem in fine shape."

"Yes, sir," Douglas agreed. "But, to tell you God's truth, I don't know for how much longer."

"All except Irena," Gavin said. "She could probably outwalk any of us if she had to."

"And that includes our horses," Douglas added with a chuckle.

They walked on in silence for another mile or so, before Douglas said, "Them Comancheros is gonna catch up with us tomorrow." The only reason he mentioned it was because he thought it necessary to discuss the trouble they were sure to face.

"Yeah," Gavin said. "That's just about the way I have it figured out, too."

"Any idea how we're gonna handle the situation, sir?" the sergeant asked.

"Not the slightest," Gavin answered. "What about you?"

"I can't think of nothing," Douglas admitted.

"Perhaps a patrol from Fort Leavenworth will find us," Gavin mused.

"Sir, you know them patrols don't come this far south o' the Santa Fe Trail," Douglas reminded him.

Gavin nodded and said, "Maybe Fort Scott—"

"Not this far west," Douglas said.

183

"I guess we don't have much of a chance, Sergeant," Gavin said.

"I don't reckon as we got any a'tall," Douglas replied.

Gavin glanced around. "My God! There is absolutely no cover or shelter out here. I can't see as much as a gully to get down into."

"We'll be spending this night in the open," Douglas said. "We'll have to keep sharing our canteens with the Russians 'til we find a creek or river."

"At any rate, let's push on," Gavin said. "There's nothing to be gained by lagging along. Who knows? We might get lucky somehow."

"Not likely, sir," Douglas said.

"Not likely, Sergeant," Gavin agreed.

The sad, tired group continued with only brief rest periods for the remainder of the day. Only when the dusk had grown so gloomy that it was difficult to see, did Gavin order a halt. He called in O'Hearn and had Douglas gather the other dragoons around him.

"We're out in the open without the slightest bit of cover or concealment as you can see," Gavin told his men. "For that reason, we're going to be on fifty percent alert all through the night, or at least as close as we can come to it."

Corporal Steeple glanced over at the Russians, who sat in a silent group in the grass. "D'ye think we could use some o' them for guard?" he asked.

Gavin shook his head. "They don't speak English, and I'm afraid that eventually exhaustion is going to set in on them. As a matter of fact, I want all our blankets to go to the women and children. Any that are left over can be used by the men."

"Be glad to, Lieutenant," Paddy O'Hearn said.

Carlson added, "Happy to oblige 'em, sir."

"Thank you, men," Gavin said. "I knew you would want to comfort these poor folks as much as possible."

Basil Karshchov joined them. "I am here to help. Did I hear you say guard duty?"

"Right, Basil," Gavin answered. "You, Carlson, Corporal Steeple, and I will be one relief. Sergeant Douglas, Corporal Murphy, Carlson, and O'Hearn will be the other."

"Mind if my group is the second, sir?" Douglas asked. "I like to be the last so's I can wake ever'body up."

"A sergeant's prerogative, hey?" Gavin said. "Request granted. I'll let you handle passing out the rations and drinks of water from canteens, too."

"Yes, sir," Douglas said. "Okay, troopers, hand 'em over and let's get a coupla cups out so's we can give these folks a few swigs o' water."

Karshchov touched Gavin on the sleeve. "Natalia has asked to speak with you, Gavin."

"I'm very busy right now, Basil," Gavin said, not wanting to get close to the young woman.

"I think it would be most unkind of you not to," Karshchov said.

"Of course," Gavin said, relenting. "I'm sorry. Let's go see her now."

The two walked over to where the Russians sat. Karshchov said a few words to them in their language. A couple of the men got to their feet and walked over to Gavin with smiles, holding their hats in their hands and bowing.

"Spasibo! Spasibo!" they exclaimed.

"They are thanking you," Karshchov explained to Gavin. "I have told them they will get a bite to eat and a swallow or two of water that you and your brave soldiers will share with them because of your goodness."

Gavin said, "You're entirely welcome." Then he allowed himself to be taken over to where Natalia sat with Irena.

"He is here, *moya lyovemtsa,*" Karshchov said.

Natalia, aided by Irena, got to her feet. "I am so glad to have this opportunity to speak to you, Lieutenant MacRoss."

"My pleasure, Miss Valenko," Gavin replied.

In spite of what she'd been through, Natalia was as lovely as ever. Her face was sunburned, and her hair had been brushed back only by Irena's strong fingers; yet her natural beauty was there to tear at the American army officer's heart. Even in her tattered and sun-faded dress, her feminine charms were wonderfully displayed.

"I wish to thank you for your kindness and bravery," Natalia said. "Basil has told me that if it were not for you, we would still be imprisoned by those horrible men."

"Basil is being modest if he hasn't spoken of his own determination and courage," Gavin said. "He is most devoted to you, Miss Valenko."

"Of course!" Karshchov agreed with a smile. "I am the man who loves her."

"Lieutenant, Basil has told me that you and he have decided to be friends," Natalia said.

"That is correct," Gavin replied. "I suppose the sharing of danger and a common goal has made us comrades in arms."

"I would like very much to be your friend, too, Lieutenant," Natalia said. "I hope you will agree to be mine."

"I am honored," Gavin said, feeling sweet misery.

"I ask an honor of you," Karshchov said. "When Natalia and I are married, I wish for you to be my—my *shafer*." He looked at Natalia and asked, "How do you say *shafer* in English? I have never used that word."

Natalia laughed. "Basil is asking you to be his best man at our wedding."

Gavin displayed a weak smile, doing his best to put more exuberance in it. "Oh?"

186

Karshchov frowned. "Of course, if you do not wish—"

"I am honored," Gavin quickly interjected. "Thank you for asking."

Karshchov suddenly stepped forward and threw his arms around Gavin and kissed him. Gavin jumped back, violently pushing the Russian away.

Natalia laughed again. "Unlike in many societies, the men in Russia kiss each other, Lieutenant MacRoss. When you agreed to be his best man, Basil was most overwhelmed with emotion. It was his way of showing how pleased he is to have his good friend honor him at such an important occasion in his life."

Karshchov laughed. "It is like shaking the hands, do you understand?"

Gavin again smiled weakly. "Well, if you don't mind, I'd like to stick to handshakes." He bowed to Natalia. "If you'll excuse me, Miss Valenko, I must return to my duties."

"I shall go with him, my darling," Karshchov said. "My friend Gayin and I are to stand watch together this very night."

"Then, we shall all be safe, I am sure of that," Natalia said.

Sentry duty didn't start until after everyone had a few bites and some quick swallows of water. Gavin and Basil went out a ways and took up a position on the defensive perimeter organized by Sergeant Douglas.

"We must sit down," Gavin explained. "During the night, one can see better by looking upward into the weak light provided by the sky. It is particularly easy in flat country like this."

"You must learn much of such things as a soldier, Gavin," Karshchov said.

"Actually, I learned it from an Indian scout," Gavin said. "Those fellows know the best ways when it comes to hunting and making war out here in the wild country."

"They sound a bit like our cossacks in Russia," Karshchov said. "They are great outdoorsmen and expert horsemen. Splendid fellows who love to fight."

"Exactly like our Indians," Gavin said.

They were silent for a while, keeping vigil without speaking as the prairie sank deeper into the night. A bright moon came out, casting shadows off the scrub plants that dotted the area.

"Gavin," Karshchov finally said. "I am asking of you another favor."

"Yes?" Gavin responded.

"I am going to save one bullet for Natalia," he said. "If I die before you, I am asking you to use one of yours."

Gavin looked at him, able to see the determination in his Russian friend's face. "Well, if the situation——"

"I am not a fool," Karshchov interrupted. "We are all going to be killed by the bad men tomorrow."

"If you really believe that, why did you ask me to be your best man at your wedding?" Gavin inquired of him.

"That was for Natalia's sake," Karshchov said. "Also, I wanted you to know that I would have asked you if there was to be a marriage. It is important that you know that."

"I understand," Gavin said.

"We are all going to die tomorrow," Karshchov repeated.

Gavin was silent for several moments; then he said, "Yes."

"Do you promise me?" Karshchov asked.

"I promise that she will not fall into the hands of the Comancheros if I can help it," Gavin said.

"Thank you," Karshchov replied.

The two sat in silence for the rest of their relief, keeping a close eye on the distant horizon to make sure no one snuck up on the pathetic little bivouac. When Sergeant Douglas and Corporal Murphy came to relieve them, the two got to their feet and walked slowly back to the area where the others slept.

Karshchov held out his hand. "We may not have time tomorrow, so I say to you my goodbye, good friend Gavin."

Gavin shook his hand. "Goodbye, my friend."

The lieutenant watched as Basil Karshchov walked over to where Natalia Valenko slept. He could see the Russian settle down and lie beside the young woman, moving close to her and putting an arm around her sleeping body.

Gavin, envying him, went back to where his saddle sat on the ground. His blankets were comforting the prisoners, so he settled on the grass and leaned back against the leather implement.

He took a deep breath and whispered softly, the words inaudible: "Goodbye, Natalia."

The lieutenant sat there all through the rest of the night, staring out into the moonlit prairie. Eventually, the sky clouded up, and a murky darkness, as if foretelling what was to be the next day, sank down over the area.

Dawn was just lighting up the eastern horizon when Sergeant Douglas brought in the second relief and began waking the camp. Within moments everyone stirred and began to prepare to meet the new day.

Sergeant Douglas reported to his commanding officer. "How's about we brew up some coffee, sir?" he asked. "There ain't much, but we can boil enough to put some perk and sass in ever'body's eyes."

Gavin, wanting to push ahead, almost refused. Then he remembered there wasn't much sense in hurrying along. "Certainly, Sergeant. It will do everyone a world of good."

"Fine, sir," Douglas said. "I'll get the boys to chip in. How about you?"

"There's some grounds in my saddlebags," Gavin said. "Help yourself."

Douglas, along with Carlson and O'Hearn, went to work. Within a quarter of an hour they had a pot of coffee steaming over their fire.

"C'mon folks!" O'Hearn called out. "Let's start the day right. There's nothing like a cup o' hot java. Come and get it!"

Gavin watched the small crowd eagerly line up for the unexpected refreshment. Then he turned and looked southward over the sea of grass. He felt someone walk up beside him, and he turned and nodded a good morning's greeting to Basil Karshchov.

The Russian also looked south. "I wonder how far away they are," he remarked.

Gavin shook his head. "They'll have caught up with us by early afternoon."

Chapter 17

The little column of American soldiers and Russian civilians, all very hungry, thirsty, and tired, moved slowly across the great expanse of the Kansas countryside. The combination of boots and hooves scuffling across the dry terrain kicked up small clouds of dust.

The going was easy in the short grass of the rolling countryside that was flat for the most part with a few gentle dips and rises. The sun, while warm, was not overwhelming. This made for a most pleasant spring day.

The women and children continued to ride the horses. Private Paddy O'Hearn, still the only mounted dragoon, acted as the group's eyes and ears as he ranged fifty yards or so to the front, picking the fastest and shortest route back to their destination of Nadezhda.

Gavin MacRoss didn't show much leadership initiative. It wasn't that his spirits had completely sunk that led him to allow Sergeant Ian Douglas to supervise the pathetically slow trek. The lieutenant's mind raced as numerous, useless and dangerous schemes flashed and died away in his thoughts. Desperation drove his concepts of escape, defense, or a combination of both. Any sort of idea he got dwindled away into bitter disappointment as countless reasons why it wouldn't work became apparent when more thought was put to it.

At midday Gavin took his horse and swung up into the saddle to make a ride southward to see if he could spot the advance elements of the Comanchero band. A half-hour's gallop showed nothing but emptiness. Now worried that a flanking movement by the outlaws would cut him off from his troops, the lieutenant swung the animal around to the north and rode back to rejoin the group.

As he closed in on them, he could easily see Paddy O'Hearn a few hundred yards away. The dragoon rode in a military manner, sitting tall in the saddle as he alertly surveyed the area toward which he led the column.

Suddenly the soldier and his horse dropped completely out of sight.

Gavin stood in his stirrups to see what had happened. To his relief a few moments later, the animal reappeared as if he were rising out of the ground. Then O'Hearn did the same, dusting off his pants while trotting over to grab the horse's reins prior to remounting.

Curious, Gavin kicked his mount into a gallop. Everyone looked up in alarm as he sped past, so he waved and smiled to let them know everything was all right. As he neared O'Hearn, the dragoon hollered.

"Hold it, sir! Don't come no closer!"

Gavin reined in, coming to a sudden halt. "What happened, Private O'Hearn? You dropped out of sight like something had reached up and grabbed you."

"There's a hidden gully there, sir," O'Hearn explained. "I rode straight into it. The thing is prob'ly a dried-up ol' creek bed. The buffalo grass is so thick that you can't see it."

The dragoon rode forward a few feet, then dismounted. He led his horse down into the deep gash and up the other side. "It's easy to see from over there."

Now Gavin stepped down from the saddle. He took his horse's reins and led the animal through the thick, tall grass and down into the incline, then up the other side. He surveyed the terrain feature for several long moments. Suddenly he became excited and agitated.

"O'Hearn! Go fetch the others. Tell Sergeant Douglas to hurry everybody over here," he ordered. "And I mean now!"

"Do you want me to get out my bugle and sound Assembly?" O'Hearn asked. He always liked to show off his trumpeting skills when he got the chance.

"No. It would make too much noise," Gavin said. "You'll have to ride over there. Be careful coming back so that nobody tumbles down into that cut in the ground."

"Yes, sir!"

Gavin waited impatiently until the group finally arrived. It took several more minutes for them all—six dragoons and twenty-seven civilians—to descend, then climb up and out of the ancient creek bed.

"We're staying here and waiting for the Comancheros to show up," Gavin told Douglas.

The sergeant frowned and looked around. "There ain't no cover here, sir. Don't you think we ought to get down in that gully?"

"No, I don't, and never mind about cover. That's the least we have to take into consideration now," Gavin said irritably. "How is our ammunition supply?"

"We got plenty, sir," Douglas said. "In all the time we been out, we ain't done no serious shooting except after them deserters."

"That's fine. Now set up a defensive line right here, facing directly south," Gavin ordered. "I'd say we're about ten yards away from that creek bed, wouldn't you?"

"I reckon so," Douglas mused. "We could cut some of this grass and set it up to hide behind if we ain't gonna get down in the thing."

"You'll do nothing of the kind," Gavin said. "I want the dragoons standing—not kneeling—standing in one rank here with the men directly behind."

"Also standing?" Douglas asked.

"Yes," Gavin replied.

"They'll be easy to spot in this flat country," Douglas said in an argumentative tone.

"I realize that," Gavin said. "The women and children may position themselves a few yards to the rear. In their case, I prefer that all of them either sit or lie down."

"Are you sure about all this, sir?" Douglas asked.

"Do as you are ordered, Sergeant," Gavin said in a terse voice. "There is no time for idle talk at this point. Those Comancheros will be catching up with us at any time."

Douglas clicked his heels together and saluted. Then he set about to put Gavin's instructions into effect. The women and children were taken back twenty-five yards and put with the hobbled horses. The dragoons moved forward with carbines while the Russian men positioned themselves directly behind the soldiers.

Karshchov, sporting the army carbine, occupied a space in the center of the line of troopers. He nudged Corporal Murphy. "What is going on?"

"Beats hell outta me, Mister Karshchov," Murphy said. "I'm just gonna do what I'm told."

Sergeant Douglas, standing nearby, said, "I wouldn't bother the lieutenant with any questions, Mister Karshchov. He's real testy right now."

Karshchov nodded. "I shall heed your kind advice, Sergeant Douglas."

Suddenly Gavin became very soldierly. "Detachment!" he called out. "Atten-hut!"

The soldiers quickly snapped into the position of attention.

"Load!"

The paper cartridges were inserted into the breeches and the blocks pushed down into proper position.

"Cock your weapons!"

Hammers were drawn back by the well-drilled dragoons.

"Target is the open country to the south!" Gavin hollered. "Fire!"

The well-trained soldiers did not hesitate to obey the strange order as seven carbines barked, sending thick clouds of smoke bellowing outward.

Douglas walked up to the lieutenant. "Sir, that's gonna attract them Comancheros right here where we are. They might be wandering off far enough to give us some more time."

"That is exactly what I do not want at this point," Gavin said, smiling. "If O'Hearn's carbine wasn't more important than his bugle right now, I'd have him sounding every call known to the United States Army."

"You mean you want 'em to know exactly where we are?" Douglas asked incredulously.

"Not only that," Gavin said. "I want them to find us as quickly as they can."

"Sir—"

"Have the men reload, Sergeant," Gavin said. "Thank you very much." He walked away toward the side of the group, pulling his field glasses to study the far horizon to the south.

There was no sign of movement for nearly twenty minutes; then Gavin spotted three riders on the skyline.

"Detachment, atten-hut!" he called out. "Target to the south! Fire!"

Once more a volley of shots streaked outward, whipping harmlessly through the clear air of the prairie country. But the trio of riders, far out of range, heard the noise. They immediately turned around and disappeared into the heat haze.

"Have the men reload, Sergeant," Gavin ordered as he kept his southerly watch through the field glasses.

In less than a quarter of an hour, distant shadows showed up in a single line across the southern expanse. Gavin counted over twenty riders.

"Enemy front!" he hollered. "Stand fast! No one will fire except on my command!"

The horsemen out on the prairie moved slowly closer, becoming easier to see as they approached. The Comancheros seemed to be studying the situation, acting in a cautious manner as they closed the gap between themselves and the thin line of dragoons.

"Cock your pieces!" Gavin hollered.

Douglas left the group to stand next to the lieutenant. "They're quite a ways out there, sir," he said tactfully.

"Aim!" Gavin ordered.

Douglas nervously licked his lips, looking out at the attackers still moving at a deliberate pace. "We can't hit shit until they're in closer, sir."

Gavin took a deep breath, then bellowed, "Fire!"

Once more smoke and flame bellowed out from the carbines as the bullets whipped harmlessly through the air to fall short before reaching the Comancheros.

"Goddamn it, sir!" Douglas hissed angrily. "Now those son of a bitches know we ain't got time to reload. They're gonna come roaring in here like a damn forest fire in August."

"That's fine, Sergeant," Gavin said calmly. He patted

196

Douglas on the shoulder in a reassuring way. "Not to worry."

Some shouts could be heard from the Comancheros. Immediately, they jumped into a full gallop coming straight at the dragoons.

The troopers all turned their heads and looked at the lieutenant and sergeant to see what they should do.

"Sling carbines and draw pistols!" Gavin barked.

"We got to get into that damn creek bed, sir!" Douglas implored him.

"Please sling your carbine and draw your pistol," Gavin said, pulling his own Colt revolver from its holster.

"Yes, sir!" Douglas said. "Goddamn it!"

Gavin spoke calmly, saying, "Look at those Comancheros, Sergeant Douglas. They've broken down into three distinct waves. Very nice tactics on their part."

"I'm just full o' admiration for them no-good buttheads, sir," Douglas said sarcastically.

By then the pounding of the outlaws' horses made the ground shake. Wild yells and yips could be heard coming from the attackers as they continued to close in rapidly.

The first wave swept in, then suddenly dropped out of sight amid the screaming of men and neighing of horses as they galloped into the invisible gully.

The second group immediately went in on the first, adding to the din of horror and fear coming from men and animals.

The third line of Comancheros, alerted by the disappearance of the first, managed to turn away at the same moment the middle line plunged into the creek bed on top of the front one.

Gavin ran as fast as he could toward the creek bed, with a very pleased Sergeant Douglas following.

"Follow me!" the lieutenant yelled.

When he reached the edge of the dry waterway, he wasted no time in firing at the crawling, moaning mass of Comancheros who were wrapped up in each other and their mounts.

Douglas quickly caught on, imitating the officer as he yelled, "Fire at will!"

The other dragoons, with Karshchov watching excitedly because he had no revolver, began to pick targets of opportunity, sending .36 caliber slugs into the heads and bodies of both injured and uninjured Comancheros.

Within moments, all had been shot. They lay still, some twitching in death, their blood now running where water had flowed in ancient times.

"By God, sir!" Douglas exclaimed. "You're one smart son of a bitch! And I mean that most respectfully."

"Thank you, Sergeant Douglas," Gavin said. "I rather appreciate being called a smart son of a bitch by another smart son of a bitch."

Douglas laughed out loud and pointed to the other Comancheros, who had drawn off. "I'll bet those bastards are about to go crazy in trying to figure out just what the hell happened."

"Lock and load your carbines, aim, and fire at will," Gavin said.

The dragoons, and Karshchov, quickly turned to loading their long arms. Within a few minutes a ragged, uneven volley leaped out at the surviving Comancheros. Two dropped to the ground while the others galloped away toward safety in the south.

"I'll call this one in our favor," Gavin said, grinning.

"Me, too," Douglas said. He motioned to the dragoons. "Get down there in that creek bed and gather up weapons, ball, and powder. Also check for canteens and rations in the saddlebags. Bring the uninjured mounts up here. Now move!"

Karshchov rushed over to Gavin, then caught himself, offering his hand. "You are to be congratulated, Gavin! A great victory! We are free!"

"I'm afraid not quite, Basil," Gavin cautioned him. "This is only a part of the Comanchero band. The leader will return to his camp to gather up the remainder and make an all-out attack on Nadezhda."

Douglas suddenly remembered something. He rushed to the rim of the old creek, shouting, "See if them two son of a bitches McRyan and Costello is down there."

A few moments later, Corporal Steeple hollered back, "They ain't in this group, Sergeant."

"Bad luck, that!" Douglas complained. "Well, hop to it, my lads. We're not at Nadezhda yet."

Canteens were gathered up first and examined. Those considered too dirty were thrown back in with the corpses. Others were looped around the saddle horns of captured horses. The Comancheros' weaponry turned out to be a big surprise. There were many types of handguns that included ancient single-shot flintlocks and a few more modern percussion revolvers. But the long guns were a pleasant discovery.

"They're all the same, Lieutenant!" Douglas happily reported.

Gavin examined the muskets and found them to be British "Brown Bess" muskets, but with Mexican stampings on the lockplates. He chuckled. "I suppose some arsenal down in Mexico was looted to get these."

"Or live folks were traded for 'em," Douglas said. He made a quick count. "At any rate, we got ten of 'em and ball and powder, too. They'll be of help."

Gavin shrugged. "I estimate that those Comancheros are going to come up to Nadezhda about eighty to a hundred strong."

"I'd have to agree," Douglas said.

"We're not out of it yet," Gavin warned.

"Sir, I never figgered we stood a snow ball's chance in hell," Douglas said. "And we still ain't!"

"You're right," Gavin said. "We've only delayed the inevitable. We could never make it back to Fort Leavenworth."

Douglas gave the weaponry another survey. "But at least now we'll be able to take more of 'em with us."

"We've still a ways to go to our last stand, Sergeant," Gavin said. "Let's get moving again. I don't want to get cut off before we reach the Russian settlement."

Douglas quickly turned to the chore of organizing the new equipment and animals. Within fifteen minutes, the little column moved out with all the women and children and a good number of the men mounted.

The dragoons, happy to be back in their own saddles, rode on as good soldiers always do, ready to accept glory or death—or a combination of both.

Chapter 18

Paddy O'Hearn was the first dragoon to reach Nadezhda, and he had Irena Yakubovski behind him on his saddle.

Gavin MacRoss had sent the pair ahead of the slow-moving column to let Count Valenko and the rest of the Russians know they were coming. As soon as O'Hearn and Irena were near enough to the settlement to be heard, the stout young woman shouted in a happy, shrill voice:

"Myeh zdyes! Kazhdye!"

At first there was no reaction. She repeated the call as they drew closer, and eventually someone heard the young woman's strong voice. A lone peasant man, carrying buckets of water, looked toward them from the interior of the settlement. For a moment he stood motionless; then he dropped his load and waved his hands over his head, yelling happily as he hopped around like a lunatic.

"Myeh zdyes!" Irena repeated. *"Kazhdye!"*

Now a group of peasants ran out toward them, shouting and gesturing in unrestrained joy. Irena once more called out the words. *"Myeh zdyes!"* Then she began speaking rapidly, gesturing and pointing toward the south.

O'Hearn didn't know what she had hollered at the other Russians, but he knew from their reactions that it was something they wanted to hear. When they reached the settlement, the people crowded around them, giving the soldier's horse such a case of nervousness that he had trouble controlling the animal.

Count Valenko, with tears streaming down his face, made an inquiry of Irena. O'Hearn heard Natalia's name in the middle of what was only gibberish to him, but he knew the old man was asking after his daughter. The answer the count received caused him to dance and sing in his hoarse, loud voice.

Other Russians, now hearing the news that all those kidnapped had survived, leaped around and broke out in impromptu dances. A mandolin and harmonica soon appeared, and everyone joined in singing.

A quarter of an hour later, when they sighted the dragoons and former captives, shouting erupted from both groups. Some of the men leaped aboard plow horses and rode the gigantic beasts out to escort the returning people back into Nadezhda.

The liberated serfs were embraced and kissed, almost to the point of creating a minor riot out on the open prairie. Sergeant Ian Douglas, never one to give into happy emotions, had absolutely no tolerance for the situation.

"Stop dancing around and move on!" he bellowed in anger. "We ain't safe yet! There's about a hunnerd damn Comancheros that want to slit your throats. Move it, damn your eyes, move it!"

He urged his mount into the crowd, forcing the people to move toward Nadezhda. Basil Karshchov, under more self-control than the others because of already liberating Natalia Valenko, began to help the sergeant. He shouted instructions in Russian, grabbing and pushing people to continue the trek toward the settlement.

More chaos erupted a half hour later when the main body reached the town. Everyone was embraced and kissed—including the disgusted dragoons—as an orgy of happiness swept across the community. Reunions were tearful and loud as husbands, wives, children, and parents reunited.

Douglas glanced over at Gavin. "Accepting things calmly ain't exactly in their nature, is it?"

"I suppose not," Gavin said.

After Count Valenko finally finished welcoming his daughter, he turned his ardent attentions onto Lieutenant Gavin MacRoss, grabbing the young officer in his massive arms and hugging him tightly to him. He planted wet kisses all over Gavin's face as the officer struggled to escape the wild expressions of gratitude being forced on him.

"You're welcome! You're welcome!" the lieutenant hollered in hopes of putting the demonstration to an end. "I appreciate your gratitude, but enough is enough!"

"You are vonderful man! Vonderful man!" Valenko yelled out between kisses and hugs.

Gavin had to literally fight off the man to free himself. He came close to using his fists before he finally broke away. He shouted out, "Basil! Basil! For the love of God, get over here!"

Karshchov responded, wisely putting himself between the blubbering, laughing old man and the disturbed young officer. He spoke rapidly in Russian, pushing the count away until finally the old nobleman calmed down enough to listen to Gavin's words.

"We are not out of this yet," Gavin said.

"What are you sayink, my brave friend?" Valenko asked. "Ewerybody is home! My daughter! My people! My future son-in-law!"

"Listen to me, goddamn it!" Gavin yelled. "Those

Comancheros are going to be here in another day or so, and they'll be numerous, determined, and mad as hell! We are in great danger! Danger! Do you understand?"

Suddenly the count was quiet. "Danger, you are sayink? Those bad men come back? Vhy? They are not defeated?"

"Hell, no, they're not defeated!" Gavin snapped. "They are far, far from being beaten, believe me!"

Gavin grabbed the count by the sleeve and pulled him along to get him out of earshot of the celebrating serfs. Karshchov helped by pushing the old man along until they were well-separated from the crowd.

Karshchov, his face serious as hell, grabbed the count by the shoulders and began speaking to him in a low, yet impassioned tone of voice. He spoke for a full five minutes as Valenko's face slowly lost its color. When he finished, the older man staggered back as if struck by some invisible club.

Karshchov turned to Gavin. "I have explained everything to him. He now knows we are doomed. I told him of our pact to make sure Natalia does not fall into the hands of the Comancheros."

Valenko looked at Gavin. "Is nothink ve can do? Ve make a pact vith them. Pay money, eh? Lots of money, I am havink."

"It won't do any good, Your Grace," Gavin explained. "I have dealt with Comancheros before, and know their customs and twisted sense of honor."

"Explain it to His Grace, Gavin," Karshchov said.

Gavin continued, saying, "The leader of the band has been doubly embarrassed and shamed by the escape then the loss of men in the attack at the old creek bed. If the son of a bitch wishes to maintain command of his men—and that also means keeping himself alive—he must wipe out Nadezhda."

"Ve can do nothink?" Valenko asked.

204

"Our only choice is how do we die," Gavin said. "Fighting or skulking like cowards."

"Russians die fightink!" Valenko shouted. Then he calmed down. "Vhy don't you ride away, Lieutenant? You can safe yourself and your men. Take my daughter vith you, eh?"

"I can't do it, as much as I wish I could," Gavin said. "There is a duty here that has been forced on me by the circumstances. To leave here would be the same as desertion in the face of the enemy. I am bound by my oath as an officer and as a soldier to defend Nadezhda. That I intend to do."

Valenko asked, "Are ve tellink the people that all vill die?"

"There is nothing to be gained by that," Gavin said. "It would make any resistance almost futile and useless if they thought they had no hope. I don't even want my dragoons to know, though they have probably figured that out themselves."

"Then, ve act like a great wictory is soon to be ours," Valenko said. "Ve are the leaders. Ve must be brave."

"There are some muskets from the Comancheros killed at the creek bed," Karshchov said. "Gavin will give those along with powder and ball to our men. He will teach them to shoot like soldiers."

"That will at least hold the Comancheros off for a while," Gavin said.

"Is good!" Valenko said. "I am former officer of Imperial Czarist Infantry, so already I am knowink what to do." He nudged Karshchov, saying, "Gather up the men. Ve must start this instruction immediately."

"Yes, Your Grace," Karshchov said. "I will have them all ready with the muskets within the hour."

"I'll get Sergeant Douglas," Gavin said. "We'll need an interpreter, Basil."

"My friend, I am at your service," Karshchov said. He rushed off to gather up the men.

"Care to join our little army, Your Grace?" Gavin asked.

"I vill fight with you, my brave friend, and I vill die with you!" the count vowed. He lowered his voice, "Now is three of us to see that Natalia is kept from those animals!"

"That's a cheerful thought," Gavin said sullenly to himself as he walked away to find Sergeant Douglas. The noncommissioned officer, knowing something would be required of him, had kept himself conspicuous. He noticed Gavin motioning to him, and he joined the lieutenant.

Gavin MacRoss and Ian Douglas sat down for a serious discussion of how they planned to handle the entire situation. Douglas agreed that the Russian peasants, in spite of their lack of military experience, could at least be trained enough to load, aim, and fire on command if a translator was available. Volley fire was the answer to delaying the ultimate defeat and slaughter they faced.

"But we ain't gonna be able to stand out there alone like a brigade o' infantry, sir," Douglas pointed out. "We're gonna need things to hide behind. Remember, too, that we'll be surrounded by them son of a bitches."

"In that case, I suggest we have our men start digging and setting up cover," Gavin said. 'We'll have to tear down some of the structures here, use over-turned wagons, and throw up dirt mounds to get behind."

"I'll go along with that," Douglas said. "But we'll have to keep the perimeter small. There ain't no way in hell we're gonna spread ever'thing out to cover the whole town. We'll just have to give up part of it."

"That area will have to be burned down, or the Comancheros can use it to put snipers behind the cabins and pick us off," Gavin pointed out. He sighed. "Doing that is going to give these folks an idea that things are extremely desperate."

"I take it they don't know we're all gonna die here," Douglas said.

"I don't see any point in telling them, or the dragoons either for that matter," Gavin said.

"Our troopers know what's what," Douglas said. "But, like any good soldiers, they figger there's hope in this mess somewheres. So they'll fight like hell."

"Those bastard Comancheros are going to pay a terrible price," Gavin said. "If nothing else, I'm sure they'll lose enough men to make them lynch that leader of theirs."

"He's Italian or Spanish or something," Douglas said. "Name o' Lazardo." He laughed. "Mister Lazardo, that is."

"I believe I spotted the gentleman right after McRyan and Costello pointed you out," Gavin said.

"That's two more that's gonna pay dear," Douglas vowed. "One of us dragoons is bound to get a shot at 'em."

"We'd better get to work," Gavin said. "I'll tend to setting up the musketry drill while you set our boys to work."

"I'm gonna need some help once we start burning them cabins over there," Douglas said.

"I'll have Count Valenko help you out," Gavin said. "He's been in the Russian infantry, so he can afford to come late to our training."

Douglas saluted, and the two parted company to set the defensive plan into action. Gavin found that all the men had been assembled by Karshchov at a spot a short distance from the village. Each held a musket along with ammunition.

"Our men are ready for to learn," Valenko said.

"Thank you, Your Grace," Gavin said. "Sergeant

Douglas requires your assistance in setting up our defensive positions."

"It is pleased I am to be helpink," Valenko said. He left the group to seek out the dragoons to find out what was required of him.

The first thing Gavin had to do was acquaint the peasant men with the workings of the Enfield musket. It was similar to their hunting muskets and blunderbusses, so they learned that part quickly. Loading, cocking, and inserting the percussion cap was easy for them. They went through some dry runs, then actually rammed home powder and ball.

"Ready!" Gavin shouted.

"Gotovyei!" Karshchov repeated.

"Aim!" Gavin continued.

"Imet!" Karshchov echoed.

"Fire!" commanded Gavin.

"Strelbai!" Karshchov translated.

A ragged, but respectable, volley blasted out of the assembled amateur infantrymen. The smoke rolled out, then was picked up by the breeze to drift away in a thick haze.

"Excellent," Gavin said, pleased at the way the Russians quickly reacted to the battle commands. "Now we'll practice while only pretending to load."

Karshchov translated the instructions. Gavin spent an entire hour repeating the procedure over and over. He finally noted that the clicks of the hammers striking the nipples had become as one noise as the coordinated effort improved with each repetition.

The training was interrupted when shouting suddenly broke out. The angry shrieking of women filled the air as a small column of smoke appeared. Then, quickly, flames erupted from the outlying buildings as the roofs ignited.

The men in the firing line grumbled loudly, turning to

Karshchov for an explanation. The Russian, feeling helpless, looked at Gavin.

"Tell them we must knock down those cabins and other structures to deny cover to the Comancheros," Gavin said. "If we do not, they will hide behind or inside them to shoot at us. We'll be like fish in a barrel."

Karshchov spoke to the men in a tone of authority, but laced with just a hint of gentleness and sympathy. They asked a few questions, and he answered, glaring at a couple of the more angry serfs.

"Basil, tell them to go comfort their women," Gavin said. "They need a rest from drill anyhow."

Karshchov sent them on their way, then walked over and joined Gavin. He pointed to where the dragoons were hard at work.

"I see our defenses are being constructed," he said. He sighed. "If only we had a chance for a miracle."

"I've seen too many slaughtered soldiers and civilians to believe in that," Gavin said. "We can only fight like hell and kill as many of them as possible."

"The serfs are very religious," Karshchov said. "They will hold a prayer session this evening and light candles. The women have already set up a shrine. Too bad we have no priest."

"Just tell everyone to pray like hell," Gavin said.

"Will you join us?" Karshchov asked. "It will please the people very much."

"I'm not much on religion," Gavin admitted. "But it's certainly not going to hurt anything. Yes, I'll be there." He looked over where the men talked to the women, many with reassuring arms around their wives' shoulders or waists.

Karshchov said, "It seems everyone has calmed down now."

"There is still a lot of preparation to do," Gavin said.

"Let's ask Count Valenko to conduct the musketry drill. I must see to the fortifications my men are building."

"I will stay and practice shooting," Karshchov said.

"Very well, Basil," Gavin said. "I shall see you later."

The lieutenant walked over to his detachment, which labored on an earthen breastwork under Sergeant Douglas's stern supervision. Gavin glanced up, noticing the sunset beginning to form. He stopped and looked at the change in the sky, appreciating both the beauty and delicacy of the colors as they blended in with the sun and clouds.

"Farewell," Gavin whispered to the natural phenomenon. "I'll not see you tomorrow, or ever again."

Chapter 19

The Comanchero camp was like a cauldron sitting on hot coals. It threatened to boil over at any moment.

When the news of the loss of over a dozen men in the dry creek bed had been spread through the camp, it caused a near revolt. In that outlaw society, failure was bad enough. When it also meant the loss of comrades, then tensions could run extremely high. Risk was something all Comancheros were willing to take, but they would not tolerate deaths brought on by ineptness or bungling. Such brutal men, angered by what they considered incompetency or bad luck, would soon turn to violence for satisfaction.

Misadventure also offered an excuse for a rebellion to be organized by the more ambitious in the group who had a yen to be the big leader. That was easy when there were plenty of angry individuals ready to join in a serious threat to authority.

Guido Lazardo was no fool. He knew he faced an uphill task in not only maintaining his leadership position, but also in avoiding having a mob of angry Comancheros tear him limb from limb—if he was lucky—or roasting him alive after some delicate and painful knife work—if he was not. He wisely gathered his Praetorian guard around him. They consisted of seven trusted and capable gunmen:

Monroe Lockwood, the large American, had the utmost faith in his leader. He had seen too many successes to allow a setback to shake his loyalty. There was no doubt in Lockwood's mind that sticking by Lazardo would pay off. He was willing to face down any number of malcontents to keep his man in office.

Big Joe, a black man who had known a slave overseer's whip on his back, appreciated the taste of freedom and even leadership afforded him by the Comanchero chief. He and his good friend Lockwood saw eye-to-eye on most issues, and that included trust in the luck of Guido Lazardo. He, too, would not tolerate any rebellion in the ranks.

Crazy Fox, a Comanche brave driven out of his own tribe for murder, well appreciated being welcomed into the band led by Lazardo. As a previous member of a fierce but undisciplined tribe of warriors, he saw no problem with errors in judgment or tactics. Any mistakes were the result of bad medicine, which could plague anybody as far as he was concerned.

Tarheel from North Carolina was a natural follower raised in an area where every town or county had an undisputed leader or patron. He found those same qualities in the Sicilian. Breaking in a new chief was something he didn't care to go through, so he threw in his lot with Lazardo.

Another steadfast follower was a Kiowa-Apache named Runs Fast. He had held a position of honor in his tribe as a leader in war and hunting parties, but found that being with the Comancheros offered more of what he craved—murderous forays and almost unlimited plundering. He gave Lazardo full credit for this improvement in his life. Runs Fast would be happy to take

212

the scalp of anyone attempting to destroy the Coman-chero chief.

Lefty Dan, an escaped convict from Massachusetts, felt safe here from the law. The faith he had in Lazardo matched that of his friends Monroe Lockwood and Big Joe. Whatever those two decided was all right with him whether it be to support Lazardo or gun him down.

A one-eared fellow named Lop-Head by his less than sympathetic outlaw brethren downright worshiped Lazardo. He had never known such success and power in any other criminal group in which he had traveled. As far as he was concerned, no matter what the setback, somehow Lazardo had what it took to come out even better than before.

In addition to those faithful few, Lazardo could also count on the loyalty of the army deserters Jack McRyan and Dennis Costello. They were not particularly trust-worthy individuals, but both knew quite a few in the Comanchero band considered them responsible in a small way for bringing the army down on them. With-out Lazardo's protection, the pair would end up with flame-blackened skulls.

The first problem Lazardo faced was caused by a woman named Molly. Her man, a half-breed called Mi-chael, had been gone for more than a week with some other Comancheros. Upon hearing of the deaths of the men at the creek bed, Molly had set up a shrieking howl accusing Lazardo of bringing about unnecessary deaths within the group. Only when she heard that the Co-manchero chief himself would be coming after her, did Molly finally stop her yowling. The frightened woman wisely gathered up her snot-nosed, filthy offspring and crossed the river to hide in the trees on the other bank.

Lazardo sent Lockwood to look for Molly, but when he couldn't find her, the gang's chief decided to forget the woman and concentrate on the bigger task at hand—regaining complete leadership and fear over the Comancheros. That was the reason he called a conference of war in his quarters to which he invited Monroe Lockwood and Big Joe.

Big Joe wasn't too worried. "All we got to do is go out there and shoot one or two of them sumbitches," he said. "Then they'll forget they's mad, and things'll get back to normal."

Lazardo shook his head. "We'll need every gun if we're going to wipe out that town. I don't want any unnecessary gunplay that would kill any of the men. Besides, more deaths might cause the situation to get completely out of control."

Lockwood dared to grumble a bit. "Wiping out that damn town is what we shoulda done in the first place."

"The reason I didn't want to stay there long enough to kill or capture everyone was because we didn't know the area," Lazardo explained. "There could have been an army post or another settlement close by as far as I knew. But now we know there isn't, so we can take our time and destroy the place."

"I understand, Mister Lazardo," Lockwood said. "This time we better kill or capture ever' one of 'em and let the boys have a good time with them women."

"That is what I intend to do," Lazardo said. "But there may be trouble in getting the men to follow us. They are very unhappy."

"Things ain't getting no better out there, Mister Lazardo," Big Joe warned him. "I still think we're gonna have to kill a couple of 'em to get things calmed down."

"Big Joe's right, Mister Lazardo," Lockwood said.

"I have a better idea," the Sicilian stated. "We are going to give the men a chance to get rid of some of that anger toward me, yet still have enough left over to wipe out that town and those soldiers."

Lockwood grinned. "I knowed you'd come up with something. I sure did."

"Me, too," Big Joe added. "What're we gonna do, Mister Lazardo?"

"We're going to give them somebody to beat up on and get rid of their anger," Lazardo said.

"Who?" Big Joe asked.

"Our latest members," Lazardo answered.

"You mean them two deserters?" Lockwood asked. "McRyan and Costello?"

"The very ones," Lazardo said. "Call those two idiots in here and prepare them for the sacrifice. I got to think careful of what I'm going to tell everybody."

"We'll take are of it right away," Lockwood said. He went to the door of the hut and found Tarheel and Lefty Dan on guard duty. "Fetch them two deserters and bring 'em here pronto."

"You bet, Monroe," Tarheel said.

Lockwood went back and sat down to wait. With Lazardo now deep in thought, both he and Big Joe knew better than to disturb his mental processes.

Ten minutes later, Jack McRyan and Dennis Costello, followed by Tarheel and Lefty Dan, stepped into the inner sanctum of the gang leader. Before they could speak, Lockwood and Big Joe quickly overwhelmed them, shoving the pair face-first to the earthen floor.

McRyan, terrorized, turned his head to one side and screamed, "Hey! What's the idea?"

When Costello freed his face from the dirt, the best he could manage was, "We didn't do nothing!"

"You brought the army down on us!" Lazardo growled.

The two luckless deserters were jerked upright as their pistols were taken and their hands tightly tied behind them with rawhide.

"We didn't bring nobody down on this camp," Jack

McRyan protested. "That sergeant was trailing after you fellers, not us!"

"We didn't do nothing!" Costello yelled one more time.

"I want a confession from you," Lazardo said. "A loud one." He nodded to Lockwood and Big Joe.

Immediately, the two Comancheros got serious about beating them up. Fists and boots collided with the hapless victims as they wailed and shouted in fearful pain at the cruel pummeling. The thrashing went on for almost a quarter of an hour.

"That's enough!" Lazardo ordered. He addressed the prisoners. "If you had enough, all it takes is for one of you to just yell out that you brought the army down on the camp."

Costello suddenly bellowed, "We brung the army down on the camp! We brung the army down on the camp!"

McRyan hissed at him. "Shut up, you stupid, yellow bastard!"

"We brung the army down on the camp!" Costello yelled again.

Lazardo smiled and gestured at Lockwood and Big Joe. "That's what I wanted to hear."

"That's what you wanted ever'body to hear," Big Joe added.

McRyan and Costello, held by their tormentors, were untidy messes. Blood flowed from cuts on their faces as bruises and swelling visually spread across their battered features. Neither one was able to see because of their eyes being swollen shut.

"Follow me," Lazardo said. "And drag those two along."

The spectacle of the Comanchero chief striding through the camp with Lockwood and Big Joe dragging the bloody army deserters behind him quickly drew a

216

crowd. Having heard the confession that Costello yelled, nearby Comancheros quickly passed the word around the camp. Curious, but still hostile, the outlaws gathered around and followed after the strange procession.

When Lazardo reached the stump of a felled tree, he immediately leaped upon it and looked around.

"Everybody!" he yelled. *"Todo el mundo! Tutti! Tout le monde!* Come here and listen to me. Everybody!"

Grumbling but curious, the Comancheros stood ready for anything out of the ordinary as they waited to see what Guido Lazardo had to say to them.

"Do you see these two miserable pieces of shit?" Lazardo bellowed. "I have just cleverly drawn full confessions from the both of them about leading soldiers to our camp. Some of you heard it, didn't you?"

"Yes, sir, Mister Lazardo," a Comanchero said. "I heard one of 'em yell that they'd brung the army here."

One gutsy Comanchero pushed his way to the front of the crowd. "I suppose you're gonna tell us that them two yahoos let them prisoners a-loose, huh?" He smirked and looked round. "I wonder how many of us is gonna believe that, huh?"

"They did not turn them loose personally," Lazardo shot back. "But they helped." He knew full well that McRyan and Costello had been with some of the other outlaws at the time the prisoners fled. There would be shouts of disagreement if he said they'd taken part in the actual escape. "We found they had spied on the stockade and snuck out word to the soldiers of the best way to let those slaves out."

That made sense. Several members of the crowd began nodding to each other in belief. But most still looked at Lazardo with blank gazes.

"How'd you find that out?" somebody hollered.

"We've been talking to them," Lazardo said. He

laughed and pointed to the battered pair. "Can't you see."

Several members of the crowd, appreciating the humor of someone being beaten half to death, joined in the laughter.

Lockwood, hanging on to McRyan, leaned toward Lazardo and whispered, "Tell 'em that these two know about some dead scouts of our'n. Hell, some o' the boys ain't come back yet. Might as well figger they're dead."

"Another thing, my brave people!" Lazardo said, taking the advice. "These rotten bastards have told us of how the soldiers killed some of our scouts. They followed their trail back here, and that is how they found us."

A few more of the Comancheros began to come around. They shouted abuse at the nearly unconscious prisoners still held up by Lockwood and Big Joe.

"I didn't trust them in the first place," Lazardo continued. "So I had both Lockwood and Big Joe keep a sharp eye on them. In fact, it was them that kept these two bastards from escaping just the other night. That's when we decided it was time to haul them in and have a little talk, which we did a couple of hours ago."

Now the Comancheros began to believe what they wanted to. A couple of ambitious fellows who had their sights on leadership shouted questions and expressed doubt, but soon they shut up as the crowd came around to the chief's line of reasoning.

"I am going to give you a choice," Lazardo said. "I will let Lockwood and Big Joe take care of them, or hand them over to you. Which is it?"

As an answer, about a dozen men swarmed forward and grabbed the prisoners, who had begun to regain consciousness. Shouting at and roughing them, the Comancheros dragged McRyan and Costello away toward the stockade.

The Indians Crazy Fox and Runs Fast shared a few moments of confusion. Not coming from a society in which lying and falsehood were in abundance, they believed their leader, even though neither could recall any long interrogation or particular attention given to the two unfortunates about to be sacrificed to save Lazardo's life and leadership. But, as far as they were concerned, if the Comanchero chief said the deserters were spies, that was good enough for them. Whooping and hollering, they moved off to join in the fun of the executions.

Lazardo, Lockwood, and Big Joe watched the mob pull the now wildly protesting ex-soldiers out of sight. Lockwood laughed. "I reckon that's that."

"I must plan out the best way to make quick work of that Russian town," Lazardo said.

"I reckon there ain't no rush, Mister Lazardo," Big Joe observed. "Them folks in the settlement ain't going nowheres, and that crowd o' riled Comancheros is gonna take their time in killing them two."

"I still must destroy that town," Lazardo reminded him. "If I don't, then I'll be going through what those wretches will soon be suffering."

The three walked back to Lazardo's quarters. A few straggling women and kids, finally hearing of what was going on, ran past them to join in the fun that was about to start.

"I'll tell you something," Big Joe said. "I ain't one to pay too much mind to what other folks goes through, but what McRyan and Costello is about to put up with makes my blood run cold."

"I'll say!" Lockwood said with a gruff laugh.

"We must see that it is over by dawn," Lazardo said. "I want to make an early start for that settlement."

"If the killing is still going on up to daybreak, me and

Big Joe will go up there and bring it to an end," Lockwood said.

"They might get mad at us, Monroe," Big Joe warned him.

"I don't think so," Lockwood said. "They'll be pretty tired by then and getting bored, too, I reckon."

"I suppose you're right," Big Joe said. "You can only torment somebody for so long afore it ain't fun no more."

Lazardo led the way into his cabin and settled down. Lockwood fetched tin cups and a jug of tequila while Big Joe made himself comfortable by settling down on a blanket and leaning against the log wall. Within moments, each man had taken several deep swallows of the Mexican liquor and uttered their approval with belching, licking of lips, and, in Lockwood's case, by emitting a loud fart.

They drank in silence for several moments; then the first shriek echoed out over the camp.

"That would be McRyan," Big Joe observed.

"I think you're right," Lockwood said, passing the jug.

Another, higher-pitched, lingering scream sounded. It ended in a sobbing wail.

Lazardo laughed. "Better them than me!"

"I'll drink to that," Lockwood said, raising his cup.

Now the screeching and howling came in pairs, keeping up a continuous sound as the evening's darkness closed in.

"The boys is letting the Injuns do the tormenting," Lockwood casually observed.

"They're the best at it alright," Big Joe said.

Lazardo took another drink. "During my days at sea, I heard that the Chinese are particular good at making painful deaths linger. A couple of sailors I knew claimed they had seen something called the death of a thousand cuts."

Lockwood guffawed. "How can anyone count when they're having so much fun?"

The trio fell into silence, sometimes paying attention to the sounds of agony, and other times either lost in their own thoughts or dozing. Lazardo did not sleep. His mind raced with making the plan to overrun the Russian settlement.

The outlaw leader had started life a bit dull-witted, but days of living in the dangerous Sicilian bandit world, the violence of forecastles at sea among rough seamen, the criminal world of southern Europe, and now the Comancheros had sharpened his mental capacities to the fullest. He brought all his cunning and acquired wisdom into the process.

Finally, as the sky began to lighten, Lockwood got to his feet. "Time to end the fun," he announced. He looked at Lazardo. "If we still want to make an early start, that is."

"We certainly do," Lazardo assured him.

"I'll go with you, Monroe," Big Joe said.

The two went across the camp in time to see the crowd beginning to break up. The Comancheros had begun to drift away from their night's activity.

"All done, huh?" Lockwood asked Lop-Head.

"Yeah," the man answered in angry disgust. "The Injuns was doing right good; then a coupla Mexicans wanted in on the fun, and they got carried away. Killed 'em off in about an hour and a half. Damn!"

Lockwood glanced over to see the charred hunks of flesh that had once been Jack McRyan and Dennis Costello.

"Fun can't go on forever," he observed.

Big Joe took a deep breath. "Now listen here, y'all! We're moving out to get that town. Mister Lockwood wants ever' swinging dick mounted, equipped, and armed at the shallows within a half hour. Now move!"

With Lazardo back in firm control, none wanted to cross him. The men hurried away, their women following to help in preparing for the trip. The entire camp hustled as horses were fetched from the corral and saddled. Haversacks and other carrying implements were stuffed with everything from powder and ball to food and extra moccasins. At the appointed time, the entire gang of Comancheros sat in their saddles as their leader, Guido Lazardo, galloped in front of them.

"Now!" he shouted. "We go to make the final vengeance. When we are finished I want everyone in that Russian village—no matter whether man, woman, child, or soldier—to be either dead or a prisoner. Do you understand?"

The outlaws shouted their comprehension and vows to exceed anything they had ever done in the past.

"Come now, *mes braves!*" Lazardo shouted. *"Valientes mios!* My brave men! *Coraggi!* Follow me!"

The Comanchero chief kicked his horse's flanks and led the way across the shallows, turning north as his men followed after him, roaring their battle lust and waving their long guns over their heads.

A few moments after they left, one of the village dogs, with others of its kind closely following, ran along the riverbank with something in its jaws the others also wanted.

No one could tell, as the curs snarled among themselves, whether the hand clenched in the animal's teeth belonged to Jack McRyan or Dennis Costello.

Chapter 20

In the twenty-four hours since the return of Lieutenant Gavin MacRoss, his dragoons, and the captives to Nadezhda, the Russian settlement took on a decidedly different appearance.

All outlying structures and buildings, including outhouses, had been either torn down and hauled away, or put to the torch. Even the prairie grass had been fired in the concentrated effort to make sure there was nothing left to give any attackers or snipers cover to approach close enough to effectively fire into the town without risking their lives. A blackened, flat area of empty plains country stretched out for a minimum of a hundred yards around the entire perimeter of the community.

Within the defensive area, all wagons and much of the debris from the hard work of destruction had been combined with shoveled piles of dirt to construct a circular barricade. The dominant feature inside this crude fortress was the village's central building constructed of logs previously cut in New England and brought out to be used for that structure. It was a strong edifice, offering cover and protection to the noncombatants and any wounded moved inside.

All of the surviving Russian men were positioned around the entire defensive position. Each had plenty of powder and ball along with drinking water and eating utensils if it became necessary to take meals on line. Their posts were to be permanent during the upcoming battle. The dragoons, on the other hand, were to be a flying squad, ready to rush to any portion of the defenses where extra firepower—or carbine butts, knives, and fists—would be needed.

Basil Karshchov, grim and determined, had the responsibility of making sure firing orders would be shouted in the Russian language. Valenko, because of his age, would be in a stationary position to either help Karshchov or take his place if he were killed or wounded.

Those two, along with Gavin MacRoss and Ian Douglas, each kept one bullet back for Natalia. This was a secret kept by the four men. If word of their impending plans for the young woman were known, then all the people in the settlement would be cast into despair.

That first night after all the construction was completed, every man slept at his post. A fifty-percent alert was in effect so that every portion of the perimeter had at least a couple of men awake and alert. Strict light and noise discipline was observed to ensure that nothing would attract attention to that exact spot in the expanse of prairie where the settlement was located. If the Comancheros were going to locate the place, Gavin was determined to make them work at it.

The women and children bedded down in the main structure, also keeping quiet. The women gossiped in whispers, shushing the kids whenever any got too rambunctious. Fussing babies were quickly nursed without regards to feeding schedules, for the sound of a squalling baby would carry far out into the open country. The sky was cloudy that night, obscuring the moon. Nadezhda was almost invisible and soundless in the darkness.

The night passed without incident, the hours marked

only by the changing of the guard and restless slumber as the people in the town prepared for the fight of their lives.

The first hint of dawn brought everyone on full alert without having to be urged into wakefulness. Water had been drawn from the new well and placed in buckets in the main building. An area for any wounded was set aside, and food was ready for everyone. The men took turns going in for bowls of thick *supu* and fresh-baked bread along with cups of hot coffee. With Sergeant Ian Douglas moving things along, the meal didn't take long. In twenty minutes, every man was back at his post, fed and anxious.

A period of waiting began. The sun grew warmer as birds flitted and scolded each other, and insects buzzed in the balmy air. A few people, tired from loss of sleep the night before, drifted off when it wasn't their turn to be on alert.

"Enemy south!"

Sergeant Douglas's shout as he stood atop the barricade with field glasses startled everyone. Karshchov reacted first, repeating the warning in Russian. All the men leaped to their positions, and any woman or child outside rushed to the main house as per instructions.

"Stand steady!" Gavin warned everyone. He hurried over and climbed up on the over-turned wagon to join the sergeant. He took a look. "That'll be the advanced scouts."

"Yes, sir," Douglas said. "They've found us."

"It won't be long now," Gavin said.

"O'Hearn was wondering if he should get out his trumpet," Douglas said. "He's always anxious to show off with it."

"That's right," Gavin said. "I remember when he was the company bugler. A pretty good one, too, as I recall."

"He figgered he could make more rank as a trooper," Douglas said. "He still practices now and then."

"I'm sure he's still an excellent field musician," Gavin said. "But we've more use for his carbine than his bugle, even though I'm sure the music would encourage everyone."

"I'll tell him to keep it in his saddlebags," Douglas said. He took another look at the Comancheros. "We're just about to get into the fight of our lives," Douglas said. "Or the last."

"You're right on both counts," Gavin said. He held out his hand. "Good luck, Sergeant Douglas."

Douglas took it in a tight grip and grinned. "Same to you, Lieutenant."

"Let's go to work," Gavin said, jumping down from the barricade.

"I'll tend to the dragoons," Douglas said, also leaping to the ground. He walked off to where the five dragoons, with carbines and pistols charged, locked, and loaded, waited for the fighting to begin.

A few moments later, a murmur arose from the Russians. They had all been watching the horizon where, quite suddenly, more than a hundred riders appeared.

Gavin joined Douglas. "Those cursed Comancheros know they're easy to spot against the skyline. They're just putting on a show for us."

"They won't stay out there long," Douglas said.

"You're right," Gavin agreed. He waved to Karshchov. "Tell the men to make sure they're locked and loaded, Basil."

Basil shouted out at the Russians in their language. All waved back at him and displayed the Enfield muskets to show the weapons were ready for action.

Some distant shouting and taunting could be heard; then suddenly the ground rumbled as hundreds of Comancheros kicked their horses into action. They quickly went into a full-speed gallop as they charged straight at the settlement.

"Dragoons to the south side!" Gavin ordered.

Douglas and his troopers immediately responded, moving into position between the Russians there.

"Stand steady and wait for orders!" Gavin yelled.

Basil Karshchov beside him made a quick translation for the serfs. The Comancheros were fifty yards away and closing fast.

Gavin hollered, "Cock your pieces!"

Yelling in several languages, the Comancheros had closed the distance to within twenty yards.

"Aim!"

It was easy to see the battle lust in the distorted features of the attackers as they roared straight at the south side.

"Fire!"

Smoke, flame, and ball ammunition blasted outward, plowing straight into the Comancheros. Men and horses screamed and tumbled to the ground. The many survivors quickly turned away, riding back out of range to leave a dozen dead and maimed scattered less than ten yards away from the defenses.

"Reload quickly!" Gavin urged his men.

Douglas, who kept his carbine slung across his back, held his smoking revolver. "That was just a test on their part, sir," he observed. "Now they know we can bite."

"They'll adjust their tactics to allow for that," Gavin said. "You can bet that Comanchero chief didn't put his best men to the front for that little escapade."

"I didn't get to know Lazardo too good," Douglas said, "but there ain't no doubt in my military mind that he's got the skill it'll take to break us here."

"If he's willing to pay the price," Gavin said. "Which, of course, we know he is."

The dragoons pulled back to reposition themselves in

their waiting area. The professional soldiers, quiet and ready, were in direct contrast to the happy, chattering Russians. Count **Valenko**, the ex-infantry officer of the czar, quickly got them to shut up and turn their attention toward the enemy.

Barely fifteen minutes went by before the Comancheros made their second appearance of the day. This time, rather than massing for a single, overpowering charge, the outlaws were strung out in a line, with plenty of space between them to make difficult targets. They sauntered along at a center, circling the settlement from left to right. They stayed just beyond rifle range for three complete circuits. Then they moved closer, kicking into a gallop.

"Don't fire until ordered to," Gavin urged everyone.

Suddenly a group of twenty Comancheros dashed toward the barricade. They unleashed an uneven volley, then turned and rode out of range.

One of the Russians staggered back from his position and collapsed. A quick check by Valenko showed the man to be dead. The old count ordered the others who had come to help him to return to their posts.

Another attack hit the north side of the line. Bullets zinged over the defenders and slapped into the main building, sending showers of splinters flying outward. But there were no casualties.

The Comancheros went back to circling, yelling taunts at the defenders. The dragoons, ready, stood tensely waiting for something to happen. The last two probes had been too quick for them to reach the affected areas.

Sergeant Ian Douglas spat. "By God! I'd give my left ball for a cannon full o' grapeshot."

He'd no sooner spoken, than a group of fifteen outlaw horsemen swept in close. Several Indians were among

228

the group, and arrows along with bullets flew into the defensive compound.

Gavin, not wasting any more precious seconds than necessary, managed to get the men to loose a fusillade at the attackers. One of the enemy fell, but a Russian was taken from the fight, too, moaning in agony with an arrow in his right shoulder.

"Attack on the east side!" came the call from Corporal Murphy, who noted a sneak move immediately after the previous assault.

This time the outlaws rode in closer, going straight at the defensive positions. A ragged volley did them no harm, and they turned away—all except one.

A Mexican, yelling in grotesque fury, rode straight at the barricade. His huge sombrero, hanging down his back, flopped in the wind as he jumped across the defenses and rode through the compound. He held a revolver in his hand, firing and yelling. The Russians on the far end of his charge turned and shot at him without waiting for orders. But, in their haste, they missed the fierce attacker.

But the shots unnerved the Mexican's horse, causing the animal to hesitate and slow down considerably.

The rider pulled on the reins and began a wild gallop toward the spot where he'd entered the settlement. He'd gone no more than ten yards before a large Russian left his position and ran after him, catching the Mexican by the arm and pulling him out of the saddle to crash heavily to the ground.

The Russian was a big, heavy, strapping peasant and the Comanchero a small, thin fellow. But he was full of fight. He snarled and hit and kicked at the man who had grabbed him. The serf tried to hold on, but the Mexican broke loose and made a run for the barricade. He fired at the men in his way as he raced for freedom.

But after three pulls on the trigger, his weapon was empty. Now, pulling his knife, he continued his escape.

Sergeant Douglas grabbed a loose piece of log from the barricade and hurled it at the running man's feet. It struck true, tripping him into a hard fall. Before he could get up, the American was on top of him, grasping the Comanchero's wrists in tight grips, shaking hard. The knife came loose; then Corporal Murphy and Paddy O'Hearn moved in to complete the capture.

The captive's hands were quickly bound, and he was dragged over to Gavin MacRoss and Basil Karshchov. The Mexican cursed them, their mothers, and their grandmothers as he stood before the defenders. A hard slap across the face from Gavin calmed his down. He shut up and looked around. Then he laughed out loud as he surveyed the small settlement.

"You are all going to die!" he said in English.

"I reckon you figger we ain't got much of a chance, huh?" Douglas said, cuffing him.

The man spit blood. "You ain't got no chance, gringo. No better than me now."

Douglas looked at Gavin. "What're we gonna do with him, sir."

"First, take him around the barricade for all the men to see, then drag the son of a bitch inside the main building and show him to the women," Gavin said. "That should dispel any notions about these Comancheros being super humans."

"That'd cheer ever'body up alright," Douglas said. "Then what am I supposed to do?"

"Sergeant Douglas, I don't give a damn," Gavin said. He turned his attention back to the job at hand.

Douglas, along with O'Hearn and Corporal Murphy, dragged the outlaw around where he got a few more punches from the Russians. A tour through the building where the women were proved worse for the prisoner.

The females clawed, scratched, and kicked the Comanchero while he did his best to twist away. After enduring that pain and indignity, the fellow was taken back to the barricades and thrown over on the other side. He jumped up and, rather than making an attempt to flee, turned and faced the defensive line.

"I ain't gonna run from you *hijos de tus chingadas madres!*" he bellowed in defiant anger.

Douglas, with his carbine, took steady aim and fired. The outlaw pitched over on his back. The sergeant calmly reloaded, saying, "I'll say one thing for the Mexican race. I don't think they ever sired a coward."

A fresh attack swept in on the west side, then another on the south. Bullets and arrows zapped through the air into the interior of the defensive position. When the Comancheros rode back out of range, three more Russians lay on the ground—one dead and two wounded.

The dragoons had been able to help turn away the attack on the west side. Reloading and preparing for the next bit of action, they gave the area a professional appraisal.

"We've lost five Russians and this here fight has just begun," Fenlay said to his pal O'Hearn.

"Maybe I should've stayed a trumpeter," O'Hearn observed as he worked on loading the breech of his carbine. "I could be back at Fort Leavenworth about now sounding Mess Call."

The Comancheros stepped up their efforts for the rest of the day. The attacks grew so numerous and lengthy that the defenders lost track of time. Volley fire blasted out at the attackers as showers of arrows and swarms of bullets slashed the air on their way into the settlement.

It became dangerous to draw water from the well by the main building, so by late afternoon, everyone on the firing line along with the dragoons were parched. The Americans helped the Russians by teaching them

231

the Indian trick of keeping a pebble in the mouth to induce the flow of saliva. It gave some relief but not much.

The sun, though far from gaining the intensity it would have in the summer, had grown extremely warm. Its rays battered down on the battle scene, adding to the discomfort of attacker and defender alike.

Blood, along with sweat, also was spilled during the long day's fighting. The dragoons were lucky, managing to remain unhurt except when Paddy O'Hearn ran face-first into the barricades during one particularly hot moment during the fighting. The Russians, on the other hand, did not fare so well. Two more of them died, and another, suffering a facial wound, was taken in to join the other three injured being tended to in the main building.

Then Basil Karshchov took a hit. He staggered backward under the impact of the bullet and fell flat on his back. But he quickly rolled over and pushed himself to his feet.

Gavin and Douglas rushed to him. While Gavin held his Russian friend, the sergeant ripped open the shirt where the round had entered.

"Please!" Karshchov said. "Let me go!"

"Just wait for Sergeant Douglas to check you over," Gavin said. "It won't take long."

"It don't look too bad," the sergeant said. He made a more careful examination. "But I can't find no exit wound. See if you can move your arm."

Basil complied, exhibiting no problem in swinging the arm around. "How is that?"

"That's good," Gavin said. "At least there're no broken bones."

"I don't feel so bad," Basil said. "It doesn't hardly hurt."

"Go inside and get bandaged up anyhow," Gavin said, glad to see no heavy bleeding had started.

"I must stay and fight!" Karshchov exclaimed.

"If that wound stiffens up, you might not be able to fight anymore," Gavin cautioned him.

Basil reluctantly turned and hurried over to the main building to get the medical treatment over with as quickly as possible.

The action began to taper off at that point, and dusk brought about a strange quiet. The shooting and bellowing, which had gone on for hours, suddenly stopped. No Comancheros showed up as the defenders anxiously waited. After an hour slipped by, it was obvious the outlaws had called it a day.

"I reckon they're in no hurry," Douglas caustically observed. "Why wear theirselves out when they can finish us off in the morning."

Gavin MacRoss, sweat-streaked and powder-stained, took a grateful drink of water that Irena Yakubovski offered him. He put the ladle black in the bucket as she went off to tend to others. "We've already lost almost half our men on the line to death or injury. Tomorrow, our troopers will have to man those positions."

"That means the dragoons will begin to die, sir," Douglas pointed out. He looked around. "Hell! We won't make it much past noon."

"What do you know about that Comanchero leader?" Gavin asked.

Douglas shrugged. "He runs his outfit by keeping his gang scared. If he catches a bullet, they'll turn and run. But there ain't no way we're gonna get a chance to get him. His most loyal men won't let him take no chances. They got a lot to lose if the son of a bitch dies."

Gavin was thoughtful for long minutes. Then he spoke with a new freshness. "Have the men saddle their horses."

"Sir?" Douglas asked, confused.

"I said to get the troops ready to ride," Gavin said. "Tell O'Hearn to get that bugle of his."

"Begging you pardon, Lieutenant," Douglas said. "But what the hell for?"

"We're getting the hell out of here," Gavin said.

Chapter 21

Count Vladimir Valenko, the wounded Basil Karshchov, and the other Russians watched incredulously as the dragoons mounted up.

"Lieutenant MacRoss!" the old nobleman cried out. "What are you doing?"

Gavin ignored the question. "The only thing left for you at this point is to man those barricades. Fight as I taught you and pray to God for deliverance."

Karshchov, his arm in a sling, looked straight into Gavin's face. "Whatever you do, I am your friend and I understand. I know there is goodness and bravery in your heart." He started to sob, but caught himself, although tears streamed from his eyes. "Live long and be happy, my friend Gavin."

The lieutenant motioned to Douglas. "Move out!"

The troopers, in file, rode to an opening in the defenses past the dismayed Russians, who stood in mournful silence. None of the serfs said or murmured a word of complaint or condemnation. Being stoic no matter what the situation was an ingrained characteristic of the peasantry.

Gavin avoided looking at the main building in case Natalia Valenko might be standing in the door or at one of the windows watching him and his men depart. He would never be able to bear a look of disapproval or contempt from the woman he loved.

The lieutenant led his men out of the settlement, breaking into a canter as they entered the open country of the Kansas prairie.

"Where do you think those Comancheros are camping?" Gavin asked Douglas.

"Only one place around here, sir," Douglas answered. "At that bend in the Republican River to the south."

"Then, we'll head north," Gavin said. "Gallop, ho!"

With increased speed, the dragoons separated themselves from Nadezhda. After going a bit more than two miles, Gavin made a leisurely turn toward the east and Fort Leavenworth. He continued in that direction for five more miles. Then, with a waving signal, he made an abrupt turn to the south.

The pace was slowed as the journey continued with more deliberation. After nearly an hour of southerly travel, Gavin raised his hand.

"Detachment, halt!" The lieutenant turned his horse and signaled his men to ride closer to him. As they came to a stop, he glanced at O'Hearn. "Is that bugle handy?"

"Slung over my shoulder as you see, sir," O'Hearn reported. "Remember, sir, you told me to take it outta my saddlebags."

Next, Gavin spoke to Corporal Murphy. "You did a fine job on that corral at the Comanchero camp. We'll be depending on your timing again."

"Don't worry, sir," Murphy assured him. "I'll have ever'body ready, and O'Hearn is gonna play the sweetest bugle music since Gabriel."

"I'm not going to lie to you," Gavin said. "We don't have much of a chance as it is. If you fail, or are even the slightest bit late, there will be absolutely no way that Sergeant Douglas or I will return to Fort Leavenworth."

"I know that, sir," Murphy said.

"If something happens to foul up your part of this mission, you are free to head straight for the fort," Gavin said.

"We'll go back to Nadezhda," Murphy said.

"That's certain death," Gavin said bluntly.

"Hell, all us lads always knowed that, sir," Murphy said. "But I'll guarantee that we're gonna do our damndest. Sometimes stubbornness can win over anything."

"That's all I can ask of you," Gavin said. He nodded to Douglas. "What about you, Sergeant?"

Sergeant Douglas said, "I'm ready, sir. May I respectfully remind the lieutenant that the rules of chivalry ain't gonna get us shit in this mission."

"I know, Sergeant," Gavin assured him. "It's down and dirty from this point on."

"You might even call it murder, but we can't give 'em the slightest benefit of the doubt," Douglas observed.

"I realize our backs are against the wall," Gavin said.

"Anyhow, what the hell's the difference?" Douglas remarked. "If we don't go to our maker over there, we would've done it in the settlement anyhow."

"Right," Gavin said. "What the hell."

"We'd best leave, sir," Douglas said. "The men all know what's got to be done. So let's do it."

Gavin waved at his men. "Good luck, everybody!"

"Good luck, sir!" they replied.

Gavin and Douglas left the others, riding off to the south in the moonlight. The two rode silently, keeping a sharp lookout around them. Finally the moonlight waned, and it was so dark they had to bring their horses to a slow walk to avoid any prairie dog holes or other natural obstacles. But the young officer had anticipated this, and allowed time for moving along at reduced speed.

They continued on into the night before reaching the Republican River. They followed the waterway to the west, glad to have the sound of the rushing waters cover the noise of their horses' hooves.

"Ho!" Douglas said.

"I see," Gavin assured him.

The pair of dragoons could observe the flickering light of campfires over the distant horizon. Now, going even slower, they pressed on until they could see the source of the light spread out along the riverbank.

Douglas forced a grin. "It seems you and me been riding up to Comanchero camps quite a bit lately, Lieutenant."

"I hope we don't develop a habit of doing this," Gavin said. He pointed to some trees twenty yards from the river. "There's a good place to wait."

"I don't see anything better," Douglas said in way of agreement.

They rode over to the stand of oaks and cottonwoods, easing inside the treeline before dismounting. They could hear shouts and laughter coming from the camp less than a half mile away.

"They're really looking forward to tomorrow," Gavin observed.

"The son of a bitches," Douglas said.

"If you were a Comanchero and figured you'd be having your way with at least three women tomorrow, wouldn't you be excited?" Gavin asked.

"Hell!" Douglas said with a chuckle. "I'd feel that way anyhow."

The night grew cooler in spite of the warmth of the previous day, making the two soldiers glad they had their blankets to slip around their shoulders. Neither felt the least need of sleep as the hours crept by. When dawn began its daily appearance, both noted it at once.

"Shall we go?" Gavin asked.

"Yes, sir," Douglas replied. "I'm in a real hurry to die."

"Keep up your optimism, Sergeant," Gavin urged him as he mounted up.

Douglas swung himself into the saddle. "I ain't never been happy about nothing. That's natural for sergeants.'

Both pulled their revolvers and rode straight at the camp. As they entered, the dragoons passed a startled trio of Comancheros beginning to cook an early breakfast. Douglas, standing in the stirrups, pointed over in one direction.

"There he is," he said.

Gavin and Douglas rode straight over to the lean-to where Guido Lazardo and his personal guards slept. The dragoons leaped from their saddles and pounced on the sleeping Sicilian, pulling him to his feet as they shoved the barrels of their revolvers under his chin.

Lazardo yelled out, *"Che cosa—"*

"Shut your goddamned mouth!" Gavin interrupted. "Or we're going to send bullets up through your jaw and blow the top of your skull off."

Monroe Lockwood and Big Joe rolled out of their blankets and stared at the sight for one unbelieving moment.

"Don't make no moves, fat man!" Douglas warned him. "Or we'll kill your boss."

"Do what he says!" Lazardo said.

"Sure, Mister Lazardo," Lockwood assured him.

Big Joe grinned at the soldiers. "Now, just what the hell do you two think you're doing, huh?"

Gavin shouted, "Everyone in this camp is under arrest in the name of the United States government!"

Now the entire band was up. The rest of Lazardo's five most loyal men drew in closer. The Indian Crazy Fox strung his bow and walked deliberately toward the three people.

239

Douglas immediately fired, the bullet knocking the Indian flat as the arrow whipped harmlessly straight into the air. Then he quickly shot Lefty Dan and Lop-Head. Both men collapsed to the ground in death.

"You listen to me, you dumb son of a bitches!" Douglas bellowed. "You draw off or die! You make it tough for us and we'll kill your boss."

The majority of the Comancheros, not giving a damn whether Lazardo lived or died, simply stepped back to watch what would happen.

Lockwood, poised for action, glared at Gavin. "There's only two o' you. You're gonna lose out eventually." He turned to the other Comancheros. "We'll take care o' these two pecker heads right quick, so don't nobody get no ideas."

"Are you stupid enough to think we came in here alone?" Gavin asked him. "There's a troop of dragoons from Fort Leavenworth just over the horizon."

"So why didn't you bring them in with you?" Lazardo asked.

Douglas kicked the Sicilian in the crotch so hard the man had to bend over to puke.

"I owed you something," the sergeant sneered. "I talked the lieutenant into letting me have some fun before the rest of the troops got here."

Gavin gestured with his pistol. "Nobody is to leave the camp. Remember! I have put you all—everyone—under arrest. You'll be taken in for trial."

"Then hanging," Douglas added.

For several long moments nothing happened. Then the distant sound of a bugle could be heard.

Some talking broke out among the Comancheros. Suddenly there was a flurry of activity as they immediately ignored Gavin's order and began preparing to leave. Only Lockwood, Big Joe, Tarheel, and Runs Fast stood their ground.

The bugle, closer now, sounded again, and a large cloud of dust could be seen on the horizon.

"There's gotta be a coupla hunnerd of 'em!" a panicky Comanchero yelled at his friends. "Haul ass, boys!"

Within moments, most of the Comancheros were aboard their horses and scrambling toward the ford in the nearby river. Abandoned shelters dotted what had been their camp.

In spite of his swollen testicles, Lazardo finally felt himself ready to talk. "You cannot get away!" he wheezed painfully. "I don't care if a thousand of your soldiers are coming here!"

Tarheel and Runs Fast looked at each other as the bugle could again be heard. As if on signal, both bolted away, heading for their horses.

Monroe Lockwood spun on his heel, dragging his revolver from its holster. Two quick shots in the back ended the attempted escape as the two Comancheros stumbled, then went facedown into the dirt.

Gavin shot Big Joe, the force of the bullet's strike doubling him over. The large man gamely tried to get to his feet, but it was no use. He sat down. "I ain't got no fight left in me," he said in a mournful tone.

Lockwood made another turn, this time only to catch a head shot from Douglas that made the back of his skull explode in a messy spray of brains and blood.

Big Joe sat in silence, looking up as he heard the approach of horses. When he saw the five dragoons dragging dust-spewing bundles of branches behind their horses as one of them trumpeted a bugle, he frowned at Gavin.

"You'd never have did this to us in our reg'lar camp," he said.

Gavin released Lazardo, pushing him so hard the Comanchero lost his footing and sprawled to the ground.

241

"You're right," he said. "That's what occurred to me as I was mulling this situation over yesterday."

Douglas's revolver fired again, putting a killing shot into Big Joe's neck. The Comanchero slowly rolled over and died.

"Would you call that murder sir?" Douglas asked.

"In this case, I call it good riddance," Gavin said. "I agreed that we wouldn't take any chances by showing mercy, so I won't offer you any complaints. Gather up our prisoner and let's get back to Nadezhda."

Murphy and the others galloped into the camp, still kicking up large clouds of dust. "How'd we do, sir?" he asked.

Gavin pointed to Lazardo, the dead men, and the empty camp. "You did damned good!"

"Stop grinning like shit-eating pigs!" Douglas snapped. "We got to get back to the settlement."

The bundles of branches were cut loose, and the men formed up. Carlson caught a horse in the camp for Lazardo. The Comanchero, with his hands bound behind his back, was roughly lifted up into the saddle.

"My faithful men will be back!" he screamed in rage and pain as spittle spewed from his mouth.

"You ain't got no faithful men," Douglas said. "They was nervous enough being up this far north in country they didn't know. None of 'em has the slightest idea of how near the closest army fort is."

"They'll not chance a return here," Gavin said.

"That's right," Douglas went on. "That whole bunch is gonna be down in Texas before the end o' this week."

Lazardo swung his hate-filled gaze at Gavin. "You are lucky! Damned lucky!"

"I didn't have a thing to lose," Gavin said. "If this had failed, my men and I would have been dead. If we'd stayed at the town to continue the fight, we'd have died before this day ended anyhow."

Suddenly, Guido Lazardo broke out into chuckles, then outright laughter, his eyes watering with emotion. When he finally regained control, he said, "I just recalled the many times when I stood with my back against a wall. With nothing to lose, I became brazen and clever. Thus, I won everything. I respected you from the way you fooled us with that false trail after freeing our prisoners. You are clever. I should never have pushed you against a wall."

"Enough talk!" Douglas barked. "Let's get the hell out of here."

The column, with their prisoner, rode north. In less than a half hour they could see a hazy image of Nadezhda dancing in the early morning haze on the horizon. As they drew closer, the dragoons waved and hollered. Within moments they could hear the shouts of the Russians coming back at them.

When they rode up to the barricades, Count Valenko looked at them in happy astonishment. He climbed over the defenses and rushed out, slapping the dragoons on the legs in greeting.

"My friends! My friends! You are not desertink us! You vill fight vith us!" he yelled.

"There will be no more fight," Gavin said. "The Comancheros have left, but we have their leader."

Valenko looked up at Lazardo and spit on him. When Lazardo spit back, the Russian dragged him out of the saddle and flung him to the ground and began kicking him. Valenko, with tears now streaming down his face, bellowed in rage as he continued booting the squirming Comanchero.

Finally, Gavin slipped from his horse and pulled the count away. "We have won. Let the United States government punish him." He looked carefully at the old nobleman. "Why are you weeping, Your Grace?"

"I cry like a baby in both happiness and sadness,"

Valenko said. "I am happy because the bad men have gone avay. I am sad because Basil Karshchov has died."

"Basil died?" Gavin asked in astonishment. "But he had only a shoulder wound that wasn't too serious."

"He bled to death in the night," Valenko explained. "Ve lost him vhile he slept. The bullet did not come out. It vent down into his body and caused much damage vhen it slipped around vhen he moved. But he vas not knowink nothink as his life ended. He vent to God in his sleep."

Gavin left his horse with Douglas, hurrying over to the barricades. He climbed the defenses, leaping down the other side to rush into the main building. He found Natalia kneeling beside Karshchov's corpse.

Gavin sank down and looked into the pale, cold face of his friend. "Oh, Basil!" he exclaimed. He reached out and laid his hand on the dead man's face.

Natalia spoke in a soft voice. "Last night, before he went to sleep, he said that you would be back."

Gavin, grateful for the Russian's faith, fought back the tears. In a quaking voice, he said, "I am so glad that he believed in me."

Natalia smiled sadly. "You were the best friend that Basil ever had, Lieutenant. He loved you like a brother."

Gavin looked at the woman. "Nadezhda is safe."

"I know," she replied. "I was standing at the window while you spoke with my father. Thank you, Lieutenant MacRoss. We owe you so much."

"I've lost a dear friend," Gavin said.

"We will bury Basil shortly. Will you stay for the services? We are attending to our other dead as well."

"Of course," Gavin said, getting to his feet. "Afterward, I must return to Fort Leavenworth."

A couple of Russian men appeared. They laid out a

blanket and placed Basil's body on it. After wrapping him up, they carried the dead man outside.

The funeral for Basil Karshchov and the others was brief since no priest was available. Gavin read from a Bible belonging to Carlson, and prayers were offered for the souls of the dead.

When the ceremony was over, the lieutenant mournfully left the grave site, pausing for a brief handshake with Valenko and some of the other men before rejoining his small command.

"Form up in columns of twos!" Gavin ordered. "For'd, ho! Gallop, ho!"

The detachment rode away from the settlement, heading east across the Kansas prairie toward Fort Leavenworth.

Chapter 22

When Lieutenant Gavin MacRoss led his raggedy, tired detachment of dragoons and their prisoner into Fort Leavenworth on that spring day of 1855, the physical danger he had faced was over, but that was certainly not the complete end of the ordeal:

The post judge-advocate, who represented military law; the regimental adjutant, keeper of administrative records; and the regimental quartermaster, who maintained all government property and records thereof, all waited to pounce on him with their administrative requirements and demands.

The first was the judge-advocate. Before anything else took place, Gavin had to turn in Guido Lazardo and charge him with murder, kidnapping, sedition, and robbery. This involved identifying him. At first the prisoner refused to give his name or any other information about himself, but an evening with Sergeant Ian Douglas and corporals Steeple and Murphy convinced him of the wisdom of disclosing all facts about himself and answering any other questions that might be put to him in a proper trial. In the end, he even gave a truthful account of the deaths of the two deserters Jack McRyan and Dennis Costello.

Although Sergeant Douglas certainly harbored no

fondness for the two petty criminals, he thought the way their deaths had been arranged was a low-down, cowardly act. He demonstrated his opinion by administering a sound beating to Lazardo as the final touch on the Comanchero's interrogation.

While that went on, Gavin had to turn in to the adjutant a mountain of paperwork on the loss of the five other men. Three died as deserters while privates Anderson and Belken went to their deaths in the line of duty. A full accounting, in triplicate, of the what, where, and why of the men's deaths had to be laboriously written out and reviewed. Any pay coming, or forfeited, had to be taken care of as did the notification of next of kin where such information existed.

The most complicated area was covering the loss of equipment with the quartermaster. Two of the horses had been killed as a result of hostile fire during the siege of Nadezhda. In the confusion of events, their saddles and other equipment had been misplaced by the Russians somehow. Gavin came very close to having to pay for the losses out of his own pocket, but managed to find an obscure paragraph in the regulations pertaining to losses under fire. Once more requests in triplicate were called for, and numerous endorsements from the commanders of the company, squadron, and regiment to which Gavin belonged had to be placed in the proper place on the documents.

It took a full five days of great effort before the administrative side of the operation was completed and the angry lieutenant had finally justified how a two-week assignment had doubled itself.

After that, the wheels of military justice began to turn at a rapid speed. The Comanchero chief was put on trial in a procedure that lasted but one afternoon. In spite of facing capital punishment, Lazardo enjoyed being the center of attention. He particularly relished the way the ladies in the court room gasped during the reading of the charges against him. Loving the impression he made on them, the Comanchero truthfully answered questions pertaining to his crimes in the Kansas Territory committed against the Russian pioneers, but he pleaded special circumstances.

At that point, Lazardo began to lie and reinvent his life, being most creative with his past. The outlaw told of an affair in his native Sicily with a girl named Liliana Bonabella. Lazardo claimed he and the girl loved each other madly and she had accepted his proposal of marriage. But a wealthy old man, who paid money to her father, had received permission to marry her. He and the girl had run away to the mountains, but she had been murdered by hired assassins sent after them by the vengeful, elderly suitor. Lazardo, of course, told everyone he had killed the man and been forced to flee Sicily to escape the vengeance of an enormous gang of the dead fellow's clan.

Next he told sea stories about fighting off pirates, saving a ship during a raging storm while the captain and crew cowered below decks, and went on about his adventures of rescuing young damsels from a life of prostitution in France. A Corsican gang, in that case, had chased after him. Then once more to the life of a sailor and finally becoming a Comanchero.

That latter part of his life was something he couldn't lie about as Lieutenant Gavin MacRoss and Sergeant Ian Douglas told of the raid on Nadezhda and of Lazardo's plan to sell the prisoners into slavery in Mexico and Texas.

Lazardo pleaded that only past cruelties and bad luck had brought him into such a life. He begged for mercy, saying that he would change his ways and lead a decent life.

The presiding officer of the court-martial, a portly

member of the judge-advocate's department, was neither believing nor forgiving. He very happily sentenced the Sicilian to be hanged by the neck until he was dead.

Three days later, Lazardo went bravely to his death, cursing the hangman and the United States Dragoons with equal fervor. After Lazardo's execution, Fort Leavenworth fell into its regular summer routine. Gavin escorted several wagon trains, chased after Indians, made endless patrols, and conducted various duties in garrison as were required of him. His former good humor had gone away, and he truly mourned the loss of his friend Basil Karshchov.

The Russian intellectual, with his large, sensitive eyes and gentle manner, had proven himself a brave and dedicated man. Though no roughneck by any means, he had courageously displayed his willingness to fight— and die—making him as brave a man as Gavin ever knew in the blue-and-gold ranks of the dragoons.

As more people began to move onto the prairie, the safety of the Russian settlement was assured. A few Americans joined the settlement, giving them a blacksmith, a couple more farmers, and a shopkeeper who opened a general store a few steps away from the main building.

Paddy O'Hearn was promoted to corporal and put his bugle away for the final time as he settled in to seriously pursue his career as a professional noncommissioned officer of the United States Army. Corporal Steeple made sergeant that following August, and Corporal Murphy was broken to the rank of private for being drunk on duty. Fenlay was elevated to take his place, but didn't do much better, losing his stripes for a brawl in the town of Leavenworth.

Sergeant Ian Douglas became the company's first sergeant, when that individual deserted taking the unit's funds with him. Using his influence with both Lieutenant Gavin MacRoss and Captain Francis Hanover, he managed to get Corporal O'Hearn advanced once again, this time to sergeant, and saw to it that young Private Olaf Carlson was made a corporal.

There was no more Comanchero activity in that part of the country. Thanks to the small, gutsy detachment of dragoons, that particular brand of criminal stayed south in the Indian territories and Texas. But that didn't mean all was tranquil. Bandits, hostile Indians, whiskey and gun runners, and other law breakers kept the dragoons busy.

The fall season moved in slowly, bringing beautiful colors to the stands of trees out on the prairie country and those growing within the confines of the garrison. The weather grew crisper and finally downright cold when the first northers swept down to begin the frigid climate that marked winter in the open landscape of Kansas Territory.

Sergeants and corporals moved their bunks closer to the stoves, and the Indians went to the warmth of their lodges as once again the yearly cycle brought around the peace and quiet of what the Indians called the Moons of Snow.

Lieutenant Gavin MacRoss, unsettled and unhappy, spent many lonely and sleepless nights in his quarters, remembering a good friend named Basil, and a beautiful young woman called Natalia. He rarely went into town and turned down invitations to visit the homes of attractive young women as he withdrew more and more into himself. His devotion to duty was complete, and he even turned down a chance for furlough to visit his home town back in Pennsylvania.

The coming spring and summer promised more pioneering groups to move into Kansas Territory. People already spoke of how it would soon be settled enough to apply for statehood and within a few years the area would be filled with towns and farms.

But to a few dragoons, no matter how civilized the plains became, the area would always be known to them as the Comanchero Prairie.

Epilogue

The coming of the spring of 1856 gave Mary Hanover, the wife of Captain Francis Hanover, another grand opportunity to display her skills at organizing grand festivities to celebrate special social events.

The marriage of First Lieutenant Gavin MacRoss of the United States Dragoons with Lady Natalia Valenko was an event in which Mary Hanover outdid even herself. Only the cream of the most socially prominent citizens of the area along with ranking army people were invited to attend the elaborate ceremony, which included an arch of sabers held up by dragoon officers for the couple to walk under after leaving the post chapel.

Count Valenko, dressed in his finest formal clothing, sported the medals and decorations of the Russian imperial nobility. He gave his daughter away, then turned to his favorite pastime of downing as much alcohol as possible while lesser drinkers faltered and fell away as the evening passed into night.

Afterward, a grand reception with plenty of food and drink further celebrated the event as the crowd danced to the regimental band. The musicians, following a program set up by the hostess, played long into the wee hours.

Gavin and Natalia made an escape just before midnight. He requested the furlough he'd turned down earlier, to take his bride on a honeymoon and give her a chance to meet his family. They departed on the east-bound stage at dawn, seen off by their closest friends.

Later that summer, in a less socially ranked cere-mony, Sergeant Paddy O'Hearn married Miss Irena Yakubovski at Fort Leavenworth's chapel. First Sergeant Ian Douglas gave the bride away while Corporal Olaf Carlson acted as the groom's best man.

Douglas wryly noted that during O'Hearn's patrol duties that took him through Nadezhda, the sergeant, like Lieutenant MacRoss, certainly didn't waste his time.

BENEATH THE CALM OF THE DEEP,
BLUE SEA, HEART-POUNDING DANGER AWAITS

DEPTH FORCE

THE ACTION SERIES BY

IRVING A. GREENFIELD